# *Praise for Highland Press Books!*

**THE CRYSTAL HEART** *(by Katherine Deauxville) brims with ribald humor and authentic historical detail. Enjoy!*
~ *Virginia Henley*

\* \* \*

**CAT O'NINE TALES** by Deborah MacGillivray. Enchanting tales from the most wicked, award-winning author today. Spellbinding! A treat for all.
~ *Detra Fitch, The Huntress Reviews*

\* \* \*

**THE SENSE OF HONOR** by Ashley Kath-Bilsky has written an historical romance of the highest caliber. This reviewer was fesseled to the pages, fell in love with the hero and was cheering for the heroine all the way through. The plot is exciting and moves along at a good pace. The characters are multi-dimensional and the secondary characters bring life to the story. Sexual tension rages through this story and Ms. Kath-Bilsky gives her readers a breath-taking romance. The love scenes are sensual and very romantic. This reviewer was very pleased with how the author handled all the secrets. Sometimes it can be very frustrating for the reader when secrets keep tearing the main characters apart, but in this case, those secrets seem to bring them more together and both characters reacted very maturely when the secrets finally came to light. This reviewer is hoping that this very talented author will have another book out very soon.
~ *Valerie, Love Romances*

\* \* \*

**FAERY SPECIAL ROMANCES** - **Brilliantly magical!** Ms. Rogers' special brand of humor and imagination will have you believing in faeries from page one. Absolutely enchanting!
- *Dawn Thompson, Author of The Ravencliff Bride*

\* \* \*

**HIGHLAND WISHES** by Leanne Burroughs. This
reviewer was easily captivated by the story and was enthralled
by it until the end. The reader will laugh and cry as you read
this wonderful story. The reader feels all the pain, torment
and disillusionment felt by both main characters, but also the
joy and love they felt. Ms. Burroughs has crafted a well-
researched story that gives a glimpse into Scotland during a
time when there was upheaval and war for independence.
This reviewer is anxiously awaiting her next novel in this
series and commends her for a wonderful job done.
~ *Dawn Roberto, Love Romances*

\* \* \*

**REBEL HEART** by Jannine Corti-Petska - Ms. Petska
does an excellent job of all aspects of sharing this book with
us. Ms. Petska used a myriad of emotions to tell this story and
the reader (me) quickly becomes entranced in the ways
Courtney's stubborn attitude works to her advantage in
surviving this disastrous beginning to her new life. Ms.
Petska's writings demand attention; she draws the reader to
quickly become involved in this passionate story. This is a
wonderful rendition of a different type which is a welcome
addition to the historical romance genre. I believe that you
will enjoy this story; I know I did!
~ *Brenda Talley, The Romance Studio*

\* \* \*

**IN SUNSHINE OR IN SHADOW** by Cynthia Owens -
If you adore the stormy heroes of 'Wuthering Heights' and
'Jane Eyre' (and who doesn't?) you'll be entranced by Owens'
passionate story of Ireland after the Great Famine, and David
Burke - a man from America with a hidden past and a secret
name. Only one woman, the fiery, luscious Siobhan, can
unlock the bonds that imprison him. Highly recommended
for those who love classic romance and
an action-packed story.
~ *Best Selling Author, Maggie Davis,*
*AKA Katherine Deauxville*

\* \* \*

**INTO THE WOODS** by R.R. Smythe - This Young Adult
Fantasy will send chills down your spine. I, as the reader,
followed Callum and witnessed everything he and his friends

# An Impossible Love...

As if from a far country Grace heard a voice
murmuring to her, calling her beloved, using all
the love words she'd ever dreamed of hearing.
She wanted nothing, not even the opening of
her eyes, to interfere with that voice so deep
and anguished and filled with longing. She lay
motionless in Owen's arms
letting his love enter her soul.
His fingers touched her hair, his hand
trembling as he stroked it back from her face.
Could this man of iron fear she was badly hurt,
dying mayhap? In truth she'd
never felt so alive.

This couldn't continue. She opened her eyes
right into Owen's dark gaze.
"You love me."

As if she were a hot coal, he dropped her
from his grasp. "You're awake," he said
and scowled. "For how long?"

"Long enough." She grinned up at him.

"You're fully recovered, I see.
I'm a fool of a man."

"That is true," she said, the smile never
leaving her.

went through as they attempted to decipher the messages. At the same time, I watched Callum's mother, Ellsbeth, as she walked through the Netherwood. Each time Callum deciphered one of the four messages, some villagers awakened. Through the eyes of Ellsbeth, I saw the other sleepers wander, make mistakes, and be released from the Netherwood, leaving Ellsbeth alone. There is one thread left dangling, but do not fret. This IS a stand alone book. But that thread gives me hope that another book about the Netherwoods may someday come to pass. Excellent reading for any age of fantasy fans!

~ *Detra Fitch, Huntress Reviews*

\* \* \*

***ALMOST TAKEN*** by Isabel Mere is a very passionate historical romance that takes the reader on an exciting adventure. The compelling characters of Deran Morissey, the Earl of Atherton, and Ava Fychon, a young woman from Wales, find themselves drawn together as they search for her missing siblings.

Readers will watch in interest as they fall in love and overcome obstacles. They will thrill in the passion and hope that they find happiness together. This is a very sensual romance that wins the heart of the readers.

This is a creative and fast moving storyline that will enthrall readers. The character's personalities will fascinate readers and win their concern. Ava, who is highly spirited and stubborn, will win the respect of the readers for her courage and determination. Deran, who is rumored in the beginning to be an ice king, not caring about anyone, will prove how wrong people's perceptions can be. ***Almost Taken*** by Isabel Mere is an emotionally moving historical romance that I highly recommend to the readers.

~ *Anita, The Romance Studio*

\* \* \*

***PRETEND I'M YOURS*** by Phyllis Campbell is an exceptional masterpiece. This lovely story is so rich in detail and personalities that it just leaps out and grabs hold of the reader. From the moment I started reading about Mercedes and Katherine, I was spellbound. Ms. Campbell carries the reader into a mirage of mystery with deceit, betrayal of the worst kind, and a passionate love revolving around the

sisters, that makes this a whirlwind page-turner. Mercedes and William are astonishing characters that ignite the pages and allows the reader to experience all their deepening sensations. There were moments I could share in with their breathtaking romance, almost feeling the butterflies of love they emitted. This extraordinary read had me mesmerized with its ambiance, its characters and its remarkable twists and turns, making it one recommended read in my book.
~ *Linda L., Fallen Angel Reviews*

\* \* \*

*HER HIGHLAND ROGUE* by Leanne Burroughs. In a stunning sequel to Burroughs' HIGHLAND WISHES, the reader will find a powerfully emotional and passionate love story that focuses on Duncan Macthomas, who was introduced in that novel.
Against the sweeping backdrop of Scotland's war of independence, this author continues an epic of a heart wrenching and positively beautiful love story. Duncan and Catherine were painstakingly developed with such realism that you'll be sharing their emotional journey. At its very heart you'll share the love, the joy, the anguish, and the tears. Along the way, you'll revisit old friends, gain new ones, and thoroughly wish the story would never end. Burroughs gifts you with a terrific story, straight from her heart to yours! A most excellent novel that I whole-heartedly recommend!
~ *Marilyn Rondeau, The Best Reviews*

\* \* \*

*RECIPE FOR LOVE* - I don't think the reader will find a better compilation of mouth watering short romantic love stories than in RECIPE FOR LOVE! This is a highly recommended volume – perfect for beaches, doctor's offices, or anywhere you've a few minutes to read.
~ *Marilyn Rondeau, Reviewers International Organization*

\* \* \*

Christmas is a magical time and twelve talented authors answer the question of what happens when *CHRISTMAS WISHES* come true in this incredible anthology.

*CHRISTMAS WISHES* shows just how phenomenal a themed anthology can be. Each of these highly skilled authors brings a slightly different perspective to the Christmas theme to create a book that is sure to leave readers satisfied. What a joy to read such splendid stories! This reviewer looks forward to more anthologies by Highland Press as the quality is simply astonishing.

~ *Debbie, CK2S Kwips and Kritiques*

**(\*One story in this anthology was nominated for the Gayle Wilson Award of Excellence\*)**

\* \* \*

*HOLIDAY IN THE HEART* - Twelve stories that would put even Scrooge into the Christmas spirit. It does not matter what *type* of romance genre you prefer. This book has a little bit of everything. The stories are set in the U.S.A. and Europe. Some take place in the past, some in the present, and one story takes place in both! I strongly suggest that you put on something comfortable, brew up something hot (tea, coffee or cocoa will do), light up a fire, settle down somewhere quiet and begin reading this anthology.

~ *Detra Fitch, Huntress Reviews*

\* \* \*

*BLUE MOON MAGIC* is an enchanting collection of short stories. Each author wrote with the same theme in mind but each story has its own uniqueness. You should have no problem finding a tale to suit your mood. *BLUE MOON MAGIC* offers historicals, contemporaries, time travel, paranormal, and futuristic narratives to tempt your heart.

Legend says that if you wish with all your heart upon the rare blue moon, your wishes were sure to come true. Each of the heroines discovers this magical fact. True love is out there if you just believe in it. In some of the stories, love happens in the most unusual ways. Angels may help, ancient spells may be broken, anything can happen. Even vampires will find their perfect mate with the power of the blue moon. Not every heroine believes they are wishing for love, some are just looking for answers to their problems or nagging questions. Fate seems to think the solution is finding the one who makes their heart sing.

*BLUE MOON MAGIC* is a perfect read for late at night or even during your commute to work. The short yet sweet stories are a wonderful way to spend a few minutes. If you do not have the time to finish a full-length novel, but hate stopping in the middle of a loving tale, I highly recommend grabbing this book.
~ *Kim Swiderski, Writers Unlimited Reviewer*

\* \* \*

Legend has it that a blue moon is enchanted. What happens when fifteen talented authors utilize this theme to create enthralling stories of love?

**BLUE MOON ENCHANTMENT** is a wonderful, themed anthology filled with phenomenal stories by fifteen extraordinarily talented authors. Readers will find a wide variety of time periods and styles showcased in this superb anthology. *BLUE MOON ENCHANTMENT* is sure to offer a little bit of something for everyone!
~ *Debbie, CK²S Kwips and Kritiques*

\* \* \*

**NO LAW AGAINST LOVE** - If you have ever found yourself rolling your eyes at some of the more stupid laws, then you are going to adore this novel. Over twenty-five stories fill up this anthology, each one dealing with at least one stupid or outdated law. Let me give you an example: In Florida, USA, there is a law that states "If an elephant is left tied to a parking meter, the parking fee has to be paid just as it would for a vehicle." In Great Britain, "A license is required to keep a lunatic." Yes, you read those correctly. No matter how many times you go back and reread them, the words will remain the same. Those two laws are still legal. The tales vary in time and place. Some take place in the present, in the past, in the USA, in England... in other words, there is something for everyone! Best yet, profits from the sales of this novel will go to breast cancer prevention.

A stellar anthology that had me laughing, sighing in pleasure, believing in magic, and left me begging for more! Will there be a second anthology someday? I sure hope so! This is one novel that will go directly to my 'Keeper' shelf, to be read over and over again. Very highly recommended!
~ *Detra Fitch, Huntress Reviews*

# The Barefoot Queen

## Jean Harrington

Highland Press

High Springs, Florida 32655

# The Barefoot Queen

For information, please contact:
Highland Press Publishing,
PO Box 2292, High Springs, FL 32655.

All characters in this book have no existence outside the imagination of the author and have no relation whatsoever to anyone bearing the same name or names, save actual historical figures. They are not even distantly inspired by any individual known or unknown to the author, and all incidents are pure invention.

ISBN: 978-0-9800356-6-7

PUBLISHED BY HIGHLAND PRESS PUBLISHING

An Eire Book

# Dedication

To Mary Ann
Of County Cork, Ireland,
And her son,
My beloved husband,
John

# Grace Notes

Thank you to my wonderfully supportive husband, John, and to my insightful critique partners, Sharon Yanish and Susann Devine; to my encouraging early readers, Grace Dowling, Kati Griffith, and Ramona McNicholas; to my 'Irish connections'—for their knowledge of Ireland's customs and lore—Eileen Swift, syndicated travel reporter of *Newsday*, and editor Kemberlee Shortland; to senior editor Patty Howell for really *seeing*; to publisher Leanne Burroughs for enjoying and publishing this story. And to Julie Palella who plays the computer as if it were a Steinway

# PROLOGUE

*B*allybanree, Ireland, 1665

"Hang him!"

"But my lord—"

"No buts, Frazer." Cutting short his gamekeeper's protest, Lord Rushmount prodded the bloody deer carcass with the toe of his high, polished boot. "You see the evidence. You know the law." He shot an irritated glance at Red Liam, the poacher. The man stood tall, his arms bound behind his back, his eyes staring calmly into the distance. "Have you anything to say for yourself?"

Red Liam's gaze swiveled to meet his own. "The people go hungry. Does that change my fate?" His lips quirked up with the hint of a smile.

Amused, was he? Rushmount's jaw hardened. He was the master here. The forest and every creature in it, human and subhuman, were his to command. To hell with the deer! He'd hang the man for insubordination alone.

"You heard him confess, Frazer. There's the tree. You and the others do what the law dictates."

Rushmount turned on his heel, his boots digging deep into the dusty lane. He seized the chestnut's reins and swung into the saddle. As he rode off, the dust rising like a tail behind him, he heard a woman scream.

He galloped on without a backward glance.

# CHAPTER ONE

"The law be damned, Liam! They murdered him." Grace's voice, sharp as a flung knife, sliced through the air.

Liam jumped up from the bench and closed the cottage door.

"You needn't bother," Grace said. "No one dares come near us. We're alone. As we deserve to be. That's true justice."

"They caught Da poaching, not us. We've done no wrong."

"Nor did he. What was his crime? Feeding the children?" Too agitated to sit, Grace paced the hard dirt floor. "I should have been with him that night. I might have given a warning, drawn them away somehow." She sighed, the sound filling the room. "Da knew I could use the weapons, but he said 'twas not women's work."

Liam nodded and went back to his seat by the table.

Grace sank onto the stool opposite him, her bare feet wide apart. Tossing her mane of red-gold hair away from her face, she hiked the wool skirt to her knees. Why cover up in front of her brother? What did niceties matter now? She glanced over at him. A big man, thickened about the neck and shoulders, he was strong as a bull, but peaceable, without a bull's willful ways.

"Liam, will you look at me?"

"You have enough lads looking at you already. You have no need of me doing the same."

"Oh, but I do. You above all." She leaned forward and grasped his hand. "We must release him. It's been three days now."

He pulled his hand free and reached for a piece of skillet bread.

"Help me," she pleaded.

"Sure and you've gone mad."

"'Tis madness to leave Da hanging like carrion for the dogs. He lived a good life. He deserves burial in hallowed ground. Next to Mam."

Liam shook his head and bent to his food.

Grace leaped to her feet. "May the devil take them all." She kicked the stool across the floor, ignoring the stab of pain in her foot. "Good God, Liam, we're descended from great grandmother, Granuaile O'Malley. We've the blood of a pirate queen running in our veins." She whipped around, sending her skirt flying about her ankles. "She savaged the whole English fleet."

"That was then, and this is now. Her ships and treasure are long gone." Liam lifted his eyes from his meal. "You're wearing yourself to a shadow for naught."

She stopped so abruptly her skirt tangled in her legs. "For naught? Da was naught? He was the bravest man on earth. They caught him unawares."

"Your senses have left you, lass. Lord Rushmount had his men combing the countryside. Da knew the chance he took, and he paid the price. If I cut him down, they'll string me up in his place."

"Not if they can't prove it."

Liam snorted his disdain. "You know better."

Grace crossed the floor in a few swift steps. "Cut Da down, and we'll see to the burying together. Afterwards, spend the night in the village pub. Pretend you're drunk and sleep on the floor. You'll have a dozen witnesses. I'll swear you were there as well."

Liam rose from the bench and picked up his field hat. "I'll go back out now and hope to everything that's holy I'm left to work the land in peace. Be careful, lass, in your keening. We could join Da on that oak. It has many branches."

"Coward," she whispered.

Liam's hat hung in his work-roughened hands. He looked down at it, twirling the brim around and around in his fingers. "You have the truth of it," he acknowledged and, shoulders bent, walked out of the cottage.

Grace ran to the door. "Liam, help me!" Her cry followed him into the open air, but no answer came back to her.

She turned from the doorway and sank onto the floor in front of the smoldering turf fire. A wisp of smoke trailed lazily up toward the vent hole in the thatch.

Three days since Da had been hanging among the oak leaves, and none of the villagers had come near the farm. Not even the suitors who, from the time of her fourteenth birthday, had been swarming about her thick as bees on a whitethorn blossom.

Seventeen now, she'd held them all off, pretty boys and slovens alike. None of them had Da's courage. None would dare defy his lordship as he had. None, except one. The one she longed for, Owen O'Donnell, five years older than herself and the stubbornest man in the world.

She stared at the faltering flames. In all of Bally-banree, Owen alone might help her. But God forgive him, he spurned anyone who offered him a kindness, or a loving glance, or a sweet word. If she approached him, he would likely rebuff her again, as he did each time she tried to speak to him.

Her mind in turmoil, she took the soiled wooden plates from the table and rinsed them in the bucket of water. A thick scraping of porridge remained in the iron pot. She covered it with a clean scrap of linen and set the pot on the shelf by the wall.

In the firepit, red winks still glowed in the ashes. Before banking the peat, she kicked at the edge of the crumbling bricks with her bare foot, defying the flames to burst free, but all she had for her trouble were soot-blackened toes.

'Twas no lady's foot clothed in white hose and shod in leather with grand, silver buckles over the arch. A lady she would never be except in her own heart. She accepted that as her lot in life, but with Lord Rush-mount's harsh rule she would never be at peace. Never. Not as long as the vision of Granuaile lit her imagination.

Grace let out a long breath. Liam was right. The glory had fled long ago. Unlike Granuaile, she had no sailing ships to defy the invaders. She had nothing. It had all been stripped away. The land. The cattle. The freedom.

She stared into the dying fire.

If not Owen, Dillon might do what she asked...she liked his laughing face. He could make a woman smile, but he was so full of himself, life to him seemed ever joyous...denying the reality of it, he was. What of Hugh? Dour Hugh...hating the usurpers as much as she, but afraid to say so outright, even when he came courting. The McElroy brothers? Hard working, yet year after year their acres failed, and the defeated look etched into both of them. Young Connor Mann, the bailiff's son? Handsome and strong...but his father a toady to Lord Rushmount.

She revisited the list over and over, taking up a possibility, only to put it aside, and go on to another name and yet another. In the end, she returned to the one name. Owen. She needed him. And Da needed him. But would he dismiss her with a cold word, or worse, none at all, and walk away, rewarding her with the sight of his retreating back? Hurt to the quick by his last rejection, she'd vowed never to approach him again.

Without the fire, the room had turned dark and cheerless. Chilled and shivering, she wrapped her arms about herself for a bit of warmth. What if Granuaile's father, Black Oak, had been killed for taking a deer? What would she have done?

A peat brick crumpled into dust.

*Act!*

Aye. Grace scrambled to her feet.

The vow she'd made would have to be broken.

# CHAPTER TWO

The moon rode high in the night sky. On his pallet near the hearth, Liam slept, his breathing quiet and steady.

*Now!*

Slipping out of her bed in Da's old room, Grace stole to the cottage door. If Liam stirred when she lifted the latch, he'd think she'd gone to relieve herself and turn back to sleep. Should he worry when she didn't return, he'd never find her, never suspect that to Owen O'Donnell she had gone.

Luck and God and moonlight were with her, guiding her way to the village. She avoided the rutted lanes, for even at the midnight hour, someone might be traveling along, a drunkard, a tinker. An armed patrol.

At the edge of the village, still hidden by the trees, she waited, peering about, looking for the slightest movement, the slightest sound. Hardly a rustle came from the sleeping forest. Not a single dog barked. Forcing her mind from the thought of the dogs, she moved out of hiding.

Owen's blacksmith's forge stood apart, the last in a cluster of low, thatched huts, their doors closed against the night, their windowless stone walls blind to her presence. Like the clamor of his forge, Owen's bitterness kept the villagers at bay. Unless, of course, they had need of his skill.

Tonight she needed him for far more than mending a leaky pot or patching a turf spade. Outside his door, in the open lean-to that housed his forge, she glanced from right to left and back over her shoulder. No one. Nothing. As fast as quicksilver she moved and, in an instant, stood inside his cottage.

The banked hearth fire in the center of the room gave off a soft glow. Along a side wall, she made out a workbench, its surface scattered with tools and a broken plowshare waiting for repairs. She stepped farther into the room. No one stirred. He must be asleep behind the rough curtain separating the workshop from his living space.

"Owen," she whispered. "Owen O'Donnell. Are you here?" Her heartbeat filling her chest, she paused to listen.

"Am I dreaming, lass?"

At the deep voice behind her, not ahead as she'd supposed, she gasped and whirled to face the sound. "Holy Mother! You nearly gave me my death!"

He lurched forward out of the gloom near the doorway, his crippled leg making a travesty of every move as he dipped and swayed with each step, his shoulders rocking with effort.

For ease, he must have removed the high wooden boot he'd fashioned for himself. His gait was worse than she'd ever seen it.

In the dim firelight, he glowered at her. All the lads smiled and called her Grace the Fair, yet from Owen, not even a smile.

"I need something," she said.

"A pot patched? 'Tis the wrong time of day."

"What I want is different entirely."

"I know what you want." He stumbled closer. His scowl deepened.

"One of these days, your face will freeze like that."

"'Tis my dearest hope. Then the urchins will stay clear of me."

She'd known the village children mimicked his clumsy walk, but not that they did so in his sight. She gazed into his face. Despite the scowl, it was handsome enough, dark complexioned with black hair falling close to his deep-set eyes, beard stubble covering the crag of his jaw.

Unlike Liam and the other men in the village, he didn't favor a mustache. She liked the look of his clean upper lip, just as she liked the look of him when he stripped to the waist to work the forge. Surely he had the most powerful body of any man in Ballybanree, except for the withered leg that had been crushed in boyhood.

"Will you help me?" she asked.

Owen stared into her eyes, unsmiling, unbeguiled. Was he not happy to have her here alone in the middle of the night? Or was he afraid, like Liam, of what she would ask? Ah, surely not. When they were young together, he'd been the bravest of the brave, always defying the other lads to climb higher, ever higher, on the rocks by the cliffs.

"I'll gladly give you everything I have if you'll help me," she said.

"You'll *pay* me?" he scoffed. "Did your da leave you a tuppence, then?"

"He left me my own self." She moved closer to him, his for the touching.

Though his hands never left his sides, he gazed at her long and hard. After a full minute of staring, he glanced away, his eyes seeking out some spot on the far wall. Then his lips lifted and throwing back his head, he roared with laughter. Great gulps of it spewed out of him loud enough for the whole village to hear. But as suddenly as it began, the laughing stopped, and the familiar scowl returned.

"Don't fret yourself, lass. I've already done what you ask for."

"How do you know what I would ask?"

"Only one thing in this world would bring my beautiful friend Grace, the Queen of Ballybanree, to the house of a cripple." His voice came down hard on the word 'cripple' emphasizing it cruelly.

"And what would that be?"

"Your father's rotting body."

"You'll help me?"

"I cut him down an hour ago."

Relief washed over her. Da, her beloved da, no longer swung like carrion in the wind. Tears of mingled sorrow and joy pricked her eyelids. How Owen had managed with his withered leg she didn't know and wouldn't ask. He'd managed. Nothing else mattered. She moved even closer to him.

"Where is he?"

"In his grave. Safe."

"You'll tell me where?"

"'Tis better you not know."

"Is the earth hallowed?"

His lips lifted as if he would laugh once more, but he didn't. "All earth is hallowed."

She nodded. He spoke the simple truth. "I knew I could trust you, but I didn't know how much."

She closed the small distance remaining between them, standing near enough to reach out and touch the roughness of his canvas shirt.

"No," he said, his voice hoarse with vehemence.

Surely he didn't mean it. "But—"

"I want no charity from you, Mistress Grace."

"'Tis not what I offer—"

"You would never have come here without a purpose. You would never have come for me alone." He stepped back. "Give your gift to another man. The one you'll marry. Not to the village cripple. Now go home, out of harm's way."

With a hasty step, his shoulders swaying with effort, he reached the door before turning toward her one last time. "If they come for Liam, tell him to say he came here this night. That I repaired his spade. The villagers will agree. I made enough noise earlier to disturb the dead."

Already halfway out the door, he stopped and glanced back, his scowl easing. "Ah, I am truly a stupid man. Now get home, lass, to your own bed."

Before she could reply, he closed the door behind him, leaving her alone in his hut.

An angry flush heated her cheeks. He'd looked at her and laughed and walked away, leaving her untouched. How dare he?

She blew out a breath. 'Twas his pride. A rare thing in men living under a vicious rule, even rarer, surely, in a man with a crippled leg, the butt of coarse jests. And worse, she realized of a sudden, the object of pity from girls like herself who would never see him whole and a man fit for mating.

But he was! Somehow, she'd known so from the time she was a tiny child and he a stripling with two sound legs. She sighed, remembering.

After he'd fallen between the rocks, he'd withdrawn his friendship from one and all, even from her. No more bantering and running about the hills in fair weather and foul, no more telling her she was the fairest lass in the village and they would marry one day. Sure, and he'd forgotten all about that promise. Or buried it beyond recovery.

Her eyes had become accustomed to the half-light, and she glanced about. She'd never been past the curtain hanging at the back of the workshop, and curious, she went up to it and drew it aside. Within, she found a narrow bed as neatly made up as if she'd smoothed it herself, a blue blanket tucked under the pallet, a second cover folded at the foot. A stool beside the bed held a book. A book! Imagine! A Bible by the look of it. *Where did he get something so rare? Can it be possible he's learned to read? So few people can.*

Her gaze roamed the small space. He had a table with a second stool pulled near. A few bowls were piled atop the table, a half-eaten oatcake in one of them. No hearth in here. There would be plenty of heat and warmth from the shop for whatever cooking needed doing...the curtain could be pulled by in the evenings...

An impulse seized her. Untying the kerchief holding her hair from her face, she folded it into a small square and opening the book, placed it inside the cover. The odor of the heather sprigs she tucked among her things still clung to it. Though not the gift she wished to give him, it would be something to remember her by, a thank you for honoring Da.

The flush she'd felt earlier began rising again. Dear God, here she was, spying on Owen's possessions, and he waiting somewhere nearby wondering why she hadn't left. Her cheeks hot, her shawl slipping off her shoulders, she dashed past the curtain, and hurrying through the workshop, ran out into the night.

# CHAPTER THREE

"'Tis grand news I have for you, Grace," Sean McElroy said the next morning, his face lit with a rare smile. "Lord Rushmount's gone to England to claim his bride."

"Gone for good, has he?" Grace asked.

Sean's faint smile faded entirely. "For two months only, Connor Mann says."

"Well, if anyone knows for certain, Rushmount's toady is the one."

A man of few words, Sean nodded and left, his news passed on, his excuse for dallying ended.

Perched on the stone wall in front of the cottage, Grace watched him amble down the lane toward the village, his shoulders bent in their usual slump.

Rushmount, a bridegroom? A killer was more like it. The worst kind. He had the law on his side.

*And she had Owen on hers.*

The realization warmed her. In his defiance of the hangman, he'd been magnificent.

But now that Da was safely in the ground, would he be forgotten? And the vicious way he'd been killed?

No!

She got up from the wall to pace the greensward fronting the cottage. When Granuaile's father, Black Oak, died, she'd captained his ships, fearlessly raiding any vessels daring to enter Irish waters.

With no ships, no coin, no men at arms, 'twas impossible to do what Granuaile had done. All she could do was dream of the glory of such deeds. Then, with the force of a hammer blow, a powerful thought struck her. Even without ships, she could take up her father's crusade! Retaliate against his killers in the only way open to her. Become what Da had been—a deer slayer— a prick in Lord Rushmount's side. Each deer taken an act of defiance, a strike against injustice.

Her thoughts in a whirl, she strode back and forth, her movements finally catching Liam's attention. He came to the open door, pipe in hand. "If you're not wearing out the floor inside, it's the turf outside. Come in, lass, and rest from whatever's deviling you."

Sitting by the fire to please him, she watched the peat burn down into embers, then into ash. A quiet satisfaction filled her. Her skill with the weapons would be put to good use after all. She would strike first at the next full moon, the raiding time Da had always favored.

The air grew cold, and with a 'good-night' for Liam, she sought the warmth of her bed. But as she lay there, sleep eluded her. Truly, revenge would be sweet, but her heart remained heavy. And empty. Aye, she would take up her father's crusade, and glory in the doing, but could she not also win the man she loved? Granuaile had done so—marrying Donal while remaining a warrior in both heart and deed.

Yet how to win Owen? How to tear down the wall he'd erected around himself? She only knew what *not* to do. No trips to the village to seek him out where all could see, no standing close by him at Sunday Mass, or worse, going to his forge again in the night. What then? What?

After hours of restless tossing, a plan, simple and direct, came to her. She must be daft to have taken so long to see it, but now that she had, she resolved to waste no more precious time setting it into action.

The next evening as she picked up the wooden bucket, Liam asked, "Where are you off to so late in the day?"

"I'm after mussels," she said. "If the tide is low, they'll be plentiful."

"A stew tomorrow?"

She nodded. At the door, to allay his suspicion, she

turned back. "Will you join me?"

"I'll sit for a while. The day's been long."

She let out a breath at the answer she'd expected—and wanted. She hurried away, the brisk salt breeze beckoning her toward the green hill sloping down to the rocky shore. On the stony path that ran to the water's edge, she slowed her pace. Even on her toughened soles, the way proved slippery, the rough, blackened pebbles tending to slide from under her feet.

Larger stones, some nearly boulders, towered on either side of the narrow pathway. Climbing among them years ago, Owen had fallen. The boulders had shifted, catching him fast in their grip, crushing the growth from his left calf and ankle.

'Twas a wonder Owen came back to this place, but if what she'd heard had truth in it, he swam here nearly every evening in summer, at dusk when his day's work ended.

The briny smell grew stronger. Her step quickened, and she slipped and slid the rest of the way until her ankles were awash in cold water. The tide surged high. No shellfish would she get this night.

She dropped the bucket and focused on the sea. With her eyes never leaving the water, she held up her skirt, ignoring the wet hem dripping down her legs. She paced along the shore, picking her way with her toes, letting them find the smooth stones that wouldn't bedevil her soles. A dark head is what she searched for, black hair slick with sea water and strong, sweeping arms.

Nothing.

A few paces from the wave's lapping, she chose a spot that looked dry and sat gingerly among the pebbles, hoping her bottom would find some that were smooth and rounded, worn by eons of rubbing against each other. By eons of caresses.

*Such a foolish idea. What brought that to mind?*

As if in answer, pebbles flew up from the path knocking against each other as they rolled down the slope. Someone was coming!

She lay down on the stony shore, trying to be as invisible as possible. With luck, the visitor would be Owen, and with more luck, he wouldn't see her right off.

She rolled onto her side facing the sound. 'Twas him!

Clumsy with hurrying, he scrambled into sight. At the water's edge, not wasting a second, he began stripping off his clothes. He pulled his shirt over his head before sitting to remove his boots, the high wooden one first then the other, and stood to shrug off his breeches. She gasped at what no one had seen since his childhood. His left leg, the thigh strong and intact, had withered below the knee to little more than a slender bone housed within a coating of scarred flesh.

He turned and she gasped again. Clearly, nothing had harmed him *there*. With his white buttocks facing the shore, he limped into the sea. When the water came up to his hips, he dove, his arms cutting through the cresting waves.

Fascinated, Grace eased herself up on her elbows and watched. Keeping a steady pace, he rode the water out so far and so deep she feared he would drown. Just as she was about to leap up and scream out a warning, he swam back toward shore where he lay floating on the surface like a sea otter for long, endless minutes.

*Will he never come out? Will he stay until the cold seeps right through to his center?*

She pulled herself upright. He wouldn't see her. Engrossed in a freedom impossible for him on land, he wouldn't be caring who might be about. In the water, he was whole and could move with ease. That had to be the reason he dove into the chilling deep. None of the villagers went into that cold, salt water on purpose, only if their curraghs failed, or a wave swept them, cursing, overboard. But here was Owen loving it.

Why should she not as well? Excited, she stripped off her garments as he'd done. Once free of her clothes, she eased her way into the sea. She let it lap at her

ankles and calves and thighs, let it come up to her waist
before diving into the surf with a cry of shocked surprise
at the frigid touch of it. Within seconds, the water no
longer felt cold but delicious, like silk she imagined,
smooth and clinging, yet light as air.

Air! Suddenly her lungs were bursting. Try as she
might she couldn't feel the stony bottom or upright
herself against the current. It sucked at her, keeping her
submerged. Frantic, she opened her eyes to the salt
sting, but saw only a liquid green haze. She had nothing
to cling to, nothing she could grasp to pull herself up to
the surface. Death awaited her in this cold, silken grave,
and she fought the water as if it were a wild beast,
flailing against it, kicking out. Her effort gained her one
quick shot up to the surface. She took in a hasty gulp of
air and went down again covered over, hidden from
view. The green veil enveloping her began to turn black.

Out of the sea, an arm seized her in a hard grip,
lifting her up, up to the blessed air. She spat out the
brine, then inhaled in great, shuddering gulps.
Suspended in the water, Owen kept them both afloat
until her breathing gradually slowed to an even, steady
rhythm.

His grip still tight about her, he said close in her ear,
"You damned fool. You could have drowned. What in
the name of God were you thinking?"

She couldn't turn in his grasp to face him, nor did
she want to. His scowl would be in place topped with his
anger. That display she could do without, but not the
strong arm holding her from death or the heat flowing
from him despite the cold of the water.

He moved toward the shore, towing her behind him.
Like so much baggage, she thought, once the fear passed
and she knew she would be safe. Using his free arm, he
swam with powerful strokes, the muscles in his back
pressing against her, his body as he kicked, touching
and retouching her own.

She began to relax, enjoying sensations she'd never
known. Too soon he stopped, in chest-high surf, and let

her go. She cried out at the sudden release, but her toes felt the slippery stone bottom. She righted herself and, with her breasts skimming the top of the water, stood facing him.

Except for the night at his forge, they'd never been so close. She could see the stubble on his chin and his white teeth before his lips clamped together. His dark eyes bore into her. "You damn near drowned out there. Never do that again. I might not be here the next time."

Her breath, so newly even and steady, started up ragged again. Did the man have no knowledge of why she'd risked herself? None at all? Pig-headed he was, for fair. As she went to move away from him, her feet slipped on the stones. He reached out and grabbed her wrist, steadying her.

"Why?" he asked.

"Why what?"

"I'll not repeat my question."

Dusk had nearly ended. Soon the night would begin to settle in around them. Exposed to the air, her shoulders and arms erupted into goose flesh. She shivered.

"We can stand here all night if you prefer," he said.

She stared into his eyes, but didn't answer. There had to be a jewel the exact color as his eyes, but for the life of her she couldn't name it. Here they stood, naked in each other's arms, veiled only by the water of the great ocean swirling about them, and his sole reaction was anger. Again she could be his for the taking, but again he was refusing her gift. Her chin jutted up. She said nothing.

"You saw me." He released her wrist.

She nodded, silent and shivering.

"You saw me go into the water. You saw it, then."

She grinned. "I did, indeed."

His scowl deepened.

"Is there no humor in you, man?"

"None where you're concerned. Go and dress yourself. I'll swim a while longer."

She didn't move.

"Go, I'll turn my back."

"You needn't look away from the sight of me, Owen O'Donnell." Her chin rose up and so did her voice. "I'm proud of the body God gave me."

"As you should be." His eyes glanced off her breasts before he turned and headed out to the deep water.

# CHAPTER FOUR

Grace shivered into her clothes. Eager to be warm again, she pulled them on over her wet skin. The sky had begun to grow dark. Before long, it would be lit only by the crescent moon and the stars and the dim white waves looming in from the deep. Though she soon felt warm enough to climb up the long slope to the cabin, she couldn't make her feet turn homeward and lingered on the sand, peering out over the ocean. What wondrous worlds lay beyond the horizon? In her whole lifetime, she would never know. Without a ship, it was impossible to sail the deep. With a shrug, she turned away.

She might as well go home. As she picked up her empty bucket and walked toward the path, she spotted a bundle crumpled on the shore. Owen's clothes! A devilish idea possessed her, making her smile. She'd hold his clothes in her hands and be waiting for him when he came out of the water. She could give him a merry chase along the shore and up the path to the soft grass, refusing to release his things until he caught her and held her.

Ah, no. The unfairness of it, the humiliation Owen would feel in front of her. She couldn't do that to him.

She glanced back over the water hoping he would come rising out of the waves like a sea god, but in the gathering dark she saw nothing. Only white waves crashing on shore. Finally, slowly, she wended her way home.

For a fortnight, though the air stayed warm and balmy, and though she visited the shore each evening, staying late and long, she caught no further sight of

Owen. Nor a bundle of clothing left piled on the shore.

The realization that she'd spoiled his pleasure in swimming filled her with shame. Very well. She'd make amends by staying away from his special stretch of beach. He needn't worry that she'd see his leg or any other part of him. She touched the sudden heat in her cheeks. What would his leg matter when they were lying down together? Hadn't he thought of that?

'Twas his pride again. The quality she loved most about him. It had given birth to his courage. And his scowl. She loved that, too.

If only she could convince him they belonged together. Even though his strength had saved her life, he saw himself as weak in her eyes. The problem was he'd not rescued her on his own two legs, but with his arms, in the water like a sea creature. Of course! He would have to prove himself on land, and she would have to think of a way he could.

Digging turnips alongside Liam, she hugged the insight to herself in silence, and in an hour, working feverishly, she pulled up more than she had all the morning long.

Once out of the ground, the harvest had to be put down in straw against the cold and the verminous wee animals bent on survival, too. She feared this year's crop wouldn't be as plentiful as last year's when both Liam and Da had worked the land together.

At day's end, Liam piled up the mound. It did indeed look smaller to her than the previous year's. And that yield had been smaller than the season before. She watched him, frowning.

"Liam, small men make small sons, it seems to me. Could the same be true for turnips? So many of them are runted. If we let the field lie fallow for a year, next season it might produce a better crop. 'Tis worth a—"

Liam stopped his sorting and glared at her. "This is men's work, lass."

"It would seem—"

"Your work is waiting in the house. I'll finish here."

"But—"

Liam bent over the pile again. He'd not change his thinking any more than he'd helped Da defy the patrol. She tensed at the thought of the patrol, yet wouldn't give in to the stab of anxiety waiting to slice into her. The moon would be at the full this night. The time had come to make a strike in Da's memory.

She filled her apron with enough of the new turnips for their next meal. Boiled with onions and carrots, they would make a fine dinner. Judging from the year's yield, she doubted it would last until the next crop came in. And almost for a certainty the following year's harvest would be smaller yet again.

All the more need for a poacher's skill.

\* \* \*

The moon had traveled high into the sky, its light clear and unshrouded by clouds or rain. Grace silently made her way from tree to tree. The old hollow oak in the center of the copse held her bow and the sheaf of arrows Da had made for her—the bow he'd matched to her height and the reach of her arm. Each arrow he'd carefully weighted to give it a long, straight flight to its mark. 'Twas a noble gift, one no other woman of her acquaintance possessed, and she treasured it.

When she reached the old oak, she paused, listening. Only the soft woodland sounds of night came to her. The hoot of an owl, the whisper of the leaves. Nothing untoward.

She withdrew the canvas case from the hollow trunk, removing from it the sleek yew wood bow and one arrow. One would do. There would only be time for a single shot, for the deer were fleet of foot and quick to panic.

She moved from the tree to a low stand of underbrush and crouched, waiting. This was the difficult part. The quiet patience, the struggle to stay awake in the predawn stillness, but she'd taken her vow and wait she would.

The sun had begun its ascent, fading the moon into

obscurity, when she spied a young buck. He stepped lightly between the trees, an easy shot. Grace stood noiselessly and took careful aim. *Guide my arm, Granuaile.* With one fluid motion she let fly and the arrow plunged into the deer's throat. Down he went, bringing the underbrush with him. Stretched out on the ground, he lay still, hers for the taking. Granuaile had heard her plea. There'd be meat aplenty to share with the villagers. Da would be pleased if he knew. And Lord Rushmount furious. Both thoughts made her smile.

As she hastened to her prize and pulled her arrow free, she heard male voices moving in her direction.

"I heard something, Frazer. This way!"

With weapon in hand she fled, as silent as the deer she'd taken and just as quickly lost.

* * *

"Will you stay out and look at the sunset, Liam?" she asked the next evening. "I'm after a good wash. I have the soil from the fields in every crease of my skin."

"You worked hard all the week long." He went outside with his pipe to take his ease on the stone step and watch the sun fade.

Grace closed the cottage door. How long would Liam be content to sit alone without the comfort of his own woman? If he didn't have a sister to provide for, he could afford to take a wife and start a family. With sons to help him, the fields would produce more. And as of yet, her skills as a poacher had produced nothing, she acknowledged ruefully.

Last night, in her first attempt, she'd barely escaped with her own skin, though the deer had not. In the brief glimpse of him she'd had before Rushmount's men were nearly upon her, she'd known him to be beautiful. A pity to take his life. Even worse that his death served no purpose for her people. Undoubtedly, the gamekeeper had brought him to Rushmount Manor. Aye, the beast wouldn't be wasted. His lordship's men would feast well on her work of last night. The thought would drive her mad if she dwelled on it.

She sighed out loud in the cabin's quiet gloom. Her first mission had failed. Was she destined to be nothing more than a burden then? The question hung in the silent room as she stood still, the wet washrag forgotten in her hand dripping cold water down the front of her shift. After a moment, her back stiffened and she flung the rag into the bucket. No, she was not a failure. She was Grace the Fair, a gift for a man too stubborn to take it when offered. And a good shot who would try again!

The water in the kettle began to boil. She added it to the wooden wash bucket sorry she didn't have enough to sink into and cover herself from head to toe.

The night she'd bathed in the ocean every inch of her had been submerged. Not wanting to invade Owen's private place and his pleasure in swimming, would she ever feel that again? She wanted to. And she'd give anything to be in his arms once more—the two of them lapped by the waves, far removed from the toil and dirt of the fields. And their clothes.

With a scrap of rag and the sliver of lye soap she hoarded from week to week, she ran her hands over herself rubbing off the fatigue and the traces of soil, readying for Sunday Mass...readying for Owen O'Donnell.

Liam rose early the next morning, working his hair flat to his scalp with a comb before raking it through his lip hair, then donning the clean shirt she'd washed for him earlier in the week.

"Will you be strolling by for Brigit Fallon on your way to Mass?" Grace teased.

He grinned then walked off alone, not inviting her to join him. A robust, hearty lass with long, brown hair and a high, rosy color to her cheeks, Brigit would be good for him and for the farm as well. She would cause him to smile more often, and work by his side and, in time, God willing, bear him strong sons.

After Liam disappeared from sight Grace picked up her shawl and left for St. Mary's. A small church in the center of the village, it would be crowded with the faithful. Now that Cromwell had met his fate and Charles II sat on England's throne, worship had become easier. Lord Rushmount had restored the church roof Cromwell's troops had burned and allowed Father Joyce to practice the faith openly. Fine gestures that did little to fill empty bellies, she thought, bitterness rising again.

Grace slowed her pace to a leisurely stroll down the lane. She didn't want to be early, before the church filled up or the altar boy lit the tapers for Mass.

Just moments before Father Joyce strode out from the sacristy, she slipped into the church undetected and bowed her head in prayer. As she blessed herself, she spied Owen's craggy, unsmiling profile two rows ahead. She stared at his dark, unhappy face. What a difficult, troubled man he was. Still her heart leaped at the sight of him.

As the priest, accompanied by the Doyle boys, began Mass, the parishioners riveted their attention on the altar. Grace suffered through the service impatiently, her eyes never leaving Owen's well-shaped head and broad shoulders.

Before the final blessing, Owen left church, his wooden boot though softened by a leather sole reverberating on the floor's stone pavers. No one, not even Father Joyce, looked to see the source of the noise. It was only Owen O'Donnell departing with his usual awkward haste. Since boyhood, he'd walked out before the last prayer refusing to limp down the length of the village in the sight of all, falling behind as his neighbors hurried past him.

She waited until the congregation stood with heads bowed for the blessing, then followed Owen out of St. Mary's, taking the path he always took, the one leading from the nave to the old graveyard. Some of the markers on the gentry graves had tilted with age, and more than a few had fallen and lay flat, their names and death dates no longer visible. Only an unshaped lump of stone marked Mam's resting place, but Grace would never forget its location.

Each Sunday after Mass she knelt to say an *Ave* by the grave. But not this morning. "Forgive me, Mam," Grace murmured as she hurried along the side of the church without stopping. This morning belonged to the living. Mam would understand.

Owen's gait might be ungainly—she could see his shoulders heaving as he moved—but he covered the space fast enough to make her hurry her step. At the copse beyond the open meadow, he disappeared between the trees, and she ran to catch up. None of the other villagers took this route home, only Owen. God, he was stubborn. She stubbed her toe on a stone, but continued to stumble after him.

Why didn't the man take a civilized path like everyone else? Because he wasn't like everyone else. He was different, better. He'd already proven that, though not to himself.

Maybe he'd buried Da in these woods. Would he ever tell her? Some day, she vowed. A few paces ahead she caught a glimpse of him, his glossy black hair tumbled down to his collar. The trees here were thick, the low branches reaching out to tangle in her shawl or snatch at her hair.

She was gaining on him. A little deeper into the trees, a step or two more and she'd call out. When he turned to face her, she'd pretend to faint. Down she would go fast as a thrown rock and lay there like one of the dead until he came to her rescue. For surely he wouldn't leave a helpless woman alone in this isolated place. Anything could happen to her here. His conscience would never allow it.

After he bent over her desperately trying to rouse her—and she'd make that very difficult for him, keep her eyes closed, her body limp—he'd have to touch her and hold her. When she felt his arms around her, she'd moan a little, reach for him, and with only the space of a heartbeat between them, she'd slowly open her eyes. Before he knew what had happened, she would kiss him full on the lips. And she'd not let go. The work in the fields had made her strong, too. She'd hold him to her until—

Now! She'd call out his name now!

She didn't see it coming. Too late the branch she'd shoved out of her way snapped back with a vengeance. Like a whip in a malevolent hand it struck her head a fierce blow. She cried out, just once, in surprise and pain, then fell to the ground, the bright morning a void around her.

\* \* \*

Owen heard a strange outcry and whirled to face it. Wolves were rare, but a wild dog might have followed him. And he without a stick or a weapon to defend himself. A dead branch that looked stout enough lay near his foot. He picked it up and stood motionless. The sound didn't come again, but he'd heard something. A cry out of the ordinary.

Armed with the stick, every sense alert, he retraced his steps. And then he saw her.

*Oh my God!*

He dropped the stick and hurried to where she lay. For it could be no one else but Grace. That flowing hair was unmistakable, like sunlight shining brighter than the crucifix in St. Mary's or the lighted candles on the altar. It drew him, that shining hair. He always saw it first, and her smile and...

She lay face down as if she'd been struck from behind. But by what? He saw no weapon, no animal about. A wren trilled from a branch, then the copse returned to its silence. Had she tripped? Did she ail?

He knelt beside her, feeling the rise of a hot spurt of anger. What the devil was she doing here in the woods? Following him? What perversity would cause her to do that? She'd seen him truly as he stumbled into the sea. How pathetic he must have looked to her eyes. The thought of it ate at him like acid. So why was she here, knowing what she knew?

She hadn't stirred. He reached out to her hair, stroking it gently. It felt crisp and alive under his hand.

It clung to him, the curls wrapping themselves around his fingers. But his caress caused no stirring. She didn't move at all.

He took her shoulders in his hands and turned her onto her back. Her beautiful face was scratched; the damp remains of fallen leaves clung to one cheek. He brushed them off. He'd never seen her so still, so white and quiet. Always, when she came near, the flash of her green eyes filled his vision. He wanted that green fire now as proof she was unhurt. But she lay as motionless as the dead.

Ah, surely not. To be certain, he lay his head on her breast. Its softness beneath her clothes cushioned him as he listened. He could stay there forever he realized, and then he heard the steady beat of her heart. The sound thrilled him. Like music it was. Elated, he raised her in his arms and held her against him willing her back to consciousness, willing her to awaken to him.

With his upper body swaying to a new, unknown rhythm he rocked her, crooning unintelligible sounds to try and reach her through the hurt. He held heaven in his arms, everything he longed for. But she could never be his. He'd not allow himself to even consider the possibility. Why tempt a starving man with the food that would save him and then snatch it away without giving him a taste?

A taste is what he wanted, just one. He lowered his face to hers. Her mouth had parted slightly, inviting him. No, he couldn't. Lower, lower he bent until he touched the satin of her cheek with his lips and found he had to have more than a single taste. He kissed her cheek again gently, ever so gently.

That brief contact, sweeter than any he'd ever known, still wasn't enough, not with her limp and unfeeling. In the kiss he'd dreamed of, God help him, she met him fully, her passion as powerful as his own. He must be a fool for letting sleep bring her to him that way. She would never want him, Owen the cripple.

He looked down at her pale face. If only she would

open her eyes and come back to her senses...but when she did, would she recoil at his touch at finding herself held to him?

The night in the sea had been an accident. She'd thought herself alone and had taken a mighty risk in the undertow. The little fool. Thank God he'd been there. Again he bent and grazed the scratches on her soft cheek with his lips. These stolen moments had to last a lifetime.

He brushed her hair from her forehead. She felt nothing, not his lips, not his warm breath, not his hands. Oh God. He clutched her tight, frightened for her. A blow to the head could be death dealing. The horror of that possibility overcame him. Anything but that. Let her live with another man, let her love him with every fiber of her being, but let her live. Lord, let her live.

"*S gra geal mo chroi thu, mo mhurnin.* You're the bright love of my life, darling...*mavourneen... mavourneen*...darling...darling.

* * *

As if from a far country Grace heard a voice murmuring to her, calling her beloved, using all the love words she'd ever dreamed of hearing. She wanted nothing, not even the opening of her eyes, to interfere with that voice so deep and anguished and filled with longing. She lay motionless in Owen's arms letting his love enter her soul.

His fingers touched her hair, his hand trembling as he stroked it back from her face. Could this man of iron fear she was badly hurt, dying mayhap? In truth she'd never felt so alive.

This couldn't continue. She opened her eyes right into Owen O'Donnell's dark gaze. "You love me."

As if she were a hot coal, he dropped her from his grasp. "You're awake," he said and scowled. "For how long?"

"Long enough." She grinned up at him.

"You're fully recovered, I see. I'm a fool of a man."

"That is true," she said, the smile never leaving her.

He reared back ready to stand, but she reached up before he could and pulled him to her. The surprise took him off guard, and as he tumbled down, she locked her hands around his head. His mouth open and ready to protest was exactly what she wanted. The kisses the village lads had stolen from her had been instructive. She did as they'd done, let her tongue dart out and slide between Owen's parted lips. He rewarded her with a quick gasp. Before he could exhale or pull free, she increased the pressure. She kept her lips firm against his, her tongue soft.

He pulled away a little.

*Oh no!*

Then raising her, he put his arms around her, his hard blacksmith's arms, and gathered her to him, his mouth and lips commanding hers, kissing her over and over until she thought she'd go mad with joy.

No one had ever kissed her like this, each kiss a promise that another would follow, and another, and another without end. Finally, with a muttered oath he pushed her away and moved to get up from the ground beyond the reach of her eager mouth and hands.

"This is a crazed game," he said, raising himself to his feet. "Go home, Grace. Follow me no more."

He couldn't be saying this, not after the words she'd heard him murmur. What was the matter with the man? Was his pride so strong it would destroy both their lives?

Aye, unless she could convince him otherwise. Ignoring the soil and leaves that marred her skirt, she scrambled to her feet. Surprisingly swift on his legs, he turned from her, heading toward his forge on the other side of the copse.

"I love you, Owen O'Donnell," she said to his retreating back. "I love you. I always have, and now more than ever. Would you let your leg keep us apart? Is that all you are, a crippled leg? You have nothing else to give me? Just that?"

In the quiet woods, her questions hung unanswered in the air. "You bloody arse." Her voice like a banshee's ripped into the silence. "It doesn't matter!"

He turned to face her. "It matters to me."

There was no reasoning with him, none at all. Grace sank to her knees. Tears came to her eyes filling them, running down her face into her neck. He would throw away everything with two open hands as if their being together, their longing, had no value.

She bent over and concealed her face in her skirt. Let her weeping be hidden. Only cowards cried at disappointment, no matter how bitter.

\* \* \*

The cursed leg did matter, Owen thought, as he stood wretched in the path his own feet had created through the woods. He wanted to come to her whole and intact, a man on two strong legs, or not at all.

*Not at all?*

Like one of the trees he remained rooted in place and, spellbound, watched her bowed head, her hair glinting in the sun. All he could see of the rest of her was a crumpled skirt and a shawl slipping from her shoulders.

He couldn't believe those tears were for him, but the proof lay before him. She was crying her eyes dry when only moments before she'd been wild in his arms.

*What do you want, Owen O'Donnell, your cold, hard-edged pride, or Grace beside you? Grace loving you?*

He needed to think no more. Good God, she was right. He *was* a bloody arse.

# CHAPTER FIVE

"Why me, lass?" Owen asked.

At the sound of his voice so close to where she sat crouched and huddled into herself, Grace looked up, startled.

"Why me?" he repeated and knelt before her. It was difficult for him to kneel, but he did so anyway.

She sniffed away her tears, swiping at the last few trailing down her cheeks. His finger went out to catch one as it dropped off her chin.

"I'm waiting," he said.

She took a steadying breath. The rest of her life depended on the next few words. They had to come out of her mouth entirely perfect. "Every man I know is a sheep that follows, but never leads," she began. "Except for one man, and that is you, Owen O'Donnell. All the sheep that come courting me have round, stout legs on them and withered spirits. They live in fear of the English. They accept everything. They protest nothing. What kind of man is that? Besides," she grinned over at him, "I've seen you stripped to the waist working the forge. 'Tis a powerful sight."

He grinned back. "You've seen quite a bit, I grant you."

As he took both her hands in his, a frown clouded his face once more. "I can't believe you want me."

Her tears threatened again. "Believe it. 'Tis the truest thing I've ever said."

He scrambled to his feet. "I have another question for you." This time he was smiling.

"Ask away."

"Do you wish to be a virgin on your wedding night?"

Grace raised an amazed, tear-stained face. "Indeed not. Do you?"

At that, he threw back his head and laughed, great gulps of laughter that amazed her even more than his question. She loved the sound and sight of his merriment. Since his childhood days, he'd seldom even smiled.

"You *are* a virgin, I'm certain of it," she added.

Again his laughter rang through the woods. "You're certain are you? Well, I'm not so certain you are."

"What!" Outrage brought her to her feet. Amusement crinkled the corners of Owen's eyes and lifted his mouth. "I've not had the lasses trying to seduce me. None except you." His expression threatened laughter again. "But you have the lads panting like dogs on a hot day. Maybe one has had success with you."

"You will never know that, Owen O'Donnell."

"You are mistaken. I will know today."

She put her hands on her hips letting the shawl fall to the ground unheeded. "Until this moment you wouldn't put a finger on any part of me, and now you, you, you—"

"Want my fingers everywhere," he finished.

"I am not sure, after all, that is what I want."

"Oh, but you are."

He stepped nearer. When she pretended to move away, he enclosed her in an embrace she couldn't escape and pressed her close. She felt his unmistakable arousal.

Despite their many attempts, she'd never allowed any of the lads to press themselves against her like this, and she glanced up at him, knowledge and uncertainty coming together in her face.

"You have seen me as I am," he said.

She nodded.

"So you know what I am and what I will never be."

"How can I know that if we're to stand here all day staring at each other? And doing nothing more."

Another laugh burst free from him. "God, what would life be like with a hellion like you?"

"Heaven on earth," she said, "no matter how much Father Joyce might deny it."

"And a bit of hell from time to time?"

"To make the heaven sweeter."

"Come," he said, picking up her shawl and placing it gently over her shoulders. "I know a place."

He took her hand and led her along a barely discernible trail through the oak grove. It lay in the direction of the shore. It must be the way he took on those nights he swam in the sea. Surely he didn't expect to swim today in the broad sunlight and the air chill with autumn.

"Where are you taking me?" she asked.

"Not to the forge. We could never slip in unnoticed." He turned suddenly and kissed her breathless. "Your good name would be sullied."

"*My* good name? What of yours?"

"That's not the way of things, and you know it."

"Bloody hell. It should be. Besides, since Da was killed my name is suspect."

"Not for the reason I have in mind." He gave her an impish smile that showed his white teeth. The turnabout in the man astonished her.

He grasped her hand again and moved forward, in his eagerness the awkward rhythm of his steps covering the ground rapidly. They came to the grassy slope above his stretch of beach and scrambled down the pebbled path to the shore. He moved quickly along its uneven surface, stumbling over rocks he ignored in his haste. Up ahead, the beach curved around a bluff and narrowed. He let go of her hand. "Follow me," he said. "'Tis not far."

A few feet beyond the curve, he stopped. "We're here."

It made no sense. "Where?" Grace asked.

He didn't answer, but pulled her along until they were halfway up the slope from the beach. Then he let go of her hand, disappeared behind a gorse hedge, and vanished from the face of the earth.

Grace peered into the thick shrubbery the wind had twisted into wild, unnatural shapes. From behind it, she heard Owen's muffled voice. "Come. I'm in here."

Following the sound, she squeezed into the small pocket of space between the gorse and the slope and then she saw it—an opening! A broad smile lit Owen's face as he helped her step down into the cave.

Light filtered through the branches, enough so she could see the place was dry and bare except for a blanket folded in a corner.

"I come here some nights to get warm after I swim. Sometimes I fall asleep." The grin left Owen's face, the old, familiar scowl replacing it. "I'm sorry 'tis not a feather bed." He didn't come closer or touch her. "There's time yet to change your mind. We do not have to—"

"Oh, but we do." Grace closed the distance between them and brought her mouth to his. When the kiss ended, before another could begin, her eyes sparked with mischief. "Are you afraid, then?"

Solemn, not matching her banter, he nodded. "Of how much I want you? It terrifies me how much I do."

He pulled her closer. As she had earlier in the woods, she felt the same hardness come between them. She remembered the night he went naked into the water and flushed, heated by the memory. She wanted it, that hardness.

His grasp on her tightened. With his mouth never leaving hers, his hands slid down her back locking their bodies together hip to hip.

She freed her lips from his kiss. "I feel you right well," she whispered.

He groaned and grasped her skirt, raising it until his hands encountered her bare flesh. He stroked her as if he never wanted to stop, but in moments, his breathing ragged, he let her skirt drop back to her ankles. Reaching behind him, he spread out the blanket before turning to her again.

"I saw you in the water, but dimly," he said. "Show

me, Grace."

An unexpected shyness took hold of her, and she hesitated.

In that moment, his hand reached out and caressed her breast. "Show me this."

Even through her clothes, she felt her nipples spring erect. His touch, the merest flick of his finger, meant that much. It wasn't to be denied.

All shyness gone, she tugged the linen waist out of her skirt, flung it to the ground and shrugged the shift off her shoulders and let it fall. Her uncovered breasts quivered before him. Then, as she wanted him to, he began to caress her.

A sound began deep in her throat as he stroked her. When he bent and pressed his open mouth to her breast, taking one nipple and then the other between his teeth, she gasped at the sensation that blazed its way to the cleft between her legs. His lips opened wider, and he began to suckle. She thought she would go mad if he stopped. Or if he continued. Either way, these emotions couldn't go on, not like this in an aroused torment she'd never dreamed possible.

She wrapped her arms around his head. "Don't stop," she whispered. "Oh God, stop."

He heard the anguish his mouth was causing and knew, despite her earlier bravado, that no one had ever evoked this volcano of feeling within her. And except for dreams and his own furtive touch, no one had caused the same tumult in him.

He fumbled for the string that held her skirt in place. She stayed his hand with her own. "I'll do it," she said. In an instant, the skirt and the shift beneath it fell away, and she stood proud and perfect, his for the seeing—and the touching and the taking.

"Now you," she said.

The cursed boot. That had to come off first. "Lie on the blanket," he said.

She obeyed, all the grace in the world in her movements.

Without taking his eyes from the sight of her spread out like a feast before him, he sat and pulled off his boots and stripped off his shirt and breeches. The leg didn't matter, he realized with a surge of joy. Grace, enthralled with the sight of his maleness, didn't so much as glance at his leg. *It doesn't matter!* The exultation of that filled him as he lay down and took her in his arms and began to teach them both what they most needed to learn.

* * *

Later, Owen raised himself on one elbow studying Grace's face as she lay by his side. Beautiful, she was, her skin so smooth, her lips full and slightly parted, the lashes fanning her cheeks like spikes of gold, her glorious hair. He reached out and wound an errant curl around a finger. How in the name of God had he ever won such a treasure?

His glance left her hair and moved back to her face. As if in response to his silent question, her lips opened wide in a smile that tore him in two.

"Your hair is like a halo around you," he said.

"Am I a saint then?" she asked, knowing the answer, but asking anyway.

"Thanks be to God, no!" He laughed and held her to him before giving her a soft feather of a kiss. The smile fled from his face.

"What is it now, Owen, that makes you frown? Is there no pleasing you?"

He'd been pleased to the depths of his soul, and she knew it. Bantering with him, urging his responses, making him smile, or better yet having him shout with delight would be the purpose of her life. She vowed from this day forward nothing else would ever be as important as turning his sorrows into joy. That and defying the yoke of the English oppressors would give her life purpose. Like Granuaile before her, she would live her time on earth to its fullest.

She reached up and stroked his cheek, the stubble across his jaw raking her fingers. "I'm waiting, Owen, to hear what troubles you."

His eyes, darker than ever, stared into her own. "I'm sorry I wasn't more skilled."

So that was it! She grinned up at him. "You soon will be."

\* \* \*

Owen awakened Grace from a sleep so sound she moaned in resistance.

"Come, lass, you need to get home. Liam will be watching for you."

Liam! She fought her way to consciousness an instant at a time. Once fully awake, she wanted to weep. With evening about to descend, the most wondrous day of her life had come to an end.

Owen had pulled on his breeches and sat beside her.

"Are you happy?" she asked.

He made no move to touch her, but his words uttered in a deep, quiet voice caressed her anew.

"I never knew such happiness. I never expected it. Not in this life. Or in any other." He turned from her slightly, showing her his craggy profile. "Now you know all there is to know," he said.

She shook her head. "Surely there is more I need to know."

"I love you," he said. "But you knew that already. You've known that for years."

"There's nothing like the telling, Owen. Nothing like the music of the words."

Would he ask her about her love for him? The silence gathered about them. No. She'd proven what lay in her heart, but he, too, should have the spoken words. "I love you, Owen," she whispered.

"You're daft, lass. Which means I'm in love with a mad woman. Is there no reasoning with you?"

"None at all." She loved having the humor flare up between them.

Her clothes lay in a heap on the cave floor. She stood and shrugged into them.

"You must cover your hair and your waist with your

shawl," Owen said. "Few know of this place, and now more than ever, I want no company here."

"You're not coming with me?"

"I'll have a swim before I go home."

She shivered and pulled her shawl tightly about her. "The water will be fearsome cold now."

As he got to his feet, she swore she could hear his smile. "'Tis just what I need—the cold. Besides, we shouldn't be seen together at this hour."

Why didn't he want to be seen with her? Surely they were as one now, married in the sight of God. What did the sight of anyone else matter?

Stung, she went to leave. She'd reached the mouth of the cave before he asked, "Tomorrow? In the evening?"

"Perhaps," she said, darting out before he could stop her.

# CHAPTER SIX

"**M**ay the devil take the man!"
Grace scrambled up the slope, fuming all the way. At the hill's crest she drew in a deep gulp of salty air and stood still for a moment letting the steady beat of the sea calm her.

By the shore a few reckless terns skittered ahead of the surf, ignoring the waves and the gulls screeching overhead. The last hour of sunlight gilded the water. Soon the moon would begin its ascent as it had done last night and the night before. But with the gamekeeper alerted to the poaching, she wouldn't risk another strike so soon. She'd let a few weeks go by, let the passage of time lull Rushmount's men into believing the defiance had ended. Then, when their vigilance had waned, she'd go hunting again.

She glanced down the slope. Owen had not yet emerged from the hidden cave, and she turned toward home. "Ah, Lord knows I don't mean for the devil to have him," she said, blessing herself to ward off the evil. "I love him so."

A damp breeze came blowing raw across the fields. She clutched her shawl against the chill. Her magical afternoon over, she'd best get back to Liam.

Once on the path for home she let her mind play with a reason for her long absence. One that would satisfy her brother. The simpler the tale the better—no fancy lies.

Sickness had visited the village of late. It always came with the changing seasons, an ague that brought misery along with it. She'd tell Liam she'd lingered to nurse Gram O'Neill. Quickly, she blessed herself again.

*In ainm an Athair, agus an Mhic, agus an Spirid Naomtha, Amen* In the name of the Father, and of the Son, and of the Holy Spirit. Amen. That would keep the evil from her despite the lie.

And she would meet with Owen again tomorrow. How could she not? He was her life. This time she'd bring along the blanket that had been Da's and wrap a bit of food in it...for after...they had much to talk about and to plan for. Heartened, she increased her step, so caught up in her dream world she didn't hear the carriage in the distance.

\* \* \*

Sir Ross, Lord Rushmount to all but his intimates, craned his neck out of the swaying carriage. Could they go no faster?

He peered up at his liveried driver, a recent Dublin hireling, his face coarsened by the elements and by drink, no doubt, although he'd been sober enough when they'd left Dublin.

"Put it to them, man!" Rushmount shouted. "Faster! My lady is fatigued."

The lout muttered and flicked his whip over the horses' straining backs. The lazy scut. All of them useless good for nothings. What a mongrel race these Irish!

Ross drew back into the carriage. He'd overlook the man's insolence—this time—pretend all was well and under his control, but the small prick of insubordination irritated him.

He masked his rising anger with a smile. His bride, Lady Anne, returned his smile, her wan, pale face strained white. He took her hand in its sleek traveling glove.

"Not long now, my dear. I've persuaded the driver to hurry, so we shall see Rushmount Manor sooner than you think. I can hardly wait to show it to you."

"We're bouncing so hard I fear my very bones will shatter," she said, her voice an exhausted thread of sound that trailed off into a sigh.

"It's these cursed Irish roads. We could travel more slowly, of course, but I'm anxious to get you home and into our own bed this night."

Her face paled even more.

Hell's fire! Who would have thought an aristocrat's daughter could be so fragile? And with William the Conqueror's blood flowing in her veins.

Ross forced his frustration away and concentrated on Anne's delicate beauty, which, along with her dowry and her well-connected family, had propelled him into marriage. As well as the need for a son and heir.

Under his gaze, she flushed, the blood flooding her cheeks with pink, and turned away to stare out at the green landscape.

"My dear," he began, "you are so lovely. "

She said nothing, but closed her eyes and leaned against the cushions. Her breasts partially hidden by the fichu of lace tucked into her bodice rose and fell with each breath.

Ross reached out and placed a hand on her quivering flesh. "Anne."

She recoiled at his touch, pressing further into the cushions, inching away into the corner.

All the irritations of the journey—the lurching of the ship in the rough sea, the revolting food, the driver's insolence, the rutted, nearly impassable road, and above all, this frightened woman—came together in a red haze behind his eyes. Under the law she belonged to him, and by God he would have her. Enough of delicacy and swooning. He would...

His outrage went no further. Without warning, the carriage careened into a crater. The sudden jarring flung Lord Rushmount against the door and knocked Lady Anne to the floor in a flurry of silken garments. She screamed once and then lay still.

He fell to his knees in the jolting space and went to lift her to him. As he reached down for her, the carriage hit another rut. Judging from the vicious shock, a crater larger than the last.

At this rate, the driver would break a wheel or worse, an axle, the stupid fool.

Anne moaned. Ross cradled her in his arms. By God, this was the closest he'd gotten to her since they'd left England. Too bad he couldn't take advantage of the moment, but the carriage continued its madcap pace as if the driver had lost all control.

Ross eased Anne back to the floor and for the second time in a fistful of minutes thrust his head and shoulders out the open carriage windows.

"Slow down, you fool," he shouted. "You'll destroy the carriage and all of us with it!"

"I cannot!" the driver shouted back. "The horses have gone mad."

"You whipped them too hard," Ross called into the wind, cursing himself for trusting an unknown servant in his haste to get Anne home and bedded. Her slim, white body had been hidden from him too long. It belonged to him now. He wanted it. And soon. His anger mounting, he called out again. "Rein them hard. They'll give way."

The man, his arms straining at the reins, didn't answer. The frightened horses unused to savage beatings kept up a wild race desperate to escape the cause of their pain, galloping out of terror, out of mind.

It would take the strength of more than a single driver to halt them. A stab of fear slid through Rushmount as he bent down to Anne. They could be maimed or killed on this insane ride.

But if the steeds tired and gradually wound to a slow gait, all would be well. Then he would force the lout to halt, take over the reins himself, and leave the useless fool by the side of the road. The man could consider himself lucky to escape with his hide, never mind recompense.

If they'd traveled with his escort, this would never have happened, but the pace would have maddened him in his haste to possess this woman. She'd better be worth the trouble she'd caused.

She moaned. He heard her over the sound of the air rushing past, and the driver's shouts, and the frantic pounding of the hooves. Then with a sole scream of agony for warning, the horses careened to a stop as suddenly as if they had hit a brick wall.

Inside the small space, Ross and Anne were tossed from wall to wall like dice in a cup. Ross' head struck the ceiling, the opposite seat, then finally came to rest on the door handle. The pressure knocked him senseless and forced open the carriage door. Anne catapulted out the opening, sliding like a log down a slippery bank into the ditch beside the road.

*  *  *

The shrieking of a wounded animal tore Grace out of her reverie. *God in heaven, listen to that! The agonies of hell!* She lifted her skirt to her knees and ran toward the sound.

Two horses lay in a great tangle of flailing hooves and heaving withers. A chestnut, pinned under by the weight of its teammate, kept rearing its forelegs upward in a frantic attempt to free itself. To no avail. Its anguished cries mingled with the screams of the injured roan. Altogether, the worst sound Grace had ever heard.

The poor creatures. As much as she wanted to, she couldn't quiet them or help their pain. She rounded the place where they'd fallen, putting a distance between herself and the powerful thrusts of their limbs. With one clean shot from her bow, she could at least put the roan out of its misery, but her weapon lay hidden in the hollow oak, a far distance, and to use it here would be to give herself away entirely. But use it she would if she could, anything to end that unholy screaming.

Briefly, a vision of the buck she'd taken flooded her mind. He'd fallen gracefully, giving himself up almost like a gift to her. How unfortunate his lordship's game-keepers had come sniffing about before she could make good use of her kill. The next time she would be more cautious, more wary, so the meat could be distributed in the village before it was seized.

A few paces away a shiny black carriage adorned with gilt ornament lay on its side, its lead shafts snapped off by the crash. Two of its wheels whirled uselessly in the air. Another had flown off its axle and lay flat in the center of the lane. Ah, they must have been dashing along not knowing the autumn rains had worsened the ruts.

This was not a road for racing. What farmer hereabouts had a creature bold enough for that? None in Ballybanree, for sure, nor a high speed carriage, either. So the Englishman at Rushmount Manor—for this rig could belong to no other—was a fool as well as a usurper.

A groan deeper than the high pitched screams of the horses came from the edge of the road. "My head, my poor head. 'Tis knocked open."

No mistaking the lilt in that voice. He was one of their own. She hurried to the man. He sat with his knees bent, a gash spilling blood down onto his orange and green livery.

An Irishman dressed up like a tinker's monkey. Disgust filled Grace's throat, but she forced herself to ask, "Are you in one piece, man?"

"Who knows? It's been a devil of a ride. 'Go faster,' he says, 'go faster.'"

"Who says?"

"His Lordship."

"Rushmount? He's with you?"

The man nodded, too busy fingering his wound to answer.

Every instinct Grace possessed told her to travel on. Go home safe to Liam and leave the accursed Englishman to his fate. He'd hounded Da to his death. For that alone she would hate him until the day of her own death. But to leave with no one about to help him would be to act like a woman without a conscience. And she wasn't a woman without a conscience; she was an Irish lady. Bolstered with that certainty, she approached the toppled carriage and peered inside.

*Himself! Lord Rushmount.*

He lay crumpled and unmoving, his head on the floor, his long legs in high leather boots, beautiful, glossy boots, sprawled on the carriage seat. Too bad. She'd hoped he could put the injured horse out of its misery. Its screams of anguish continued on and on.

*'Twas enough to raise the dead. Where were the villagers? All deaf, unable to hear the unholy shrieks and come running with help? Or unwilling to?*

Just as Grace was about to climb through the upended carriage door, she spotted a figure lying in the ditch beside the road. A woman!

Ignoring the muck that would cling to her skirt, Grace slid down the bank and stared at the sight in front of her. She'd never seen a woman the like of this one, not up so close at any rate. A lady. An English lady. The worst kind. Grace bristled at the idea, but she couldn't leave her helpless in the dirt.

"Lady," she whispered. "Madam."

No response.

"Mistress." What did one call a female member of the gentry?

She knelt by the woman's side and picked up a hand in a leather glove, a glove as thin as paper. She pulled it off, one finger at a time and began chafing the hand that lay limp and lifeless in her own.

If only she had a dash of cold water, something to sprinkle on the woman's face and the bosom half exposed under a piece of lace. It had to be lace. Grace eyed it with wonder. So that is what such finery looked like, a web of intricate threads as delicate as gossamer and the sky blue gown so slippery smooth, silk surely.

But the lady's shoes were what caught her attention and held it. The shoes of her dreams they were, with heels so high and buckles of silver.

*Ah, to have shoes so fine!*

The envy left her in an instant. For shame—people hurt, the horses in agony and herself enthralled with fripperies. She looked down at the lady. How could she stay so still through that horrific din? She began to pat the young woman's cheeks, her touch gentle, but firm.

God in heaven, what would she do if the woman remained unconscious? See to the man in the carriage. Perhaps he could help. The driver moaning by the road was useless. Even the screaming, flailing horses failed to rouse him from where he sat. But if neither passenger awoke, Grace would have to leave him here as a poor kind of guard and go to the village for help. 'Twas her Christian duty.

*  *  *

Ross opened his eyes and lifted his head off the carriage floor. The world had turned upside down. His head on the floor, his feet on the cushions. He pulled himself to a sitting position and fingered his throbbing skull. He felt a knot over his left temple. No wonder his head throbbed.

What was that maniacal sound? Like voices from a thousand hells. Oh my God, the horses! And Anne? Where was Anne?

He swung his legs off the upturned cushion. Ignoring the pain that flamed in his left arm, he scrambled out of the wreckage and glanced about frantically. He spotted her lying in a ditch with a peasant woman bent over her. He hesitated, but Anne would go nowhere for a moment or two, and the horses' agony had to be stopped.

Was the pistol he never traveled without still safe in the door pocket, or had it flown out of the carriage? He reached in and found it where he'd hidden it. With all the bouncing around and a ball ready to fire in the chamber, he was lucky the damned thing hadn't gone off. He cocked the breech and walked over to the horses.

Though desperate to be free, the chestnut appeared intact, but if its flailing continued, it would harm itself beyond repair. The roan couldn't be saved. Each time it reared up, its legs beating the air, it screamed.

*One shot to the head.* Ross took careful aim and squeezed. The report pierced the air, and with a shudder of release, the mare stilled.

*That ought to bring the natives running.* God knows, for once he wished to see them, filthy and savage though they were. The chestnut needed to be freed from the halters before it would have to be put out of its misery as well, but unless help came he would have to wait until the horse exhausted himself. Maybe then he could free him without being kicked to pieces.

The groans of the injured driver caught his attention, but for a second only.

*Anne.*

Ross whirled around and ran to the ditch. The peasant woman still hovered over Anne trying in some fashion to bring her to. The sight of this creature's hands on his wife when his own hands had hardly touched her infuriated him.

"What do you think you're doing?" he shouted. "Get away from her!"

As if he hadn't barked out an order, the woman didn't heed him in the slightest. Anne stirred, tossing her head from side to side and moaning in a low, lost voice. The woman began murmuring to her all the while chafing her hand between her own rough paws.

*Enough.*

Ross slid down into the bottom of the ditch. With his intact hand, he grabbed a fistful of the creature's hair and yanked. The woman yowled and fell back against the clay bank.

"Anne. Dearest." He knelt by her side. How bloodless she looked. Even her blonde hair released from its bonnet had gone pale in the gloaming light.

He'd never seen her less than perfectly groomed. Now she lay in a welter of tumbled skirts, her bonnet on the ground beside her, one glove on, one off. What of her rings? The wedding emerald had damn near cost him the price of a small farm, and that peasant had been...no, it still adorned her finger. Another moment or two and who knew what might have become of it?

Where had the woman gone? He turned to check,

and at the sight of her, his breath fled his body in a gasp of astonished surprise. An unkempt, disheveled girl—with dirty feet, her hair a disordered tangle of red curls and the most beautiful face he'd ever seen—glowered back at him. As if to verify her beauty, a final ray of sun shot down and quickened her glorious hair.

In that same instant, he wondered why red hair was so despised. *Because no one who matters has ever seen this girl.*

Her eyes appeared green. For some reason, he had to be certain. He lowered Anne's arm to her side, stood and stepped within inches of the girl. Yes, green and glaring at him.

Her lips were full, the lower lip rounded and the upper a perfect bow. A short, straight nose. Not *retrousse*, the London rage. And cheekbones sculpted high with no peasant fleshiness at all.

What of her teeth? Seldom were teeth straight and white. Perhaps they were flawed. If so, her perfection would crash into nothing. He hoped that would be the case. It wouldn't do for an untutored wench by the side of the road to outshine his Anne the way a star outshines a candle.

His resentment boiled anew. "Were you about to rob her?"

The girl leapt to her feet. In her height, too, she outstripped Anne. "I am not the thief here."

Her coarse gray skirt, marred with clumps of clay, swirled around her ankles as she scrambled up the bank to the roadbed. "Nor am I the murderer here!"

*The outrageous gall of the little savage. Didn't she know he had men punished for less?*

"You vixen!" he said. "There is no murderer here."

Her eyes spat green fire. "You're right about one thing. A vixen I am for certain. Like Granuaile before me." She threw back her head and laughed. In that instant, he saw her teeth were perfect.

*Who in blazes was Granuaile?*

Ross watched her stride away on bare feet, her back

as straight as an arrow. A strange thought came into his mind.

*All Irishmen are descended from kings.*

He'd never believed that, not for a second.

Anne stirred and mewled like a kitten. He turned back to her, his wife, a descendant of William the Conqueror.

# CHAPTER SEVEN

Noon and the crewel bed hangings still closed. With a stab of irritation Ross strode to the bedstead and flung open its draperies. Nestled in embroidered pillows, Anne moved slightly, but her eyes didn't so much as flutter.

She's pretending, he thought, feigning sleep, feigning illness. But why? The answer came fast, so obvious it galled him. Other than fighting him off, which he couldn't imagine her doing, pretending to ail kept him out of her bed as it had last night. He walked around to the other side of the four-poster and snapped open the hangings, then the heavy draperies that covered the windows, keeping the room enshrouded in darkness. A twist to the casement lock and it flew open. Good. The salt breeze would revive her.

At the sudden rush of air and light, Anne moaned and tugged the coverlet up to her eyes. "No, Ross, no," she murmured.

"Anne, it's late in the day. You must rouse yourself, my dear."

"I'm ill. I can't."

"Nonsense. You're not ill, and you must."

As she watched, her eyes wide blue, he shot the bolt on the chamber door. "It's time," he said.

By God, he'd never meant anything more in his life. A wife was for touching, a wife was for using, a wife was for... He pulled off his doublet and shirt and flung them over a chair. His boots next. Each one hit the floor unheeded, then his breeches. As he went to remove his smallclothes, he heard a cry of shocked disbelief from the center of the bed. He glanced over at her. Perhaps she'd leap up and try to flee, forcing him to pursue her about the room until he could topple her. That would add...but no. One look at Anne's eyes, all he could see of her, told him differently.

All right, then. He stripped naked and approached the bed. Her whimpers of fear had begun to excite him. He needed release. He needed an heir. He needed a wife.

He yanked at the coverings that hid Anne from his sight. Her blue eyes had looked their full on him. His turn, now.

Grasping her bed gown, he raised it to her chin.

\* \* \*

A pity he'd had to insist. Yet how else would the act have been accomplished? Through an age of tender wooing? That called for more patience than he possessed.

Beside him, Anne lay in an exhausted slumber. He gazed at her porcelain face, enjoying the sight of the breeding that revealed itself in the fineness of her features, in the delicacy of her bones, in the pale sheen of her hair. Above all, her breeding had shown itself earlier. She'd received him without complaint. Or enthusiasm. He knew she hadn't enjoyed the experience. While this first time didn't matter, what of future times? Would she always lie unmoving and lack-luster beneath him? Well bred even then?

A cold draft from the open window sent a shiver over his skin. If what he suspected became reality, he would have to seek compensations. That red-haired beauty with fire in her eyes could well be one.

Comforted, he eyed the ornate French clock on the mantelpiece. A wedding gift from Anne's cousins in Normandy. Those powerful cousins were now his as well. Without doubt, marriage had definite rewards. It was three by the clock. He tossed off the covers and got out of bed.

At the sudden cold, he saw Anne open her eyes then shut them as quickly. Ross had no intention of letting her revert to those pillows. Whether she knew it or not, her married life had begun in earnest.

"Time to get up, wife." He bent over her naked form, ignoring her attempt to cover herself with her arms, and dropped a gentle kiss on her forehead. "Your bed robe is on the chair. Let me help you into it. As soon as I'm dressed myself, I'll send your woman in. It's three o'clock. I'll expect you in my study at five. The estate manager will have gone by then, and we can share a glass by the fire."

Pleased by the domestic bliss the scene conjured up, he smiled as he helped Anne don her robe. "Shall I close the windows?" he asked.

Wordless, she nodded and tied the robe around herself. In her eyes, he read her new knowledge and her new fear of him.

She had no need to fear him. What had happened today had been necessary to their marriage. He trusted she wouldn't make him insist again. To test her, he caught her eyes with his own and held them fixed. She stared back but a few seconds before lowering her lids in submission.

No, willing or not willing, she would cooperate to the best of her ability. What that might be remained to be experienced. Nevertheless, his blood quickened in anticipation. Without wasting any time, he shrugged into the clothes he'd scattered about the room, pulled on his boots and, picking up a silver-backed brush from Anne's dressing table, smoothed his rumpled hair.

At the door, he paused. "Thank you, my dear. At five, then."

She managed a smile and a little incline of her head, causing her silver-blonde hair to dip forward and curtain her face from his view.

\* \* \*

While his lordship sprawled behind his mahogany desk, estate manager Connor Mann stood before it, a leather register clutched in his hands. Without an express invitation, he wouldn't dare sit in the brocade side chair facing the desk.

But he had no complaint to make about that or much else in his life. His expansive girth, as he knew, gave ample testimony to how well he fared in the employ of his Protestant English lord. Luckily, his father had had both the cattle wealth and the foresight to educate him with the Jesuits in Galway. They'd taught him to read and write in English, a most valuable tool for a man whose future lay with the conquerors.

To survive Cromwell's purges and retain his holdings, Connor had renounced his Catholic faith and had never regretted his decision. Church of Rome, Church of England, what did it matter in the overall scheme of things? The same God looked down on all— on the practical men like himself, and on the stubborn starvelings who refused to acknowledge the way the political winds blew.

Yet, despite his defection, as he faced his lord and master, a surge of the Catholic guilt he'd ingested with his mother's milk rose up and caught in his craw. "There is much to review, milord." He fumbled with the register pages searching for the latest entries.

"Have a seat, Con," Ross ordered.

He did as he was told and opened the book to what he knew Rushmount would want to discuss first. "Shall we begin with the rents, sir?"

Rushmount nodded.

"Most are current." He hated to go on.

"Oh? Not all?"

"The McElroy brothers couldn't meet the sum."

"Why not? Two strong men working a small piece of land. What's preventing them?"

Keeping his place in the ledger with one blunt finger, Connor got up and went over to a large wall map of the estate. He pointed to a tiny square on the north-west corner.

"This is their holding. It has the poorest soil in your entire demesne. They struggle morning to night, but—"

"What do you suggest? Eviction? New tenants?"

Connor had feared the threat of eviction would be his lordship's reaction. He resumed his seat. To hide any flow of hatred that might shine from his eyes, he lowered his face to the figures in the ledger.

"Ah, eviction. A harsh measure, if you'll pardon my saying so, milord. I know the parcel well. 'Tis not one others in the county would welcome."

"Well then?"

Connor took a deep breath. "Reduce the rent?"

"What!" Rushmount's fist pounded the desktop.

Startled, Connor loosened his grip on the ledger. It slipped from his fingers and thudded to the floor.

"Don't come to me with suggestions like that, Mann," Rushmount said. "Lower the rent for one tenant, they'll all be banging at my door for the same. I would rather evict and let the land lie fallow. In fact, that well may be the best solution. The fields have been overworked, no doubt. They might yield better after a time of rest. Like all of us, hmm?"

Connor nodded and picked up the book. "Better half a loaf than none, sir," he replied mildly.

"Hmmm." Rushmount drummed the desktop with his long, tapered fingers.

Connor felt beads of sweat stand up on his forehead, but the moment passed, and he swiped at the damp with a sleeve when his lordship said, "Very well. Add what is owed to next year's debt. We'll discuss this again in twelve months' time. What else do you have to tell me? There must be much to report. I've been off the estate for weeks."

He might as well have out with it. If he held back, it would be worth his hide. "There is news of a sort. A suspicion, no more."

"Ah, where there's smoke..."

"Several nights ago, in the woods to the north, your gamekeeper found evidence of poaching."

Alert, Rushmount leaned forward across the expanse of his desk. "Give me the details."

"Frazer and his men were scouting north of the

estate proper and came across a dead hart. Pierced in the throat it was. An arrow perhaps. Although Frazer can't be certain."

"An arrow! Clever. The thief didn't risk the noise of a shot."

"Apparently not, milord, although I doubt there is any such weaponry about the village."

Rushmount cleared his throat. "You're right, of course. Not even a snare...interesting...a good marksman would make a swift job of it. Far less chance of detection that way."

Connor studied his ledger as if it contained a solution to the poaching. It didn't, but one would be forthcoming he knew, and he dreaded hearing it. If he'd found the poached deer, he would have hidden it, then informed Owen O'Donnell of its whereabouts. Though not a poacher, Owen would be sure to know the man. Despite Owen's dour face and manner, the people trusted him.

He gripped the ledger tighter. The reason for their trust troubled him more than a little. Owen they saw as incorruptible. On the other hand, how his countrymen saw himself, he knew full well. But without despised Con Mann sitting here under the angry gaze of Lord Rushmount, their fate would be even harsher, whether they knew so or not. An Englishman in his position would be savage, while he tried to do good whenever possible, so long as it didn't compromise his own welfare.

His grip on the register loosened.

Lord Rushmount got up from his desk and walked over to the wall map. He put a finger on the forest area where the deer had been taken. "Here?"

"The very place."

"It abuts the Collins' plot, and the O'Flahertys', and," he peered closer, "yours, by God, Mann. Your older son, Hugh, farms that land now?"

"True, but—"

Rushmount turned from the map and went back to

his desk. A smile played at his lips. "My idea of jesting. The proximity of the fields has nothing to do with the theft. Who would shoot in his own backyard, hmm? My guess would be someone from the far side of Ballybanree to throw us off scent. What say you?"

"Astute, milord." Connor's hands were sweating. "As always."

"What happened to the deer?"

"Your men brought it here. It's been dressed and smoked."

"That's all well and good, but by God, this proves the O'Malley hanging was no deterrent. Will these people never learn?"

Connor cleared his throat. *Courage, Con, courage.* "They're hungry, sir. 'Twas a single deer only."

"Christ, you're on their side! Of course, you are!"

Rushmount stood, six feet of outrage in high, polished boots. He glared down at Connor and pointed a finger in his face. "You're a good steward, Mann. Don't force me to let you go. Understand this. The deer means nothing. The forests are full of them. But if this incident remains unpunished, there will be no end to the thieving and no fear in the hearts of these...these..."—he looked straight into Connor's eyes—"these *natives.* Without fear, how can I rule?"

Rushmount expected no answer, and Connor offered none. His courage had fled.

The man fell back into his chair. He lifted his feet, in the boots that were the envy of every man and boy in the village, to the desktop. "I'll send for Frazer when we're through. But first I want to hear the rest of what you have to tell. The revenues from the dairy, and the progress you've made draining that dank fen to the south, and whatever else has occurred in my absence."

For the next half-hour, Connor droned on. His figures were accurate; he knew that well enough. What had no part in his reporting was the occasional tub of butter or slab of cheese he took home, some of which he gave to the neediest of his neighbors.

He knew Lord Rushmount suspected a certain amount of such pilfering occurred. As long as Connor kept his take secret and small, his larder would remain well stocked and unchallenged. The pilfering was a part of his recompense and little enough for the thorough manner with which he kept the estate running and his lordship free for pleasanter occupations. Deer slaying, now, was a public act of defiance, a different matter altogether.

When the long, detailed recital of estate business ended, Lord Rushmount surprised him with a question.

"My bride, Lady Anne, has a request to make of you."

Connor tried not to let his jaw drop in surprise. He'd never met Lady Anne. What request could she possibly make of him? "Her ladyship has a request of me, milord?" he asked, his voice coming out of his throat in a squeak.

Ross laughed. "Yes, you. The night of the accident on the road, a local woman came to my lady's aid." He lifted his legs off the desk and stood, a signal that their meeting had ended.

Almost.

"The woman damaged her clothing trying to help. Lady Anne would like to replace it."

"Who is this woman, sir?"

"Ah, that's what we do not know."

"Then how—"

"You know everyone hereabouts. I can describe her." Connor nodded.

"Young, a mass of red-gold hair..."

"There are several redheads in Ballybanree." Ten years earlier even his hair had been red-toned.

"True enough, but this one had a face out of the ordinary and a temper to match."

*Out of the ordinary, be damned. She would have to be a stunner to catch his lordship's eye.*

"A beauty then? A red-haired beauty with the heart of a lion."

"That's it exactly. And another thing. She spoke to me in English, most boldly. Not in that damn barbaric tongue you all garble."

*Good God, the lass had challenged him!* "There is only one young woman who fits that description," Connor said. *The only one who has a face out of a dream.* "Grace O'Malley. From what you say, she could be none other."

Ross swept his arm toward the wall map. "Point out her family's plot. Lady Anne will want to know her whereabouts."

Connor put his forefinger on the O'Malley place and waited for the realization to sink in. It took only a moment before Rushmount looked at him with his mouth agape. "Christ, was her father Red Liam O'Malley? The one we hanged in the spring?"

"The same, sir."

# CHAPTER EIGHT

Ha! So he was to believe Lady Anne wanted to gift the O'Malley lass? Bloody unlikely.

Connor slogged his way across the rain-swept lawns, the cold wet lashing at him. Eager to get to his cottage on the edge of the estate, he quickened his pace. Like all such meetings, this one had left him drained. The ordeal over, he looked forward to his snug fire and the meal Kath would have waiting.

So the lass had harmed her skirts in aiding the lady of the manor? Since when had the occupants of the great stone house considered such trifles? The face of an angel the lass had, and whether that was a blessing from God or a curse, he was unable to tell. She needed to marry and soon. That would be her only salvation if his lordship tried to act on his fancy. And fancy her, he did. The gleam in his eye as he described her had the lust glow.

God, he couldn't blame the man for what he felt. Every man and lad in the county dreamed of possessing Grace O'Malley. She was the closest thing to a goddess anyone had ever seen.

Con crossed himself at the unbidden image. "Blessed Mother, forgive me," he muttered as he pushed open his cottage door. Strange how the old prayers never died away completely.

"Con!" Kath came to him as she always did, with a smile and a welcome. Whether her warmth was for him alone or the comforts his work provided, he couldn't determine. Nor did he care. He basked in those same comforts.

"Evening, Da." Young Con sat by the turf fire, a

pewter mug of ale already in hand. "Take my seat, Da, you look cold." Young Con got up and leaned against the mantel. "Was it the mists or his lordship that chilled you?"

"Both." Connor took the seat and stretched his hands toward the burning peat while he waited for Kath to serve him. "I have a task for you," he said to his son. "For Sunday next."

"More tasks, Da?"

"'Tis one you'll like. I want you to call on Grace O'Malley."

The light flew into the lad's eyes and gleamed there. Ah, Grace had the power! Let him try for her then, but Connor doubted she would have anything to do with him or his family. They worked for his lordship, whose ancestors had stolen, to her way of thinking, what had been O'Malley land. That the lass was right, he hadn't a doubt, but to what avail such hatreds? Of what benefit to recall the exploits of her pirate ancestress, Granuaile, who had run Elizabeth's navy ragged for a score of years? And then had turned on the Spanish. He grinned remembering the tale before shaking his head. Ireland had come to a sorry pass since that time, and Grace, for all her fiery spirit, had no fleet of ships to command, no way on earth to defy the powers that controlled them all. These days, it was better by far to eat well and live well.

If he continued to please his lordship, and he had every intention of doing so, in the natural order of things, Young Con would succeed him as estate manager. Grace would have no better chance at a good, decent life than one the Manns could provide. But in his bones, he knew she would be too stubborn to see that. He sighed aloud.

"You're that fatigued tonight?" Kath asked as she handed him his mug and a slab of buttered bread topped with a thick cut of cheese.

"No matter, but—"

"Something's afoot, Da. What is it?"

The lad was sharp as tongs on a pitchfork. He would

make an excellent bailiff some day. "Her ladyship wishes to send a gift to Grace."

"Jaysus! Whatever for?" Kath asked clearly stunned to her toes by such news.

He told her of the accidental meeting by the roadside.

"What is this gift?"

"A double length of cloth. Black wool of good quality."

Kath sucked in her cheeks. "A fine gift, indeed."

"And I'm to bring this cloth to Grace?" Young Con asked.

"That is my intent."

"I'll do it."

A smile played about Connor's lips. "The answer I expected, but there is more you should know."

Young Con waited while his father sipped at his ale and bit into the soft, buttered bread. Finally, impatient, he asked, "What more, Da?"

"Grace is sure to refuse the gift. You must convince her to accept it."

Kath snorted. "What woman would refuse a double length of fine wool?"

Connor took a long, satisfying swallow. "A woman the likes of this one."

"But why?" Kath asked.

"She is stubborn to a fault, Mam," Young Con said, the grin on his face taking the harshness from his words.

"And well worth the aggravation, aye?" Connor asked, leaning forward to give a slap to his son's thigh.

The lad reddened.

"Then win her, if you can. But as to this gift from his lordship, when she refuses, and she will,"—he shot a look at Kath that stilled her—"tell her it's in payment for a service rendered. Not a gift. A payment for her effort she might take. A gift from the English she will not."

Young Con's Sunday excursion would be more than a pleasant dalliance. Connor didn't have to tell him he couldn't go back to Lord Rushmount and say his ladyship's gift had been refused. Or lie and say it had been accepted if it hadn't. That would be courting dismissal. Grace had to keep the offering for the Mann family's sake, if not her own.

"More ale?" Kath asked.

Connor nodded and held out his mug. To his son he said, "On Sunday give Liam a warning and heed it yourself. Another deer's been taken. Rushmount's men will be patrolling the forests. Stay clear of the woods and tell Liam to do the same."

"I will that."

Connor got up and stretched his legs. Weary he was to the bone. He would go in to the bed earlier than usual and tomorrow tell his married son, Hugh, of the danger. 'Twould be a cautionary measure only. Life was too good for the Mann lads to risk it in poaching.

Liam O'Malley, on the other hand, had less to lose. Could he be following in his father's footsteps?

* * *

On Sunday next, Young Con stood outside the O'Malley's cottage door with a package under his arm. No one was about. In his eagerness to see Grace, he must have timed his arrival too early in the day. She and Liam would likely be at Mass at this hour. No matter, he would wait however long it took. He lowered himself to the stone slab in front of the door and watched the path for the first sight of her. Each minute went on for an hour, but finally the eternity ended, and she came toward her home at last. The walk of a queen she had, her head held high and glinting in the sunlight!

His heart pounding, he scrambled to his feet, hoping she would smile at him and greet him kindly.

She frowned when she saw him. "Young Con Mann, what brings you here today?"

He held out the paper packet securely tied with twine. "This," he said. "For you."

"What is it?"

"Payment for a job of work."

"Are you daft? I've done no work for you." The frown didn't leave her face, and she made no attempt to take the parcel from his hands.

At her tone and the stiff distance she kept between them, he knew he wouldn't be invited in to slake his thirst and have a bit of a visit. "This isn't from me. It's from Lady Rushmount."

"What!"

Her mouth that he'd dreamed of pressing to his own fell open. To kiss those parted lips now would be heaven. But he dared not. "'Tis true. Here, take it. It's yours."

"I take no gifts from the English."

"'Tis not a gift. You aided the woman and destroyed your clothes doing so. She is repaying you, that's all."

"The woman by the road?"

"The very one."

"My skirt brushed clean. I ruined nothing. Tell her ladyship so."

As Grace went to move past him, he reached out and seized her wrist. "You can't refuse."

Her look withered him. "Is there a law against that, too?"

He dropped her arm. For the first time since he could remember, he felt shame at his family's well-fed life. His full belly would cost him Grace. The contempt in her eyes told him so. He hadn't a chance with her, none at all.

"No law," he said, "but you can't refuse."

The shawl slipped down to her hips. She held it there with both hands, her elbows jutting out at her sides, her anger lighting her beauty like sparks touching coals.

*Oh God.*

"Why? Why can't I?" she asked.

"Lord Rushmount told my father to present you with this cloth. If you don't take it, 'twill reflect badly on Da. On my whole family."

"*Lord* Rushmount? I thought you said that Lady R-"

"Who knows for certain? Either way, my father cannot tell them you refused."

"And he dare not lie."

Miserable, he nodded.

"That would fail to please." She raised her chin. "Of what concern is that to me?"

She went for the latch. He didn't attempt to stop her, but before she could close the door on him, he said, "My father is a good man, Mistress O'Malley. He does much for the villagers, much that you have no knowledge of. Let him be replaced with another, an Englishman most likely, and life in Ballybanree will be harsher for all."

She stayed her hand and looked at him. He saw a glimmer of respect flash in her green eyes.

"There's more," he said. "Warn Liam. A poacher is about. The woods will be swarming with his lordship's men."

She pushed the door open, a sudden spurt of alarm coming into her face before vanishing as fast as it had appeared. "Liam is no poacher, but I thank you kindly for the warning. And for bringing her ladyship's payment."

She held out her hands. He put the brown paper parcel into them, but as he suspected, he received in return no offer of a mug of ale and a chat.

# CHAPTER NINE

Would her brother never return from Mass? Young Con had long gone, and the sun had passed its zenith. Still no sign of Liam. Deep into the afternoon, Grace ate her noon meal though it had turned cold. No matter, the skillet bread and the barley soup afloat with bits of cabbage satisfied even when not warm in the mouth.

After she and Owen were together as man and wife, she would discover all his favorite dishes and cook them for him. Some of her own favorites, too. She knew he would enjoy them as well, for they loved the same things. Alone at the trestle table, she felt the familiar heat rise in her cheeks at the very thought of him.

He'd be waiting for her in the cave, eager for her, and she for him, but she couldn't leave without warning Liam to stay clear of the woods, that Rushmount's men were searching for a new poacher. She'd tell Owen of it as well.

Both would wonder who the poacher might be, but never would they suspect the truth. And they must never know. Liam would be frightened for his life. And Owen for hers. It was her secret, and she would keep it for as long as her good fortune held. With heaven's help, that could be a long, long time.

True, she'd nearly been caught on her first try and her prize had been seized. But her next strike would be better planned, in a deeper part of the forest.

Just as she'd begun to despair of Liam's return, she heard voices outside the cottage and ran to the door. Liam, more animated than she'd ever seen him, walking hand in hand with Brigit Fallon. A love aura surrounded the two of them as clear as the halo around Saint Patrick himself.

When they saw Grace standing in the doorway, their chatter halted and their hands quickly parted company. Oh dear Mother, she'd invaded their private world and caused the magic to vanish. But she would intrude for a short while only. She longed to be off with Owen, to enter her own world of belonging.

"The meal's ready," she said to Liam. "There's enough for you as well, Brigit."

"We've eaten," Liam said. "Brigit's mam fed us at noon."

"Oh?"

Brigit nodded. "We had soda bread today. My mam's a good cook. I've learned much from her," she added before her voice went shy as if she'd overstepped herself.

Soda bread, however well baked, hadn't brought that happy pink color to Brigit's face. There would be news.

"Come in, come in," Grace said. "You must have room for tea at least. I have a few of the leaves left that Da brought home."

Liam took up Brigit's hand once again. "We're to be wed as soon as the banns are announced."

"In four weeks' time," Brigit said.

*Ah, of course.*

"How grand to have a sister as well as a brother," Grace said, hurrying to kiss Brigit's flushed cheek and embrace Liam. It was the first time they'd touched since she sobbed in his arms the night Da died. If the memory of that bitter night occurred to him, he didn't let on. Just as well. Let his happiness be as complete as possible. A person had little enough of it in life.

*Four weeks only.* Then she'd give up Da's bed in the second room to the newlyweds and sleep out in the main room by the fire. Brigit would take her place as woman of the house, as was right and proper. Nonetheless, now more than ever she needed to find a place of her own. She and Owen had been so happy living in their stolen moments they hadn't settled their future and set a time for marriage. But today, if Owen said nothing, she would speak of it.

She tugged Brigit away from Liam and drew her inside. "I have a wedding gift for you," she said. "Some fine woolen cloth. Come look."

The packet lay on the table. Grace unwrapped it and held up the length of material. It fell in a long, supple sweep to the floor. "See! There's enough for each of us to have a skirt."

Brigit gasped in delight. "A new skirt of unused wool!"

The pleasure on Brigit's face made Grace smile. "If we hurry with the sewing, we can have them ready for your wedding day."

A good thing, after all, that she'd swallowed her pride and taken the gift. For a gift it was, not a payment, and for every gift received one had to be given in return.

\* \* \*

Owen wasn't waiting in the cave. Grace sat alone on the blanket through the long gloaming hours into the full, chilling dark. Still, he didn't come. What could be keeping him away? Did he ail? Did he have work at the forge he couldn't leave? Only a dire emergency would keep him occupied an entire Sunday.

While she'd been delayed today with Liam and Brigit, had he come and gone? No, he wouldn't have done that. He would have waited for her, just as she would wait for him. Forever, if need be.

But as the night went on, she knew that whatever had happened, for now she must return home. With a bit of luck, Liam would be sound asleep and not stir when she crept in. At dawn, she'd go to Owen at the forge. The hours would be long until then, but running through the woods at night with Rushmount's men on the alert would be a stupid risk. She had too much to lose to be impatient. Somehow, no matter how difficult, she would bide her time till the cock crowed.

*  *  *

A feeble sun fingered the sky. Smoke meandering out of vent holes in the villagers' huts mingled in the air above the rooftops. The raw, cold November workday had begun.

Carefully, without making the sound of a mouse, Grace opened Owen's door and slipped inside the workshop. It took but a moment for her eyes to adjust to the dark. When they did, she blinked in disbelief at the cheerless space and shivered in the chill damp.

"Owen," she whispered. "Owen."

No answer. She glanced about. The firepit looked strangely different. She walked over to it.

*Merciful God, the coals are dead!*

She touched them gingerly, ready to pull back her hand the instant she felt heat, but the gray ashes coating her fingertips were cold.

*The fire has been out for hours.*

She ran to the curtain separating Owen's living quarters from his workshop and yanked it aside. As she feared, no dark head rested on the cot, no powerful form raised the blankets from the straw.

From the look of things, the bed, still neatly arranged, hadn't been slept in or a morning meal taken. What had happened to him? Whatever the answer, it wouldn't be a good one.

Frantic with foreboding, she paced the cold room. Surely he wouldn't swim in the sea in this weather. Oh God, may she perish for that thought. The forest, then. Resourceful and strong despite his leg, he could survive a mishap in the woods. But if his good leg had been injured, he might not be able to reach help.

Her shawl slipped from her shoulders and dropped to the earthen floor. She didn't stoop to pick it up. Where to go? Where to look? She could canvass the woods hereabouts, but he could be anywhere. She might not find him in time.

A keening voice startled her back to her senses. Wailing out her agony was she? For shame. That wouldn't help Owen. She needed to *think*.

The neighbors! Start there. Someone might know something. She ran out of the smithy, slamming the door behind her for all to hear. Let the village know she sought him. That didn't make a particle of difference now.

Still, no need to look like a wild woman. She retraced her steps, retrieved the shawl and wrapped it around herself. She'd make a calm, neighborly inquiry. There might be a pleasant reason for Owen's absence, although in her heart she doubted it.

At the first cabin with a smoke plume above its thatch, she knocked on the door. In due time, a thin-faced boy of five opened it and peered out.

"Noel Burke, please ask your mam to come to the door."

A tired woman, her hair threaded with gray, her body big with child, appeared behind the boy.

"Mary, I've come to the blacksmith, but he isn't there, and the forge is stone cold. Have you seen him?"

The woman shook her head. "My man said he was taken after the last Mass yesterday."

"Taken?"

"For questioning, Donal said. By Lord Rushmount's men. They're searching for a poacher."

"That would never be Owen O'Donnell."

"Not with that poor leg of his."

*No one sees Owen as I do. No one knows him as I do. Or loves him as I do.*

"Where did they take him?"

Mary shrugged. "That's all I heard tell of." The children behind her began to scuffle. "Will you come in and sit by the fire?"

"Another time, Mary. To see the new baby, perhaps."

Mary nodded wearily. "God willing, I'll birth this one in a fortnight or so."

"I'll be back then."

The mists had begun in earnest. Grace raised her shawl to her head and clutched it close. All warmth had left her.

Where could they be keeping him? Worse yet, what could they be doing to him? Her imagination consumed her with terror as she hurried away from the village.

Connor Mann, that toady to the English, would know what had happened to him, and somehow she'd persuade him to tell her what he knew.

Connor's holding lay close by his lordship's estate. A shortcut through the copse would be the fastest route. In the daylight hours, the patrol wouldn't stop a single woman hurrying on an errand. She put aside the worry. What mattered was to get rid of this burden of not knowing.

The trail through the woods soon gave way to the rutted road bordering the village and leading directly to Rushmount Manor. Within the hour, half walking, half running, Grace reached the start of the estate's broad gravel drive. Breathless with haste, she looked toward the huge limestone edifice at its end.

Silhouetted against the sky, its pale gray stones pierced with long glass windows sparkling in the light, the manor was the largest building she or anyone else in Ballybanree had ever seen the like of. Obscene in its splendor, the mansion filled her with disgust.

Built on O'Malley land it was, land stolen from her grandfathers and their fathers before them, stolen from her father and Liam and herself and from their future children. The ugly, cold pile of stone! She hated it.

What right had the English Henry and his daughter to reach out long arms and seize Ireland? And what right had Cromwell to maintain that theft? And a pox on Charles II. It mattered little that he professed belief in the Roman church. He'd brought no justice to her people.

Grace heaved a deep sigh. Such thoughts wouldn't help her find Owen this day. She moved on, keeping her shawl tight about her and staying near to the hedge lining the great lawn in front of the manor. The dairy was situated at the estate's southern end. Near it, Con and Kath and Young Con lived in a neat caretaker's cottage, far and away the finest one in Ballybanree.

Reading and writing had served Con well. With them as tools, he'd thrown in his lot with the English. Maybe Da had been right. Such skills bred discontent in those who possessed them. Still, she regretted—

"Halt! Stop, I say!"

Startled, Grace whirled around at the shouted command. Engrossed in thought, she hadn't heard the rider approach. Her grasp on her shawl loosened. It slipped off her hair to her shoulders. The horse was almost upon her!

\* \* \*

Ross Rushmount reined in the chestnut, his annoyance at the trespasser melting away as he looked at her. It was the girl from the road. Grace O'Malley, Connor Mann had called her, and as lovely as he remembered. He would play the game, act the courtier to this beauty in rags. Why not? He bowed slightly and touched the brim of his hat with his hand.

"Mistress Grace O'Malley, I believe."

After the initial surprise and the stab of fear he'd seen come into her eyes, she stood her ground, holding herself regally upright, graceful and confident as any high-born lady. Indeed, if he didn't know better, he would say she had the posture of a queen.

"You know my name, then," she said.

In her tone and her words, he detected none of the obsequiousness he'd come to expect from the natives. "And you speak my language."

"You already knew that."

The spark of defiance in the girl amused him. "You aided my wife the night of our unfortunate accident."

She nodded.

"My name is Ross, Lord Rushmount."

"I know who you are."

The mist, as the Irish called this damned perpetual damp, had soaked into the girl's clothes. She shivered. Except for the heavy shawl and low shoes made from what looked like moleskin, her clothes were the same as the night they'd met—a coarse linen waist and a worn skirt that couldn't possibly have come from the new cloth he'd sent to her.

Yet her radiance overcame the poverty of her clothing. A vision flashed into his head of a Grace O'Malley coifed and powdered and jeweled, wearing a gown of deep green, its low neckline revealing a dazzling expanse of flesh and full, white breasts. An emerald suspended between them.

"Did Connor Mann deliver my lady's gift?" he asked.

"Gift? You must mean the wool. 'Twas my understanding it was a payment."

"Payment?"

His puzzlement evaporated in an instant and he threw back his head and laughed. What a minx. A payment could be taken as dead-ended, a gift entailed an obligation. She was a clever girl. How he would enjoy having her return a gift to him. But he sobered quickly.

"I don't know what brings you here today, Mistress O'Malley, but for your kindness to my lady, I give you leave to trespass on my property."

She looked at him, her upturned face holding an emotion he couldn't read.

"How can I trespass on what is my own? This is O'Malley land. Our claim goes back hundreds of years. Long before King Henry. My da kept the ancient deeds that prove it."

Didn't she know he could run her over where she stood, crush her like a beetle, evict her from the land, ravish her, beat her, kill her?

As fast as the surge of anger arose, he as quickly tamped it down. She risked her life with those words and she knew it. What a woman stood before him! She would not lie limp and unfeeling in his bed. His jaw tightened. Nor would she triumph over him.

"What does this deed say, exactly?" he asked.

Silence.

"Have you read it?"

"The priest read it to us."

*Illiterate.*

A smile creased his face. He let her see it, let her know he knew. "Whatever the priest read to you is no longer valid, of course. English law has superseded it."

Christ. To think he would stoop to this dialogue with an illiterate peasant, however beautiful she might be. He increased his grip on the reins, ready to turn his mount and ride off.

"My lord?"

Her courteous tone pleased him.

"Mistress O'Malley." Once again, he touched his hand to his hat brim.

"I came to ask about your prisoner, Owen O'Donnell," she said.

"You know him?"

"I know him well."

"Ah, of course you do. You came to plead for him."

"He's no poacher."

"Do you know the man who is?"

She shook her head.

"Nor would you tell me if you did."

"I know of no such man."

"Yet you know this Owen O'Donnell is not the thief."

"On my father's soul, I swear he is not."

"I agree. The cripple didn't kill that deer."

"Cripple! He is more a man than anyone."

He glared down at her. What chances this girl took with him. Could she be enamored of this crippled blacksmith? Unlikely, but when they questioned the man, he'd shown the same stubborn pride.

"What is your interest in this Owen O'Donnell?"

"He's part of my family, a dear friend."

That was not the reason. She lied. He could see uncertainty in those green eyes. They were unused to concealing the truth.

"You've wasted a long walk, Grace O'Malley." He urged his mount forward. "The prisoner's been released."

He cantered off, taking with him the sight of the pure, unmistakable joy that had leapt into her face at his news. How ridiculous that it caused a spurt of envy to stab at him.

# CHAPTER TEN

So Owen had gone free.
And she couldn't read.

Waves of happiness and frustration washed over Grace, the emotions overlapping as they surged within her.

Love won out. Wet, angry and weary though she might be, having Owen alive mattered more than anything on earth. The reading would come later. Owen had a Bible. He could teach her to read. Side by side, they could pore over the words together in the evenings by the fire's glow.

His lordship's gift hadn't been the length of wool after all, but an insult that cut deep because she deserved it. To be enslaved by a vicious conqueror was one thing. To be enslaved by her own ignorance was another affair entirely. An ignorant lass she was in truth, but she wouldn't be so forever she vowed as she hurried back to Owen's forge.

Her resolve hardened with each step and helped her shrug off the weariness. On her way to the village, she took the shortcut through the woods, and faster than she would have thought possible, the forge loomed ahead. For the second time that day, she lifted the door latch, boldly this time, and walked in.

No burning fire greeted her with its warmth, but she hardly noticed. Beyond the curtain she'd parted earlier, she saw Owen seated at his table, his head propped in his hands.

"Owen?" He didn't lift his head. She stepped closer. "Owen?"

He raised a ravaged face, his dark skin as white as

death. She ran to him dropping on her knees next to his stool.

"They hurt you?"

"I am as intact as I will ever be."

"Then all is well. But you look so—"

"All is not well."

He made no move to touch her. She reached out to him. At the pressure of her fingers on his arm, he recoiled and got to his feet. He shifted his weight to his good right leg and leaned against the table.

On her knees, she asked, "My love, what is wrong?"

"The truth, Grace."

She pulled herself up onto a stool and sat waiting for what she didn't want to hear. From the look on Owen's face and the sound of his voice, what he was about to tell her would strike like a body blow. Against whatever it might be, she had no protection. Yet, perversely, she *must* know.

"Tell me," she said.

"I was taken by Rushmount's men."

"I heard. Why you?"

"Con Mann named me."

"But why?"

"Sooner or later, everyone hereabouts comes to the forge. He thought I might know something, might point to the poacher."

"Do you know anything?"

He shook his head. "No."

"Con should have saved his breath, the scut. Even if you did know, you never would have told them." His news wasn't so bad after all, and she heaved an inward sigh of relief. "They let you go unharmed."

"Do you know why?"

"You were not the poacher."

"True enough, but that is not the reason. Rush-mount and his gamekeeper laughed at the sight of me." Owen clapped his injured leg with the flat of his palm. "As deformed as I am, could I take down a deer and dispose of it? Not likely, they reasoned. Nor would anyone ask for my help, for of what use could I be?"

"They don't know your strength."

"They dismissed me as useless. Do you understand my meaning, Grace? They saw me as less than a man. And they're right."

"Not so! I know you in a way they do not." She got up from the stool and stood facing him. "I *know* you," she whispered.

"God forgive me, Grace, for that knowledge. For naught will come of it."

The heat drained from her body. "You can't mean that. We love each other."

She peered closely exploring his face—the dark eyes shadowed with fatigue, the full lips compressed into a tight line, the clenched jaw. She saw no yielding in that face, no agreement that she'd spoken truly for them both.

"Tell me you don't love me," she said. "Tell me our time together meant nothing."

His silence spoke for him. But his jaw hardened, and the bleakness stayed in his eyes.

"Talk to me, Owen."

More silence, and then, "For a while, you made me forget what I am."

"Please don't—"

"Hear me out, Grace. Rushmount and his men did me a kindness. They forced upon me what I wanted to forget. It was wrong of me to encourage your gratitude."

"I beg you, Owen, don't do this." She stepped closer. "Don't fling me away with both hands. We've belonged together since we were children, and we belong together now more than ever. I'm yours, Owen—body and soul. Even without the holy words said over us, I'm your wife. And you know it in truth."

He backed away as he had the first night she'd come here, as she'd begun to trust he never would again. "Find a whole man, Grace, someone other men will respect. Someone who will not limp along by your side."

"You've lost your courage then?"

"I have no fear for myself. But for you...for you chained to me, the wife of a man despised, I have no stomach for that."

He meant what he said. She could see his determination in the rigid way he held himself apart from her, the way his eyes avoided looking into hers. And to think she'd believed they had moved far, far beyond this obstacle to their happiness. She'd believed wrongly, yet she loved him still with every fiber of her being. She would love him until the day she died whether or not he ever again held her in his arms.

"You've made me yours," she said, her voice cracking under the weight of the words. "And I've made you mine. 'Tis wrong what you're doing to us this day, Owen. Wrong before God. But I will not beg for your love. I too have pride." She let tears stream unchecked. "May our pride keep us warm for the rest of our days."

Blind with grief, she ran from the forge and stumbled her way home. She avoided the cottage for hours, sitting alone against the stone wall edging their north field, too numb to talk to Liam, too numb to think of what her future might hold now that all joy had fled from it.

Days later, in her despair, she did toy with a wild, wicked idea. She would tell Owen she was with child. In the daylight hours, the plan seemed feasible and she warmed to it, but in the wee hours of the nights that followed the days, she knew she couldn't lie to him. She clung, though, to a little ray of hope, for as of yet, she wasn't sure what the month might reveal. Then, in a few weeks' time, she knew she had no news for Owen. Mary Burke's daughter, Deirdre, was the only babe born in Ballybanree that Christmas season. Deirdre and the Christ Child. Grace had no such expectations.

Barren she must be. And bitter for sure. Grace the Fair rejected by the one man she loved. How all the lads she'd sent away would scoff, not that she cared what people thought or said. But she did care that each day without Owen the minutes turned into hours, the hours into centuries. Only at Da's murder had she known such black despair. If Owen loved her in the same way she loved him, how could he endure this? A question without an answer, it added to her torment.

\* \* \*

The day after Christmas, with the winter sun shining down a meager warmth and light, Grace sat sewing by the open door. Despite her unseeing eyes, she plied the needle in and out, in and out, by some small miracle creating a straight seam. The skirt had to be ready in two day's time for Liam's wedding. Brigit had finished hers already. But Brigit had reason to make her needle fly. Soon she and Liam would be man and wife and begin their married life together here in the cottage.

Grace had washed the bed coverings and scattered dried heather sprigs between the folds. The morning of the marriage, she would make up the wedding bed with the fresh linens. That night she would lay alone, listening to their murmuring and the rustle of the mattress knowing as she hadn't known before this past summer what such movements and sounds signified.

*Oh, Owen, how can you deny us?*

"Grace."

She looked up from her work startled by Liam's voice although he'd spoken softly as always.

"I was deep into my thoughts," she said, "and you so quiet."

"We need to speak." He pulled up a stool next to hers.

"The man of few words wanting to talk. 'Tis unbelievable," she said, forcing a smile.

He nodded, sheepish at the truth, and studied his big-boned hands, collecting his words before bringing them out into the open. Finally, "You've been looking pale and ill these past several weeks."

Grace bent her head over her sewing to hide the quick tears filming her eyes.

"Are you unhappy about Brigit and me?" he asked.

Her head snapped up releasing the tears. She swiped

at them with the back of a hand. "Never think that, Liam. I am happy for you both."

"Then why so wan? Is it the giving up of Da's room"

"Ah, sure and you cannot believe such a thing. I will love having a sister here, a woman to talk to and share the day, but..."

"What?" His eyes, earnest with worry, searched her face.

"I need to find my own place. I cannot stay here overlong."

"This is your home. You are welcome forever if need be." A rare humor played about Liam's lips. "Although that would disappoint every man and lad for miles around."

"I'm the one disappointed."

Perplexed as to her meaning, Liam drew his brows together and asked, "What are you telling me, Grace?"

"The one man I want cannot be won."

"Who is this rare creature?" Liam scoffed.

She had to tell someone or burst. She bent over her work again, hiding her eyes. "Owen O'Donnell," she whispered.

"What! Owen the cripple? Grace the Fair wants *him*? You were right to keep your secret. Good Lord, Grace, pick a man in full. God knows you have your choice. Someone who can stand beside you."

Liam kicked back the stool as he stood, a big man, well muscled with brawny thighs filling his breeches, the calves below them round and hard. A powerful man who'd feared to cut down Da's body, who would have let him swing on the rope to this very day. To him, Owen O'Donnell—who'd defied the world—was less than a man.

Grace's heart flooded with new pain. How Owen suffered at the hands of all. More so than even she'd suspected. With that insight came a measure of release. The pain remained, but the bitterness ebbed. Long for him she would, but with sorrow in her heart not the hatred that had seeped in and begun to dwell there.

She stood and let the sewing drop away. "You needn't worry about Owen as my mate. He sees himself as unfit."

"In that, he's right," Liam shouted, angrier than she'd ever seen him. "No more talk of Owen O'Donnell. Find yourself a fitting husband, Grace, and soon. 'Twill be best for all of us."

He strode out of the cottage, slamming the door behind him. He'd never done so before. That, more than anything he said, told Grace she must find a new home.

# CHAPTER ELEVEN

The more Malachy Ennis nipped at the jug the McElroy brothers had brought to the festivities, the louder he thrummed the *bodhran*. By late afternoon, he collapsed, exhausted and drunk, and Dermott Doyle took over the musical tasks.

'Twas a relief, Grace thought, to have Dermott's pure tenor rise sweetly into the air, until she heard the words he sang.

Only death can set me free,
For the lad that I loved is gone from me:
*Es go deh thu, mavourneen slaun.*

I'll wrap my shawl about my head,
And round the world I'll beg my bread,
'Til I find my love, alive or dead:
*Es go deh thu, mavourneen slaun.*

The lyrics hurt her to the quick, and certain her troubled feelings showed all over her face, she was glad when the mists left off and the wedding guests fanned out of the cottage onto the surrounding greensward.

"Sunshine in December. 'Tis God smiling on the marriage," the village grannies said, carefully holding their drinks as they followed everyone out to the yard.

The food had strained the resources of every housewife in Ballybanree, but the feast piled high on the trestle table had been gorgeous. Fresh baked breads they'd had, and hard-cooked eggs, bowls of mashed turnips mixed with onions and bits of butter. Best of all, a cheese round and a ham shank with the meat full on the bone. The cheese and ham had been sent over that morning by Connor Mann, and Liam had been so pleased and proud, Grace hadn't the heart to refuse them.

Now only scraps were left for the dogs to snatch at, but while the whiskey lasted, the guests would stay singing and dancing until time for the bedding of the newlyweds.

Was Liam eager for that? Grace wondered. Remembering how Owen's hands had trembled when he first touched her, she knew he must be. And what of Brigit? Grace glanced across the green to where she stood, her face flushed rosy pink. Did Liam bring to her the same rush of anticipation that Owen's slightest touch raised in herself?

Owen. Her heart had soared at the sight of him at the wedding Mass. After Communion, as was his custom, he walked out of St. Mary's making no attempt to quiet the thump of his wooden boot on the stone floor. Almost, she thought, as if he wanted to drum the unevenness of each footstep into her mind.

He'd looked worn, the hollows in his face more pronounced than ever, throwing his cheekbones and jaw into stark relief. Making him, if anything, more arresting to her eyes. At the ravaged look of him, she knew he wouldn't come to the wedding feast, and he didn't. The stubborn fool, how she loved him.

Liam, a tin cup of whiskey in his hand, took a moment from his bride to whisper into Grace's ear. "Today's your chance, lass. The lads can't take their eyes from you. Pick out one and smile at him. Make him delirious." Somewhat unsteadily, he waved his cup at a fair-haired man sitting on the stone wall regaling a circle of men with a ribald tale. "'Twould do no harm to encourage the likes of Tim Leary. His family farms ten acres...or Young Connor Mann over there."

She glared at him ready to spit on the ground at his feet. "That English lover—"

"All right. All right. I mean no harm."

Instantly contrite, anxious not to mar his wedding

day, Grace put a hand on his arm and kissed his cheek. "Of course, you don't. Have a happy life, Liam. You're my brother and I love you."

Quick tears glazed his eyes before he could nod and hurry back to his bride.

*He will have a night to remember.*

Grace was happy for him. This night, she would sleep next to the children by the small turf fire in Mary Burke's cabin. The newlyweds needed to be alone—as she and Owen had been in the cave—with no one about to inhibit a movement, or overhear a sigh or a murmured love word...

A flurry of activity caught her eye.

*Owen?*

*Ah no. It's Father Joyce.*

As her heart sank within her, the men sprawled on the low wall sharing tales scrambled to their feet.

"Good evening, Father."

"Evening, Father."

"Good evening."

Grace's heart lurched back to its usual rhythm, and she went up to Sean McElroy who'd kept a jug of spirits tight by his side all the day long. "Will you fill a cup for Father?" she asked.

"Anything for you, Grace," he said, giving her a thin-lipped smile and pouring to the very rim of a tin cup.

With a nod of thanks, she took the cup and carried it over to the priest, taking care not to spill a drop.

"For you, Father. The food is nearly gone, but surely you will take a wee taste."

"Thank you, lass. For this special occasion, I will, indeed."

He took a tentative sip. "Ah, from the McElroy brothers. The best, the very best in the whole county."

"You know that for a certainty, Father?"

"Behave yourself, lass," he said, a grin erasing the rebuke from his words. He took a second, larger swallow.

Grace smiled at the man. Stern though he might be

and upright as to the teachings of the Church, the kindness in him tempered the laws he maintained. A learned man by village standards, he shared the hardships of the people with an added burden. He had no wife or children to ease him. Or to torment him, the sour minded would say. But looking at Liam's joyous face as he awaited his first night of love, Grace couldn't find it in her heart to be cynical.

"The whole village is here," Father Joyce observed, glancing around.

"Not everyone, Father."

"Who is missing, then?"

"Owen O'Donnell."

"Ah, Owen. He stays away from the dancing."

As he nipped at the cup, the frown that had begun to cloud his face faded away. Closing his eyes for an instant, he looked as if he were following the rare treat as it made its way down to his belly. When his eyes snapped open again, Grace could see they were an amazing blue. Strange, but in all the years she'd watched him say the Mass, she hadn't noticed the color of his eyes. But never before had they been so intent upon her.

"You have reason to want Owen O'Donnell here today, lass?"

"I do, Father."

He held out his empty cup. "I must be going. Tomorrow, come to me after the morning Mass. You can tell me what troubles you then."

"I have no—"

"Tomorrow, lass."

As he turned from her to make his way back through the gathering, Grace looked down at the empty cup in her hand. She would try the *uisce beatha* and see for herself what all the fuss was about. "Sean," she called. At the sound of his name, he got up from his seat on the wall and came over to her, the jug in his hand.

"A drop?" she asked.

"For Grace the Fair, more than that," he said.

"A drop is enough, Sean. I've not taken any before. Only a cup of ale from time to time."

He poured her a generous tot and stood back, a quizzical expression on his face. She sipped, and at the alien taste, gasped and sputtered. Good manners alone kept her from spewing the fiery liquid out of her mouth.

Sean laughed. "That is always the way the first time. 'Tis not for its taste that men love the whiskey. Sip again and you'll soon know why they do."

She did as Sean instructed, then once more, a mouthful the second time. A moment later, the magic began. Warmth spread from her middle to her heart, to her head, to her legs and arms, fingers and toes...the world had gone soft...

"'Tis a miracle what it does to one," she said.

Amusement played about Sean's pinched mouth. "The drink is a great pleasure in life."

"Some say pleasure is dangerous."

He nodded, the habitual gloom back on his face.

"And some say that's what makes life worth living," she added. The thought of Owen in her arms leaped up as vividly as if he were there caressing her.

"What does? The pleasure or the danger?"

"Both." Whiskey and lovemaking were both fraught with danger, yet each warmed body and soul. Of the two, she preferred love to *uisce beatha*. But what of her secret danger, the one she'd told to no one, not even to Owen? Was that a pleasure as well? She would have to think long and deep before she could answer her own question.

She emptied the cup and gave it back to Sean. "You and your brother Tim are miracle workers."

"More?"

"Not today." An idea formed. "Sean, have you offered your *uisce beatha* to his lordship?"

He shook his head and looked about with alarm. "Jesus, no, Grace. He knows nothing of it. No telling what he'd do to us if he knew."

"If this is as good as Father Joyce claims, Rushmount might take some in payment for the rent."

"I don't dare suggest it. There's no telling how he would react."

Be daring, she longed to say, seize your chance. Take the risk.

In the fast-gathering dark of the short winter day, Malachy Ennis started up his *bodhran* again. With a great shout of glee, the throng picked up the bride and groom and carried them to the cottage door. Before the noise and banter and jests could turn Brigit's face from pink to scarlet, she ducked inside, and Liam closed the door firmly behind them.

The racket would continue until the wee hours, but Grace knew they wouldn't care. Nor would she if she were in a bed with Owen's arms about her.

# CHAPTER TWELVE

Father Joyce kissed the stole's embroidered cross before placing the strip of purple silk over his shoulders. He sat and pointed to an oak bench opposite his own.

Confession then, Grace thought, as she took her seat. Not merely a talk about her troubles.

"Whatever you tell me is sealed, Grace. But let us speak as friends, for that's what we are above all else."

She nodded, willing away the tears that threatened. Tired she was of them leaping into her eyes lately.

He let a silence fall.

She would have to begin. Very well. "I love Owen O'Donnell."

"Go on."

"He says he is less than a man, not fit to be my husband. He will not have me."

When Father Joyce spoke, his voice came gentle into the still air.

"Has he given you reason to think he would have you?"

"He has, just as I have given the same reason to him."

"You have lain together?"

"We have."

He looked up and, like the day before, pierced her with the blue of his eyes. "You feel remorse for your sin?"

"'Twas no sin, Father. Love is no sin."

Grace saw a quick flash of anger darken his face, but he didn't unleash his wrath.

The silence thickened between them for a long,

weighted moment. Finally he said, "Your words are blasphemous, Grace, and you know it. But in my heart, I cannot condemn you. Nor can I give you absolution. Not without true sorrow. You and Owen are not man and wife—"

"We are in the way that matters."

"Lass, you are mistaken."

She stood, poised to flee.

His hand darted out drawing her back to the bench. "We are not through yet. I have a question for you."

She raised her chin, defying him. "I'm listening."

"Has this love...as you call it...caused you happiness?"

"It did."

"For a brief time. For a lifetime, you need the sacrament. Then what happens between a man and a woman becomes holy. And stable."

Grace covered her eyes with one hand, hiding the truth from him. She would go to Owen in an instant with or without holy words spoken over them. The only words she needed were, "Come to me." Or less. A gesture, an outstretched hand, a smile.

Oh God, she lived in hell.

The priest reached out and pried gently at her fingers until they fell away from her face. "I heard Rushmount's men seized Owen and something of what they said to him. The man is clinging to his pride. In his mind, it's all he has left. Would you ask him to give that up for you?"

Grace jumped to her feet and stood glaring down at the priest's white hair.

"I ask for nothing!" She would not be persuaded back to the bench nor did he make a move to detain her.

"Your pride, child, is as great as his. Of the host of sins man is heir to, pride is the deadliest. It hardens the heart and soul to the love of God. Without that love, life becomes a living hell."

So he knew. Grace drew in a deep breath and sat again. "My heart is not hard, Father. It is a gigantic ache in my body that will not stop tormenting me. That ache cannot be pride."

"All sins are proud, Grace. They tell us our desires are greater than the will of God. What they keep secret from us is the price they exact." His blue gaze stabbed at her once more. "You are paying this price now." He sighed, his breath a puff of vapor in the cold air. "Should Owen speak to me of this matter between you, I will counsel him. But he hasn't sought my counsel in years. Not since he was a lad, the summer he had the fall."

"I love that stubbornness in him, Father. Almost more than anything else about him. And there is much about him to..."

She fell quiet at the vision of a naked Owen hovering over her, his knees bent as if in prayer.

"You are kindred spirits, lass. God help you both. Now let us say an *Ave* together. This is the Blessed Mother's church. We'll ask her to bring you peace."

*Ask her to bring me Owen!* Without voicing the thought, Grace bowed her head murmuring the ancient prayer as Father Joyce intoned the familiar words. When the prayer ended, she sat still for a moment gathering her courage, then, "Father, I need your help with another matter."

"What is that, child?"

"I have a great desire to learn how to read."

Father Joyce tugged at the purple silk band until it slid from his shoulders. "For this, we won't need the stole. Reading is man's business, not God's."

"You will help me?"

"'Tis not that simple, Grace. Which language do you wish to read?"

The question stunned her. "What are my choices?"

"Three in Ballybanree. Hundreds the world over."

*The world over! The world beyond the ocean. The lands she would never see.*

A hint of a smile played about Father Joyce's mouth. Was he laughing at her and her absurd desire? She had pride, as he well knew. It took hold of her in that instant.

"Ballybanree will do for the time being," she said.

He laughed out loud. Somehow, she didn't take offense and laughed, too, at the impossibility of her knowing any other land but this Ireland of her people.

"Well," he said, wiping the wet from his eyes, "we have three ways of reading. The Latin, the Gaelic, and the English."

"Latin is the Mass talk."

"True, lass. In every country of the world, Latin is used for the sacred rites."

"It's not spoken outside of Mass?"

"Seldom now, but great writings exist in it. Our *Book of Kells,* the most beautiful manuscript in the world, is written in Latin. My lifetime wish is to see it before I die. 'Tis glorious, they say, encrusted with enamel and gold, and alive with fabulous beasts and saints that look ready to step straight off the pages."

"A wondrous book."

He nodded, unaware that his eyes were filled with dreaming.

"What are the readings in Gaelic?"

"Less, perhaps. The Franciscans printed a Catechism. I have a copy. When the monasteries were destroyed, some of the ancient myths survived the burnings. The Brehon Laws are written in Gaelic as well."

"And the deeds to the O'Malley holdings. Mam once told me they were writ in Gaelic."

He nodded. "True. Your mother had me read them to her years ago when you were a wee lass. You heard. Do you remember?"

"How could I forget?"

"Above all, do not start believing in them." An unaccustomed bitterness crept into his voice. "English law has made them worthless."

She nodded. "'Tis well I know that, Father. His lordship, no doubt he reads in the English?"

"Of course, 'tis his native language, and depending

on the extent of his education, he might have a smattering of Latin and Greek as well."

"Greek?"

"Don't worry about his Greek, Grace. 'Tis the English for him."

"Then that's what I must learn to read first."

"First?" He laughed again.

Grace smiled. Let him enjoy himself so long as he would help her. She waited patiently until he looked grave once more. "You will teach me?"

"You want to be the only woman in the village who can read?"

She nodded.

"Why?"

"Why not, Father?"

No need to tell him of her deep anger at the insult Lord Rushmount had dealt her. He would interpret her reaction as another sin of pride, and in that he would be right.

"Why not?" he repeated. "Well, for one thing, I have no book in English."

"Oh."

"I gave my English Bible to Owen the summer he injured his leg. We spent the following months reading it together. It helped him through that bad time."

"Would you ask him for the use of it, Father?"

He shook his head. "He needs it, lass. Now, I suspect, more than ever."

She nodded at the truth in what he said. Owen should, of course, have the sacred text, but her frustrated desire caused her to ask, "Is there no other book in English hereabouts?"

"There's a Catholic Bible belonging to the Mann family. 'Twas Connor's father's, printed before King James interfered with the true word of God. Connor might let you have the loan of it. I doubt he reads it often."

"Printed in English, this Bible?"

"It is."

Connor Mann of all people. To seek a favor of the panderer to his lordship galled her. But if she wished to rise from the pismire of ignorance, she would have to humble herself and ask.

"I'll speak to him, Father. If he gives me the loan, you'll help me?"

"Get the Holy Book, child, and we'll begin."

Grace left the church with her heart a bit lighter than when she'd entered. Owen had been brought no closer to her, she had no absolution from her priest, but she had a promise. Reading would be a great treasure.

And she still had her secret not yet shared with anyone on earth, not even with Father Joyce in confession. What sin had she committed that she should tell of it? The land and the creatures on it existed for the good of all, not merely for one arrogant man. But she would take care in doing what she was driven to do, not for her own sake; she had little in life to lose, but for the sake of her cause. At the next full moon, her prize would not be taken from her. Or the next time. Or the next.

She raised the shawl to her head. The winter mists had returned. On the morrow, she would speak to Connor Mann about the reading. For today, she longed for her home's turf fire and hoped to God Liam and Brigit would not hate her for bringing their brief idyll to an end.

# CHAPTER THIRTEEN

"Kathleen Mann. Good day to you."
Uncertain of her welcome in the Manns' cottage, Grace kept her voice low. Her opinion of the English would be no secret to Kath—or her opinion of the Manns themselves, either.

Kath, her hands deep in the kneading of a loaf, gave out a little surprised cry. "Grace O'Malley is it? You startled me half out of my skin. Come in. Come in," she said. "'Tis grand to see you."

All the while Kath spoke her hands kept moving, shaping the bread dough into a round, fat loaf. Finished at last, she dusted the loaf with flour and wiped her fingers on a piece of rag cloth. "Have a seat, lass, and I'll make you some tea as soon as I put this to the fire. The men will be wanting their noon meal soon. You must stay and join us."

Oh Lord, noon and her looking to eat like a poor, hungry lass. Another reason to be beholden to the Manns. She could have kicked herself. Now that Brigit was Liam's wife, she had no need to prepare all the food, and with winter holding Ballybanree in its grip, she wasn't needed in the fields. Free to leave and eager to speak to Connor, she'd ignored the height of the December sun.

Torn between leaving and staying, she remained standing uncertainly in the doorway.

"Do sit, lass," Kath urged. If she were curious as to why Grace had arrived at her doorstep midday, she didn't let on, but busied herself wiping off the tabletop and putting down plates and cups for the noon meal.

Grace came in and sat on a high-backed bench

flanking the table. She glanced about the room. It had
the same hard-packed earthen floor as her own home
and the same stone walls. Unlike her cottage, this one
had a stone chimney to carry off the fire's smoke,
keeping the walls free of soot. 'Twas a grand improve-
ment over a vent hole in the thatch. As was the glass
window that let in the clear light and kept out the cold.
How wonderful on a winter's day to have God's sun
inside the house shining on one's task. Or on one's
book.

A dark dresser of rich-hued wood stood against one
wall. It held more plates and bowls than Kath needed
for this meal and some of them pewter. Beside it, near
the fire, was a narrow bed covered with a shag rug like
the one Da used to fling about his shoulders on the
coldest days. Young Con's sleep place, no doubt—and a
warm one.

Kath's loom partly filled with linen in the making
took up most of the opposite wall. Long considered the
best weaver in Ballybanree, Kath sometimes employed
village girls to help her spin the flax and set the warp.
She paid them generously with food, but Grace had
steadfastly refused to work for the Manns.

First Da, and now Liam, brought the raw flax to the
Manns' cabin and at year's end collected a length of
linen cloth in payment. Yet here she sat in the very
house she'd refused to enter in the past. Was reading
more important than food or cloth? She would have to
think about that long and hard.

In the center of the table, Kath placed a crockery
bowl filled with boiled eggs still in their shells. She cut a
wedge of cheese from a wheel on the dresser and put
that next to the eggs.

"As soon as the bread is baked, we'll be ready for the
men. In the meantime, we'll have our tea. Real English
tea I have."

"But I didn't come to—"

"Whatever brings you here, you're welcome," Kath
said as she hung a copper kettle on the hook over the

flames.

Grace felt a heat rise into her face. Kath had a warm way with her, yet few of the women called on her except to beg for food. She might be starved for company. More comfortable with that idea, Grace relaxed at the table grateful for the warm cup Kath placed in front of her.

They chattered about the wedding and Liam's happiness, the food the guests had brought, the weather, and of everything under the sun except the reason for Grace's visit. She felt herself stiffen as plump and kindly Kath, pulled the baked loaf from its iron spider on the coals and placed it, hot and steaming with its heavenly odor, on the table.

"I'll add some water to the kettle," she said. "They'll both be along shortly."

"I'd best go." Grace went to rise from the bench.

In the act of dipping water from a bucket under the dresser, Kath said, "And disappoint Young Con?" She filled the kettle and placed it over the fire. "You must stay for that reason alone."

"I'm here to speak to Connor, your husband."

"Whatever you want to say, it'll go better after we've all partaken something."

It would be an act of rudeness to protest further. Besides, she did have to speak to Connor. She sat back, but when she heard the men approaching, her pulse began to quicken. He could not refuse her. But what if he did?

She leapt to her feet when they entered.

Connor, the first to come in, stopped still at the surprise of her. But he recovered himself quickly and turned to his son. "We have company. Beautiful company," he added with a smile.

Never strong with talk, Young Con stood silent, his mouth agape. Connor clapped him on the back. "Welcome her, lad," he said.

Young Con ducked his head at Grace in greeting. She returned the gesture, but it was to his father that she spoke. "I would have a word with you, Connor."

"Ah, business. A beautiful lass comes to see me and it's for business only."

"Oh, pish," Kath chided. "Sit everyone. 'Tis time. The kettle's going mad over the fire."

Later, with eggshells littering the tabletop and the kettle drained dry, Connor leaned back in his place and said, "You have something to speak of, Grace?"

She nodded and with her heart in her mouth told him why she'd come to his house this day.

\* \* \*

*Christ,* Connor thought, she's *the most glorious creature I've ever laid eyes on.*

And look at the lad there ready to piss his breeches over her. Not that he blamed him. If he were twenty years younger and a few stone lighter, he'd try for her himself.

Ah, the foolishness of old age. Kath suited him fine. But what a treasure the lass would be for any man. That wild hair with the rays of sunlight catching at it and those eyes aglow in the whiteness of her skin...her full bodice. Pshaw! Kath's bodice was over full. He'd leave the young goddess to the local studs. She'd have to choose among them soon. Once Liam's family started arriving, his fields would be strained to provide...babes, aye, what outstanding ones this Grace O'Malley would birth.

Connor shook himself and concentrated on what she was saying although he couldn't believe what his own ears were hearing.

"You want to read?" he asked, his voice gone high with astonishment. "And to borrow the old Catholic Bible? Why in God's name do you want to do that?"

"Father Joyce's question exactly."

"So?"

"Why not? That was my answer to the priest, and it's my answer to you."

His thoughts tumbled over themselves. He had to reply carefully. There was more at stake here than a lass wanting to reach above herself. If his lordship heard of this, what would he say? Or do? That consideration came first. Would he object? For the life of him, Connor couldn't be certain. Ordinarily, yes, he would object violently. Keep the natives ignorant would be his motto. Savages were easier to control than educated men with ideas.

But his lordship had expressed interest in the lass. Looking at her across the table, he understood why, but would his gratitude extend to *reading?* And English for Christ's sake? Of all the natives of Ballybanree, only he and Young Con could do so, and possibly Owen O'Donnell, or so rumor had it.

He himself had taught Young Con, grooming him for the time when he would take over the care of his lordship's ledgers. The lad had learned quickly. He could read as well as his da and tote up a row of figures even faster.

Ah! There was his answer.

He cleared his throat. "I cannot give you the loan of the Douay Bible."

Her face fell. "I would take good care—"

"'Tis not that. The Bible is Roman Catholic. We hid it from Cromwell's men, Kath and me together, in the walls of our old cottage. 'Twas worth our lives if it'd been found, so it's precious for that reason alone. It's also dangerous even now. The English King James had another Bible printed. The true one, he claimed."

"But—"

He held up a quieting hand. "Father Joyce can say the Mass as long as it pleases King Charles to be tolerant. Because of the king's leniency, Lord Rushmount rebuilt the church after Cromwell torched it. But it's best not to flaunt the religion about."

Never would he tell the lass Rushmount's true words. *"I'll give them a place to hold their Mass, Con. That'll keep them quiet and working. And that's well worth the cost of reroofing the old church."*

"I must learn, Con. You cannot deny me. You are Irish, too, not an English bastard."

Con eyed her narrowly. In her vehemence, she had flung an insult at him. It lay an inch, no more, under the surface of her words, and its meaning crystal clear: Irish he was in blood, but not in spirit.

He skewered Young Con with a swift glance. The lad hadn't spoken a word since Grace made her outrageous request. Nor would he. Not overly given to idle chatter, he was struck dumb in the lass' presence. Alone with her in the dark, there would be no need for words, and he was overly ripe for such experience. Intelligent Young Con was, without doubt, but strong enough to handle a woman with the fierce blood of Granuaile running in her veins? No way to know. It would be a risk for sure, but one well worth taking to have her in the family.

He leaned across the table, his elbows ignoring the eggshells scattered about. "I have a suggestion."

Grace's eyes widened, and he saw a sudden hope leap into her face.

She leaned forward, too. "Tell me of it, Connor."

"The Bible will remain here in my cottage. If you come in the evenings after the day's work is through, Young Con will teach you what you want to know."

Young Con smiled. The lad understood, and why not? They thought alike most times. He would delight, of course, to sit in the evenings by the firelight next to Grace with the holy book open before them and a bit of charcoal to write down letters on a board, his hand guiding hers with the making of those letters. If the lad kept his wits about him, he might win her yet.

She smiled, her teeth white and even. What a prize she was!

She turned to Young Con. "Are you willing to teach me as your da says?"

"Of course." He smiled back at her like a cat with a bowlful of milk all his for the lapping. "When do you wish to begin?"

"Now."

Connor laughed. "Not now. Young Con and I have an afternoon's work ahead of us. Come back tomorrow before dark. And lass, tell Father Joyce of our plan, but no one else, understand? If you do, all lessons must cease."

"No one else will know. That's my wish, too," she said.

Ah, a woman in full she was. Young Con had his work cut out for him.

# CHAPTER FOURTEEN

"'T is cunning the way the letters fit together," Grace said. Once she knew their intent, she saw how easily they could be strung into words.

"You're making good progress," Young Con told her.

To help her grasp the meanings more quickly, he had her form the letters herself with a bit of charcoal on a smooth board. So eager was she to learn, the rag used to wipe the board clean soon became blackened with soot. The logic of the reading thrilled her, and the economy of its structure. The letters, little more than a score of them, became the keys to unlocking a new world.

"It helps that your mam taught you to speak the English," Young Con said. "Reading and writing are like speaking in silence."

"Ah! A gorgeous thought entirely," Grace said, struck with the force of his concept. She looked up from the Bible spread open on the table before them and smiled at him. He moved closer, and his hand reached out to cup her knee.

So it had come to this. She wasn't surprised. It had only been a matter of time what with the two of them alone evenings sitting side by side at Kath's well-scrubbed table with the turf fire and a rush lamp lighting the pages, and old Connor and Kath in bed in the cottage's second room.

His hand on her knee was unwelcome, but she couldn't give up the learning so soon. As good as her progress might be, there were too many words in the

English that she didn't recognize, too many that sounded alike but had different meanings, and too many that had no counterpart in the Gaelic. Yet despite all the difficulties, she loved the learning. A gigantic puzzle it was to be solved one word at a time until the hidden meaning came clear as water in a rain barrel.

No, she couldn't give this up, not without a struggle. It meant everything. She'd even put off searching the woods for deer these past weeks, telling herself the villagers had no great need, that she couldn't risk being caught, not before she'd unlocked the mystery of reading. But she learned quickly, Young Con had told her so, and soon now she would go back to her yew bow and her sacred vow to Da.

Soon now.

She yawned, pretending Young Con's hand hadn't found its way to her knee and had now discovered her thigh. She stood, stretching herself as if weary from the hard bench and walked about the room for a few moments. "I'm parched, Con. Could I help myself to a cup of water?"

"To anything that's mine, Grace. You must know that."

Her ruse hadn't fooled him. The Manns were known for their canniness with Young Con the canniest of all.

"The book learning's enough to ask of you, Con. That I do need."

"Why so thirsty for it, Grace? What use will reading be when you marry and have babes clinging to your skirt?"

"How can we understand the way the English think if we don't know their language? How can we resist if we can't read the laws that enslave us? We all need to understand. All of us! The whole of Ballybanree!" She spread her arms wide, her voice throbbing with determination. "Once I master the words, I'll teach the village children to read as well."

Young Con frowned. "My father will have much to say about that, I fear."

"Resistance must come. It must. We can't continue on like this—an entire nation of *tenants*. The land belongs to us, not to the thieving landlords."

"England is here to stay, Grace. Get used to it."

"I cannot." She looked across at him, heavy-set, well fed, and knew he didn't understand.

"You'd best. King Charles will never restore Protestant-held lands to the Old Irish families. He won't risk being deposed a second time. Not for the likes of us. He's as much in thrall to Parliament as we are to Lord Rushmount."

Young Con's face had begun to turn red. Grace fell silent. Arguing with him this way wouldn't help her with the learning. She took her cup of water and sat down on the opposite bench. Maybe he wouldn't notice she'd put herself out of his arm's reach. Though his quick glance as she sat apart from him said otherwise.

Above all, she didn't want to anger him and have the lessons end. The memory of Lord Rushmount astride his horse smiling down at her ignorance still rankled. Yet she couldn't encourage Con. She swiveled the Bible around to her side of the table and turned the hourglass upside down. "Half of the glass only and then I must be going home."

She extended a finger, ready to trace the line in the psalm she'd been trying to read. He leaned across the table and seized her hand. "Grace, look at me." She lifted her glance from the page to his eyes. "You can't keep on living with Brigit and Liam. You need a home of your own."

Slowly she pulled free, letting her fingers slide out gently from under his.

"You can have a home with me whenever you wish," he said.

Grace sighed and stood. No more learning would take place this night. "Thank you kindly for your welcome, Con. But I'm not free to accept."

"Indeed you are. You're as free as the air."

Before he could rise from the bench, she seized her

shawl and ran to the door. No way could she let her love for Owen escape her lips to be bandied about by all, but the temptation to scream it aloud nearly overwhelmed her. She had to get out of the cottage before Young Con caught her. Once she rebuffed him for good, no more lessons would be possible.

She flung the door open and fled into the night. The dark enclosed her like a black glove, but she knew her way. Once past the meadow and into the woods, she darted from tree to tree, moving on her soft-skinned brogues without a sound. Behind her, she could hear Young Con calling her name as he stumbled through the undergrowth.

She could slip away from him easily enough. The woodland hid her well. Tomorrow she would ask Kath to let her read the same page alone in the daylight while her son kept busy elsewhere. Kath would be disappointed. Grace had seen the matchmaking gleam in her eyes as she and Young Con sat side by side. But Kath wouldn't refuse her the book. She was too kind for that.

The sound of her name in the distance grew fainter. She'd lost him. Good. The next time they met, she'd pretend that in her haste to be home she hadn't heard him come after her. Maybe that way she could keep at the lessons without making promises she had no intention of keeping.

Through the bare oak boughs, she could see stars pricking the night sky. Did any of them have names? Da once said they did. Even so, she could rename them as she wished. The biggest one high in the north she would call Owen. O-W-E-N. "Owen."

"You see through trees now?" a deep voice asked.

She stopped, standing still as a wild creature sensing discovery. Had she heard a voice or imagined one? The one she most longed to hear.

"Owen, is it you?" she whispered.

"None other."

He stepped out from behind a thick-trunked tree and stood blocking her path. With only the starlight for a lantern, she couldn't see him clearly, but the voice's deep timbre thrummed through her, playing at every nerve end.

"Why are you here?" she asked.

"I've been following you these past nights. There's sickness in the village. I had to see if you were well."

"You've followed me every night? Impossible. I would have heard you."

"Supposing I arrived and took up my station before you came hurrying to Young Connor Mann?"

Jealous, he was! What a glorious realization. Grace grinned at his dark outline in the starlight forgetting her anger at his desertion, forgetting his stubborn pride that kept them apart, forgetting everything but the fact of having him here within arm's reach. And jealous! Wild with jealousy he must be if he'd watched for her night after night—as she'd watched for him last summer by the shore.

He moved out of the deepest shadows, but she couldn't tell how he fared. Did he look gaunt? Had he suffered since their last meeting? If so, she couldn't find it in her heart to feel overly sorrowful for that. Still, she had to know.

"Are you well?" she asked.

"Well enough. No need to ask that of you. I saw you earlier, before dark. You look as beautiful as ever. And fevered in your longing to get to the Manns each night. You must be in love."

"I am."

"He's a fortunate man."

"He knows it not."

"You haven't told him?"

"I've told him several times over."

"That's that then. Be happy, Grace. You're the love-liest woman in the whole, wide world and courageous to boot. Young Con doesn't deserve you—only a rare man would—but he can give you a good life. And that you should have."

Without warning, not giving him a moment to turn

away from her, she ran to him, flinging her arms around his neck. The sudden move threw him off balance. His injured leg gave way and he fell. She went down, too, her arms never leaving his neck, her body sprawled on top of him.

Seizing the moment, her lips found his and refused to leave them. In search of a breath, his mouth opened under hers. She met his tongue with her own, dallying with it, sucking it, pulling it deeper into her mouth. He rewarded her with a groan he couldn't stop. When it shuddered to a close, he tugged his hands free and lofting her from him with his powerful arms, he put her aside on the hard, cold ground.

Despite the withered leg hampering his effort, he struggled to his feet. "I'm glad of Young Connor. He can do for you what I cannot. Accept him, Grace."

She scrambled up, outraged. "He can do nothing! He has no bread for my spirit. So what can he give me that matters? Nothing, I tell you. Nothing!"

Before he could voice a response, she fled sobbing, running swiftly between the trees with a skill learned from many dark nights passed in their company.

# CHAPTER FIFTEEN

Always, at Eastertide, the food supply dipped low. In the glory of the spring, with the day lilies, the whitethorn and the wild primroses at the height of their color, the women began to measure the grain left in the root cellars, calculating the amount and the weeks remaining until the next harvest.

Grace and Brigit looked to their own stores.

"For two, it might last," Grace said, "but for three there's no telling. I'm sorry, Brigit, I should take myself off to a new place, but the only way is to marry and—"

"That time will come soon enough. There's no joy in rushing to a man you don't love. Love is worth waiting for." Brigit blushed at her own words. "Besides," she added, "the cow should calf within a month and we'll have milk."

Brave talk, Grace thought, but Brigit looked worried. They needed more food, and mackerel were running now. If only Liam would go out in the curraghs with the men, that would help, but he feared the water. Many village lads had drowned over the years; their hide-bottomed boats no match for the rocks lining the shore should they be set upon by a sudden shift in the wind or a change in the tide.

A shame the men wouldn't let her join them in the boats. How different they were from the men of Granuaile's day who'd accepted a woman as their captain, the chieftain of their clan. Grace blew out a breath. Aye, as Liam had said that was then and this was now.

But what of the future? Next year they would be four and the need for food greater than ever. She glanced at

Brigit whose cheeks had gone round and full with early pregnancy. How long would that healthy glow remain if she were stinted of food? Such hunger shouldn't be. Like all the people in Ballybanree, they raised enough to feed themselves well. Rushmount's rent was the evil that kept them hungry much of the year. Da had been right to work against it in the night. And she'd been wrong to put the book learning ahead of her vow. They all needed meat to remain healthy—Brigit most of all.

"We have a little oaten flour left, and there might be hens' eggs," she said. "How would hoecakes do for the noon meal? With water in place of buttermilk?"

"Indeed!" Brigit flashed Grace a grateful smile and went to search the hens' nests. At the table, Grace kept busy with the stone pestle, mashing the grains to a fine powder for the cakes, but her mind had fled far away. This couldn't continue. The lack of food would get worse before the cow calved a month from now. The few cabbages left from fall would be gone. The wild watercress would be coming in, but that was hardly—

"I found three eggs, Grace," Brigit said as she entered the cottage. "We can add them to the cakes with a pinch of salt. We won't miss the buttermilk."

"You're just in time." Grace smiled at Brigit's happy, triumphant face. Ah, what love fulfilled can do, she thought, the bitterness rising up unbidden and powerful enough to bring tears to her eyes. "The flour's ready. Why don't you finish the cakes for Liam? I'm going to walk into the village."

"Before you've eaten?"

"I promised Mary Burke I'd stop by. The baby's been ailing."

"But—"

Quickly, before Brigit could see through her excuse, Grace hurried away. Let Liam, who worked so hard, and Brigit, with her baby making its demands, eat well. She could do without.

From the fit of her skirt, she knew she'd lost weight. Lately when she went to the Manns' cottage for the reading, Kath put something by for her. "Something to nibble on," she called it.

More times than not Grace refused the food. Although God help her, other times she succumbed, seduced by the odor of the fresh-baked bread or the pure gold of the cheese, a wedge of it waiting at her place at the table sitting next to the great book like a temptation from the devil himself.

And once she'd asked to bring home a taste to Brigit. That had to stop. The more kindness she accepted from Kath, from all the Manns, the more tightly she bound herself to them. Yet maybe that was the only way of things for her, and for Liam and Brigit and the babe to come. She couldn't keep taking the food out of their mouths.

Mary in heaven, if only Owen O'Donnell wasn't so stubborn. But that very stubbornness had her caught fast in a vise. Without it, she wouldn't love the man the way she did. The twist of it drove her frantic. She loved him for the very thing that kept them apart.

She hurried her pace. A lyrical day filled with sunlight shone down on her. If Owen was working the forge today, she would do what she'd sworn never to do, steal a glimpse of him as she passed by, see the sparks flying into the air, feel the warmth reaching out from the fire, from the metal, from his eyes that would widen at the sight of her—before he looked away—drawing her like a magnet to the lure of him. Drawing her like a willing moth to his flame.

Aye, drawn and quartered she was by his strength and her own weakness.

But the door to the forge remained closed, and no sound of metal striking metal came from within. Maybe today he'd put out to sea searching for fish with some of the villagers. She knew he had no fear of the water.

In the dirt outside their hut, Mary's children played about in the sunshine. Ten-year-old Eileen, the eldest of the five, her pinched face as smeared with dirt as her feet, hurried up to Grace.

"Have you anything for us?" she asked.

"Sorry, love, I do not."

"Ah, I'm sorry, too."

"Have you eaten today?"

"Not today. Yesterday. Owen brought us bread. He bakes it, you know, on his forge."

"I see. Play, love, with your brothers for a while. I need to speak to your mam."

Obedient, Eileen turned back to her listless game, and Grace went into the cabin. In its dim interior, she saw Mary on a stool with the infant Deirdre clasped to her breast.

Mary put a warning finger to her lips. "She's just now fallen asleep," she whispered. "Out of exhaustion," adding in a shamed voice, "my milk is failing."

Grace knelt by Mary's side and put her arms around her. How thin she was! Her bones could be counted clear through her clothes.

Grace glanced down at the baby's wizened face, so peaceful in sleep.

"No wonder you can't feed her when you have no food yourself. Where is your man, Donal?"

"He's gone out with the others looking for fish. With any luck at all, he'll come home with enough for a few days." Mary's voice trailed off.

A few days, then what? Grace wondered. A croppie who worked by the day laboring for the tenant farmers, Donal Burke earned part of the crop as his pay. With so many mouths to feed, his share never lasted from harvest to harvest. And now with the whole long summer to wait, the children were already in need.

"Mary, listen to me," Grace said, her voice hoarse with renewed resolve. "I've found a way to get food for your little ones and for others in the village, but to carry out my plan, I need your aid, for no man will agree to help a woman with this task." As fear leaped into Mary's eyes, she added, "Will you take a risk to feed your children?"

"But how—"

"If I tell you, you must swear to share what I say with no one, not even Donal."

"But he's my husband."

"Not even."

A wariness crept into Mary's deep-set eyes. "'Tis that serious?"

Grace nodded. "Do you swear?"

"On my mother's soul."

"I know of the poacher."

Mary stiffened and clutched the baby tighter, threatening to awaken her. "Don't tell me his name. 'Tis worth our lives to know."

"I'm the poacher."

Mary's arms dropped to her lap and the baby with them. Her jaw sagged, sending her mouth into an open gape of disbelief.

Grace glanced down, but Deirdre slept on. Looking at the undersized little face, she wondered if the child would ever waken.

"Jesus in heaven, I can't be hearing you right," Mary said. "'Tis unbelievable. You can't be the poacher. No lass could be."

"That's what I want everyone to think, especially the men. Them most of all."

"Close the cabin door. The children—"

Grace peered over her shoulder. "They can't hear us. I had to tell you, for I'll need your help."

"You must be mad. You know what happens to poachers. Your own da—"

Grace reached up and covered Mary's mouth with her palm. "Don't speak of him, Mary. I can't bear it."

"Then—"

"What's worse, to risk death or to watch the children fade in front of our eyes?" Grace's gaze dropped to baby Deirdre. "She will die if your milk dries."

"'Tis well I know. And she not the first."

"What of those outside the door?"

Mary's eyes flooded, the tears running down the creases in her cheeks. "Donal tries."

"I know. The fault is not with him. It's the cursed injustice we live under."

"There's no help for it. Life is harsh."

"Mary, we're starving in our own country, and there's no need. No need at all. Rushmount ships his crop to England every year for profit while we go hungry. We can't keep on like this. 'Tis a sin against God and man."

Mary clutched Grace's arm. Her bony fingers digging in hard enough to bruise the flesh. "Stop that talk. What can one lass do? Nothing at all. God has put us here to endure misery. Like Father Joyce tells us, the next life is the one we live for."

"Perhaps. But this life can be good, too. Why should we go hungry day after day, or watch the village children turn to skin and bones? We must try to help ourselves."

Grace dropped her voice even lower and leaned in close enough to whisper into Mary's ear. "I'm going out tonight. If God is watching, I'll take down a deer. The last time Lord Rushmount's men seized my prey before we could get any good from it. I know now I've waited too long to try again." Her jaw clenched. "But I'll wait no longer. Meet me an hour before dawn and tell no one. I'll be by the old oak, the one they used for Da...I'll need help butchering the meat and getting it back to the village."

Mary recoiled. "We'll be killed."

"Not two helpless women. If Rushmount's men come upon us, we'll say we found the animal already dead with an arrow in its throat. They'll believe that. It's worth the chance." She skewered Mary with a grim look. "It takes courage to stay alive."

Mary fell silent. Her eyes studied the baby's face with its dark fan of lashes brushing her pale cheeks. When open, Deirdre's eyes were blue, and they would open soon, her unfilled belly pulling her out of sleep.

"What say you?" Grace asked. "Live or die?"

"I want *her* to live."

"An hour before dawn, then. Bring a sharp knife and

some rags if you can spare them." Grace got to her feet. "Remember, tell no one. If the men learn of it, they'll stop us."

Mary nodded, her eyes on Deirdre. "I'll tell my man I ail and need to see Gram O'Neill."

Grace squeezed her hand and smiled. "Wish me good hunting."

Mary nodded, her sunken eyes filled with fear. "May God help you."

Settling her shawl over her shoulders, Grace nodded and left the cabin feeling more light of heart than she had in weeks.

* * *

Mary sat still, looking out the open doorway as Grace walked away, her stride elegant, her head held high, her hair a radiant curtain flowing down her back. Then her gaze fell to the baby in her arms. She would let her sleep as long as possible.

And keep her heavy secret as long as she could force herself to do so.

# CHAPTER SIXTEEN

Guided by the moonlight, Grace's arrow soared from the bowstring. A clear, clean shot she had, only the one, but that one sufficed. The arrow met its mark and pierced the deer's neck. The buck fell, crashing heavily through the underbrush, the sound of its fall loud enough to wake both the living and the dead.

Hidden from view behind an oak, she listened, her ears straining at every slight rustle, at every imagined footstep.

Minutes passed. At last, convinced she was alone, she stepped out and walked over to her prey. A young male by the look of the newly formed antlers. Good. At this time of year, most of the does were ready to foal. A male made a far better target.

She bent and yanked the arrow out of its neck. First, she would hide her weapon in the hollow tree trunk nearby. Then if anyone happened upon her, she could claim innocence. She'd need a tale at the ready, an excuse for being alone in the woods at this hour. She ailed? That would do. On her way to Gram O'Neill's for a stomach potion, she came upon the kill.

That might be believed. She could claim the lack of food had her benighted. Quickly, trusting the silence, she hurried to the oldest oak in the copse—the one Da once told her had stood long over two hundred years. The kind of noble tree the druids might have worshipped. Despite an opening in the trunk, its branches sprouted every spring, though less and less each year.

She reached into the narrow hollow. From it she

pulled out a canvas sleeve, reinserted the bow and arrow and closed the flap. Da may not have believed in book reading, but thank the Lord he'd believed in arms for self-defense.

She smiled at the remembrance of herself as a wee lass playing with the small bow and arrow he'd fashioned for her. What had started out as child's play soon became serious.

Why shouldn't she be able to use the bow with ease? she'd asked. "Don't tell me women can't shoot as well as men, Da. They must. They die in war, too."

He'd smiled at her vehemence and given in, finally. Over time, her accuracy had improved enough to impress even Da and outshine Liam's halfhearted efforts. They never spoke of that, nor did she display to Liam as she had to her father the sizable hard muscle in her right upper arm.

Before she dropped the canvas sleeve back into its hiding place, she reached into the opening again and pulled out a knife by its horn handle. She'd best be wary of the blade. The day before, she'd honed it to a razor's edge on an oiled sharpening stone.

No time to waste! Lying on its side, the beast appeared to weigh about twelve stone, heavier than she'd thought. It should be hung and drained of blood, but that wasn't possible. She'd have to begin without wasting any time, but dear God, she could use Mary's aid with the butchering, a job she hated. She'd plucked and dressed chickens and had helped Da when he slaughtered a pig each leaf falling time, but a nearly full grown deer, never.

Ah, well, a peasant woman should be able to do this deed without flinching. She knelt by the buck's belly and plunging the blade into the center of the gut, slit it open. The viscera poured out onto the ground giving off a mingled scent of hot blood and a sickly sweet ripeness. Ignoring the cold, she pulled off her old gray skirt and her waist and hung them on a branch. She'd work in her worn shift; the guts would befoul her clothing and her hands and arms.

No help for it. The riches that lay in front of her were more important. Working fast, she separated the heart, kidneys and liver and set them aside. The liver she'd divide, half for Mary and the other half for Brigit. The heart and kidneys would go to Gram O'Neill. Gram had to keep well. The women of Ballybanree needed their midwife.

Now to separate the haunches from the hide. She slid the blade under the pelt. When she had it well loosened, she laid down the knife and using both hands pulled at the skin until it peeled away with the sound of ripping cloth.

She picked up the knife again, working it into the flesh until it struck a thighbone. Using all of her strength, she applied pressure to the joint. When she heard the bone crack, she hacked at the last shreds of clinging flesh and cut the haunch free.

Now to make up a bundle! In the dark, wrapped in a rag, the meat could pass for a swaddled baby. She shrugged on her clothes and hurried to their meeting place. As they had planned, Mary waited, shivering with cold in the lane by the hanging oak. With any luck at all, she would get her prize home without detection.

Grace put down the bundle and hugged her tight. "I've carved up a good part of it," she said. "The heart and kidneys are for Gram O'Neill. The rest is for you. As soon as you see this home, come back. I'll have more ready by then. I'll put it in the branches of the old hollow oak."

Mary picked up the meat and clasped it to her chest. "God bless, Grace."

"He has already this night. Did you bring another piece of rag?"

"Behind the tree—"

"Good. I'll take it back with me and wrap up more. Cut it into smaller pieces and share with the neediest. If anyone asks, say you found it on your doorstep. You have no knowledge of who left it. And Mary, when you cook the meat, use the dampest peat. The smoke will help disguise the smell of the cooking."

Mary nodded in quick agreement. "I'll be back as soon as I can. Then I'll start my fire. 'Tis unlikely Rushmount's men will be searching through the village at this hour."

They might search at any time, Grace thought, but why burden Mary with more fears? Yet truth be told, Mary could be right. If Rushmount's men suspected no trouble, they might be less diligent. No poaching had been discovered for months now.

She picked up the rag cloth and hurried back to her prey before the forest creatures harmed it. She had to finish what she'd started. Too many mouths were going hungry. Owen's included. She'd leave part of the loin inside his door. It would only take a second, a quick press of his latch, to drop the meat on his workbench.

The thought cheered her and sped up the bloody task. Despite the strength in her arm, she wearied. Yet with each thrust of the blade, her determination grew. Every bit of this food would be put to good use.

She glanced up at the sky. The sun would rise soon. Still she wouldn't rest and wait for Mary's return. The risk of being seen or having the offal discovered was too great. A shame to waste the hide, but to cure it meant chancing discovery. She'd have to discard it along with the entrails and the hooves and antlers. But where?

She had no time to dig a hole. As Owen had done for Da, an unmarked grave she couldn't visit or cover with wild flowers.

She stifled the thought half formed. This wasn't the time for more grieving. The remains had to be hidden and quickly. The ravine at the edge of the woods offered the fastest solution. Too steep and treacherous for man or beast, it was unlikely Rushmount's men would venture there. She'd throw the scraps over the edge. In no time, the forest creatures would reduce them to a pile of bones, or less. The antlers were the danger, no denying their origin. But with God to help her and with spring filling in the undergrowth with fresh green, they might never be found. The bloodied ground where the deer lay she could cover with dead leaves.

Her arms straining with effort, she lifted the remaining bundles of meat into the branches of the hollow oak. That would help keep the catch safe until Mary could get back and carve it into pieces.

And give her time to wash the blood off her hands.

* * *

"Brigit! Look what I found!" The surprise in Grace's voice drew Brigit to the cottage door. "Look at this! Meat! When I went out to make my water, there it lay on the doorstep."

At the sight, Brigit's eyes flew wide open.

Grace placed the bloodied bundle on the table and unwrapped it fully. "A piece of liver and an entire haunch."

"Oh my God. 'Tis venison. The poacher's returned!" Brigit's hand darted up to her mouth. "Who would take such a risk?"

Grace shrugged. "Whoever it is, he wants us to have this. Da always shared his kills."

Brigit nodded. "Aye, many a time he left gifts of meat at my family's door. But if we're found with it—"

"We won't be. We'll eat this up as soon as we can. I'll take a bit of suet from the haunch to fry the liver. Has Liam eaten yet today?"

"He took a fistful of oat cake when he went out."

"That's all? Then he'll be hungry. You must have the largest piece, but there is plenty for him as well. And some for me, too."

"I'm afraid."

Grace paused, the carving knife in midair. She plunged it into the fat that marbled the haunch and sliced off a strip. "We're all afraid, Brigit. But we can't let our fear stop us. We'll eat this meat for the strength to go on living. And hope to everything holy the poacher strikes again soon."

She rammed the knife point into the tabletop. "And

again." She withdrew the blade. "And again." Once more, the blade struck the wood. "And again—"

Brigit reached out to catch Grace's arm and stay her hand. "You'll be destroying the table entirely," she said, a little smile lifting her mouth. "I understand. You have the passion in you."

And your husband, my brother, does not, Grace wanted to shout. Or maybe he did in ways that Brigit understood. Grace hugged her tight. "Forgive me."

"For what? You need no forgiveness." Brigit kissed her cheek. At the light feathering, like that of an angel, Grace felt tears spring into her eyes.

"You have blood from the meat on your waist," Brigit said, "and on your arms. If you want to be having a morning wash, I'll stoke the fire. Then after we've eaten the liver, I'll put the haunch on the spit. 'Twill last us for many meals."

"My intent exactly."

Grace turned from Brigit's look of surprise and went out to the wooden bucket they kept in the yard for washing. This time, in broad daylight, she would be more thorough with herself than at dawn by the stream.

In future, she would have to be careful not a single slip of the tongue escaped her. Having Mary know the truth was risk enough, but Brigit mustn't have the slightest suspicion.

Freed of the blood stains at last, she went inside and found Brigit at the table busily slicing the liver. "It parted under the knife like new butter," she said. The rendered fat in the spider had melted into hot liquid. Using the tip of her knife, Brigit eased the liver slices into the pan. Soon the aroma of sizzling meat filled the air.

"Ah, this is a million times better than a cold crust, is it not?" Grace asked.

"Indeed," Brigit agreed. "It's nearly ready. I'll call Liam in."

"I'll fetch him," Grace said.

"There's no need." Liam's big frame blocked the

light from the open door. "I could smell the cooking a field away. Liver is it?"

Brigit stooped over the fire and tried the meat with the knife tip. "'Tis ready for you, Liam."

With a swift stride, Liam loomed over her. He peered into the spider. "Where did you get this?"

"'Twas lying by the door."

"Anyone about?"

Brigit shook her head. Using a wadded rag to protect her hand, she lifted the spider off the fire and carried it to the table.

"Liam, there's venison too," she said. "I'll cook it as soon as we've eaten. 'Twill be safe enough. No one from Rushmount Manor's been about the countryside for weeks now. 'Twill do us for a long while."

Liam hurried to the open door and slammed it shut causing the walls to shake in protest. The smoke, deprived of an easy exit, began drifting upward toward the vent hole in the thatch.

He strode back to the table and banged his fist on its scarred surface. At the impact, the spider leaped up spattering the hot fat.

Grace jumped out of the way of the flying drops. "Would you scald us in grease, Liam?"

"Fools, both of you. Fools!"

Liam's angry eyes moved from Grace to Brigit, and as Grace watched, Brigit's chin started to tremble.

"Liam, for God's sake—" Grace began.

"Leave God's sake out of this," he said. "What of our sakes? Have you forgotten Da? Should we risk everything for a taste of meat?"

"Not for myself or for you. Brigit needs the meat for your son."

"Ah." He said no more, but stood with his knuckles pressing the tabletop as if the table were all that held him upright.

Brigit ran to him and threw her arms around him. Without glancing at her, he reached out to stroke her back, his eyes focused on the pieces of liver growing cold in the spider.

That would not do, Grace thought. Brigit needed the nourishment. They all did.

She took three wooden plates from the shelf on the wall and placed slices of the fried liver on each one, reserving the largest piece for Brigit.

"Here, Liam, have a bite. 'Twill do you good," she said.

"I can't. 'Tis stolen."

At his words, Grace's anger flared up as searing hot as the venison fat had been moments before. "Eat, damn it. Starving to death takes no courage."

"No one's starving here."

"Look to the root cellar if you have not already. We'll be hard-pressed to last until the new crop is in."

"Whose fault is that?" Liam asked in a voice quiet as death before he turned and walked out of the cottage. This time he closed the door without making the slightest sound.

# CHAPTER SEVENTEEN

Had he heard the door latch open and then close? Strange. Who would steal into his hut at dawn and a moment later leave quiet as a thief?

With his breeches midway to his hips and the awkward boot yet to be pulled on, Owen swung back the curtain separating his living space from the workshop. The room stood empty. Perhaps he'd imagined the sound.

He glanced about at the stone firepit where banked embers gave off a faint reddish glow, at his buckets of water for cooling heated iron, at the pieces of unshaped metal hanging on the walls, at his workbench strewn with tools from yesterday's task repairing leaks in the McElroy brothers' copper tubing.

His payment had been a rare treat, a half pint of their *uisce beatha*. If he savored only a mouthful at a time, it would last him for weeks to come.

Ah, but the magic of that mouthful! In the middle of the night, it had brought him visions of Grace. Once more, he'd held her and tangled his fingers in the silk of her hair and tangled his legs with hers only to awaken damp with his own excitement.

Alone.

*As you have chosen to be.*

He would have to have a look at Sean McElroy's jug. Perhaps he'd had more than a mere mouthful of the whiskey. But then, he needed little to bring Grace to his heart. And loins.

No sense in more looking. Nothing was amiss. The thief, if that's who it had been, hadn't taken time to seize a tool in his fist.

About to turn back for a taste of food, he spied a wrapped bundle on the floor next to the workbench. The cloth wrapping oozed blood. What in God's name? He hurried to the bundle and flung back the covering.

Ribs of meat, crudely butchered, but meat for all that. Enough for days of feasting lay at his feet.

Venison. So a poacher had gone ahunting again. Good God. After Red Liam's hanging, what other man in Ballybanree would take the risk?

He picked up the meat and carried it to the table behind the curtain. First, he'd finish dressing, then contraband or not, he'd stoke the fire and cook this gift. The skinny children next door could use a good feed and then some.

Despite the truth of that, poaching was a dangerous way to keep hunger at bay. If discovered, it would lead Lord Rushmount to further reprisals. There had to be a better solution.

An idea he'd harbored for months, ever since Red Liam's death, filled his mind anew. Perhaps he should take up his acquaintance with Father Joyce and lay his thoughts out in the open. No man in the village gave better counsel.

A twinge of guilt shot through him. He'd ignored the priest and his God for years. To keep scandal at bay, he attended the Mass each week, but with a heart of stone. Yet he knew that even with bitterness darkening his soul, he would be welcomed by the priest. At the thought, the cold iron band that kept a permanent grip on his chest eased a bit. The old priest had taught him to read, and in defiance of church custom had given him his English Bible, his only treasure, and had been treated shabbily in return. Was it Father Joyce's fault that his God would not, or could not, restore Owen O'Donnell's leg to normal?

He knew the answer, but stubborn pride had kept him frozen within himself blaming everything and everyone—God, the world, Father Joyce, and his own boyhood curiosity above all. Grace alone had shattered the ice around his heart. For the brief, wondrous time they'd spent in the cave together, her magic had prevailed and made him whole again.

Ach, the rantings of an idiot. He wasn't whole, and she was a goddess from heaven. Those shining hours she'd given him, he mustn't believe they could last. He had nothing to give her in return except his crippled self and the skill of his hands. Above all, he lacked land for her sons to inherit. His longing for her was a fool's dream.

Young Connor Mann now, he could give her so much more. His family owned their thirty acres outright, a grant from Cromwell, and their ownership left intact by King Charles...mayhap Lord Rushmount had had a hand in that. They had cattle to drive to the upland pastures every summer, and for added measure, Connor held the post of estate manager for his lordship. Indeed, the Manns were wealthy. The great beauty of Ballybanree *should* marry into their midst.

And lie in Young Connor's arms and sweep him to paradise. Bedeviled by his thoughts, Owen paced the cabin until the sound of his own uneven footsteps drove him out into the sunlight. He'd see if Father Joyce had time to listen to his ideas.

In the clearing in front of their hut, the three Burke lads ran about in the warm spring air chasing a stone with stout sticks.

"Whack!"

"Whack!"

A long shot, then "whack!"

"Not fair! You cheated. You missed the circle!"

Listen to the lungs on the lad, Owen thought. Emmet couldn't be more than five and already a fighter. Good for him. He'd need that scrappiness, a croppie's son who would soon be toiling next to his da in someone else's fields.

Eileen hurried to him as she always did. Even his deepest scowls never daunted her. Her faded blue shift hung loosely about her, but her wan, dirty face opened up like a flower with the smile she gave him.

"Owen! We will eat meat today."

"That's grand news to be hearing!"

Of course. Whoever left the loin for him, a lone man, would surely consider these needy children. God, how would Donal keep them all alive on his meager earnings? Mary had lost two little ones in the past. Babes died, oftentimes from lack of food, but not so long as the mother could nurse her babe.

*Ah!*

"Is your da inside?" he asked Eileen.

"Not today. He has a job of work at the McElroys."

*The McElroys. With the worst yielding acres in Ballybanree.*

"I'll have a word with your mam, then."

Eileen ran ahead of him and burst into the cabin. "Owen's here, Mam."

He waited for Mary's welcome before entering.

"'Tis a fine day, Owen," she said finally, "and 'tis early in it for calling."

A cool greeting. He stepped inside nonetheless. A smoldering fire filled the single room with the earthy scent of burning peat and sent a steady trail of smoke toward the vent hole.

The fuel wasn't dry enough. Mary would know that. She must be trying to disguise the cooking. Already the haunch skewered on the spit had turned brown, its succulent odors penetrating the thick air.

Eileen pointed to the meat. "See, Owen. I told you."

"Leave us," Mary ordered, her voice sharper than Owen had ever heard it.

She sat by the fire, watching the roast, the baby quiet on her lap. In the corners of the room, the children's straw pallets and their few coverings lay on the floor against the smoke-blackened walls. The firepit in the center and the trestle table with its stools and a backless bench nearly filled the remaining space.

Mary pointed to an overturned stool. "Straighten that up, Owen, and sit for a while."

"Mary, I have venison as well. I found it in the workshop earlier." She glanced down at the fire, but not before he saw a stab of fear come into her eyes. "Do you know who might have left it?" He waited, but only the hiss from fat dripping onto the smoldering peat met his question. "Do you?"

"The poacher," she whispered.

"Without doubt. Did you see him?"

Again, a strange hesitation clouded her eyes before she shook her head.

*She knows something.*

"Mary, I'm your neighbor and your friend. I would die before I would hurt you or your children. But someone's into dangerous work, and I would speak to the man. That's all. Just speak."

"I know of no such man." Her eyes met his unflinching and direct. They concealed nothing, not this time, yet he had the feeling she knew more than she told.

He righted the stool and sat opposite her. The baby on her lap stirred faintly.

"She'll be waking soon to be fed," Mary said. "I pray to heaven I can do for her."

Tears filled Mary's eyes and threatened to course down her cheeks. So that was the way of it. Good Lord, the woman was more desperate for the food than he'd known. He could have kicked himself.

"The poacher knows of your plight?"

She nodded.

"I see." He stared down at his hands. How could he look at the woman's ravaged face and say what he must? "Mary, I understand. Believe me, I do. But do you understand the poacher is risking death?"

As he looked up, her tears spilled over and fell freely, coursing down her face to drop onto the baby's head.

Another Baptism, he thought, this one as sacred as the first. "We can't have his death on our souls, can we?"

Wordless, she shook her head.

"Let me talk to him, Mary. There might be a better way for us than poaching. Let me try. Let me know the man."

"I know of no man."

"But—"

"Our dear friend, Grace O'Malley. She may know something."

Mary reached out to turn the spit. At the sudden movement, baby Deirdre opened her eyes and began to mewl.

The wee creature sounds like a weak kitten, Owen thought as he got to his feet.

From Mary's guilty tone, he was certain Grace knew who the man was. He'd have to see her then. Joy caught at his throat. But when he swallowed, fear was what he tasted.

Fear for her.

\* \* \*

She sat on the low stone wall turned away from him, the full play of her hair running over her shoulders and down to the small of her back. The sight took his breath away. Her tresses were longer than he remembered from the summer last. But he well remembered their silken feel, the luxury of probing her curls with his fingers and the way those tendrils of gold clung to him pinning his hands in heaven.

As he watched, she moved the brush through her hair lifting strands, fanning them out in the sunshine. It was like fanning flames with a bellows, the way they caught fire from the sun.

He stepped closer. "Grace."

She whirled around. Could he be wrong, or had her heart leapt into her face when he spoke her name?

She'd become thin; shadows had formed in her cheeks. Her eyes were huge, greener and more luminous than ever. But her lips, parted in surprise, were the same, and as soft he would warrant.

"I never expected company today," she said. "I'm after washing my hair. It's almost dry."

"I can see that."

She stilled the brush letting it rest in her lap and gazed down at it.

He'd never seen her so subdued. "I would have a word with you."

At that her head came up, as defiant as a queen's. "A word? Only that?"

Unable to tear his glance away, he watched as she gathered her hair's glory in one hand and bound it at the nape of her neck with a length of green ribbon. "The poacher's hunting again. He made a killing last night. Mary Burke said you might know of him."

She stiffened. "Why me?"

*She wasn't going to make this easy.* "Mary's a sensible woman. She wouldn't mention your name without a reason."

Grace jumped down from the wall and stood facing him, one hand holding the brush, the other fisted by her side. "I have nothing to tell you."

"You're lying to me, Grace. You know who it is. Tell me, lass, so I can stop him. Poaching is not the way. You, of all people, should know that. He risks death."

"Maybe he cares not. Maybe he has little to live for. Or maybe he prefers to die with courage like my da, not an inch at a time."

She turned away showing him her straight back and the bound tail of her golden hair. But she hadn't turned in time to hide her tears.

He caught her arm and spun her around. Her face was close, so close to his own, her chin tilted upward, her eyes closed, the tears squeezing out from under the lids...her lips were slightly open.

*God help me. Turn me into stone.*

With the words barely formed in his mind, before any god anywhere could grant his wish, he bent to her and took her lips with his own. She opened under his kiss, wide and then wider, her tongue meeting his as he probed her soft mouth. Ah, how well he remembered her open to him in all ways.

Abruptly, as abruptly as he'd seized her, he let her go. She staggered backward.

*This was madness.*

"No more, lass. No more."

She swiped at her wet cheeks with the back of a hand. "You don't like it?"

"I came to learn of the poacher. Only that."

"Only that? Well you'll go away unsatisfied, Owen O'Donnell. In every way. But that is your choice."

"I have no choice."

"Now it is you who lie. You could have me if you wished." She swiped at her face again. "But you choose not to."

How could he make her understand, this woman with sorrow distorting her face? This woman he loved more than life. "One thing I would have you know. The hours in the cave...they were the reason I was born."

He saw hope come into her eyes as she moved back to him.

The hope turned to resolve as she said, "Then you should know something as well. I must leave here. Liam is too hard pressed—"

"Marry Young Connor Mann."

White faced, she came so close to him he could count the light dusting of freckles across the bridge of her nose. How he longed to make a love game of the count.

"You want Con's hands on me?" she asked. "His body in mine?" She dropped her voice to a whisper and seized the front of his shirt. "Is that what you want? Tell me, is that what you want?"

His eyes betrayed him. Not since childhood had he felt them wet with tears. "I love you more than I love myself," he said. "Marriage to Connor is best for you."

She let go of his shirt and stepped back. "Can I not judge what's best for me?"

He grasped her arm to stay her until he could explain. "Grace—"

She wrenched free. "Keep away! I hate you for what

you're doing to us. Hate you! Do you hear me? Do you?"

She twisted away from his arm's reach, and with her skirt whipping about her legs, ran to the cottage and disappeared inside.

He ignored the tears that streamed down his face into the stubble on his chin.

He'd lost her utterly.

Nothing else mattered. Not even the reason he'd come here to see her.

# CHAPTER EIGHTEEN

To Ross Rushmount's surprise, that glorious redhead, the O'Malley girl, came hurrying out of the woods and ran across the meadow toward the Mann cottage. In her haste, she didn't see him riding in the distance. He reined in his mount to watch her.

Slim, with a long-legged stride, she crossed the field rapidly on her bare feet, her skirt swirling about her. She must have sewn the garment from the black cloth he'd sent and sashed it with a fringed red scarf. Her hair, caught up at the temples with a piece of red ribbon, flowed over her linen waist.

Of all the women in Ballybanree, this one, this Grace O'Malley, he encountered the most often, in the lanes, or in the fields, or on his grounds. Or was it that he noticed her the most? Like a single bright star in a dark sky she caught and held the eye.

He wondered at her haste. And her beauty. How had she sprung from these peasants? When he could insinuate the question carelessly, he'd make a point of asking Connor about her people. Con might have some tales worth hearing.

Her father, of course, he knew about. Unfortunate that of all the villagers, he'd had to scapegoat Red Liam. No doubt she hated him for it. Too bad, but absolutely necessary. She had a brother—now the tenant on the same acres—who'd recently married.

The chestnut tossed back its head and whinnied. Ross leaned over to stroke him. "You want your run, boy? All right, but a short one this morning."

Something had drawn the girl along so quickly she nearly tripped in her haste. He'd see what that might be and have another look at her up close. For pretext, though he really didn't need one, he'd claim thirst and a cup of cool water from Connor's wife.

While still a field's distance away, he dismounted and led the chestnut to a grassy plot enclosed by a stone wall. The horse could crop there in safety for a while. "I'll be back, boy. We'll have our run yet." Already busy at the grass, the horse ignored him as Ross closed the gate and strode across the field.

The cottage door had been left open to the soft spring air. He stood in the opening, blocking the light. At that, the girl looked up from her seat at the table. He heard her quick intake of breath.

"May I come in?" he asked.

"Mistress Mann is out by the hens," she said.

"Then I'll have to wait, won't I?"

As he stepped into the room, he realized he'd never entered the cottage before. Curious, he looked about for a moment. Unlike the village huts, this one had a fireplace with a chimney that kept the soot from blackening the walls. From a pot suspended above the coals, the odor of cooking—a stewed rabbit most likely—rose in the air. Against a wall cupboard, pewter plates shone softly, and in the corner opposite the fire, under the single window, a loom stood half filled with linen in the making.

He stepped farther into the room, his boots creating no sound on the hard-packed dirt floor. It was a warm, well-ordered place with a pallet bed in one corner.

The girl's eyes never left him as he looked around. He enjoyed filling her vision and her curiosity. Here in Ballybanree, he seldom bothered with the formality and discomfort of a wig. That morning he'd clubbed back his hair with a cord and had freshly shaven. For some reason, he was pleased he'd done so. As for the rest of him, like all the Rushmount men, he had a tall, angular frame with well-developed thighs from his many hours on horseback. The men in the family rarely ran to fat in middle years as his lean father and uncle had proven.

Vanity over that more than anything else caused them to order their clothes from the best London tailors. The perfect cut of his tweed riding jacket would be lost on her, of course.

She looked much as he remembered, but thinner, with strain showing in her face. Surely not from his presence alone.

"I came in to beg Mistress Mann for a drink of water," he said.

Her lips curled upward, but for an instant only. So the 'beg' had not been lost on her nor, perhaps, the cut of his clothes.

"I can get that for you," she said, "and save Kath the trouble."

She stood from the bench by the table and walked over to the cupboard, her step as casual as if he were not the lord of the manor whose every wish should be a hastily filled command. From a bucket on the floor, she dipped up a cup of well water and held it out to him without coming forward to proffer it.

*How dare she!*

And how in the world did she keep herself so *clean?*

The hand holding the cup was white, its rounded nails astonishingly free of grime. Her skin, pale against that amazing hair, hadn't been touched with powder or paint and shone, most unfashionably, with no attempt made to cover the light dance of freckles across her small, straight nose.

Very well, he'd indulge her game. He came forward to take the cup. As he did, his fingers brushed hers. He felt their touch along every nerve end in his body. He gulped down the water and held out the cup again.

"Another," he said.

She took the cup and refilled it. This time she put the cup down on top of the cupboard. So she'd felt something, too?

He sipped slowly. The bed chamber, if that's what the natives called it, must be in the small ell off the main room. He'd be willing to wager a year's rental it held a bed big enough for two.

Grace moved back to the table and took her place in front of an opened book. A Bible! What in the devil was she doing with that? He'd have sworn she couldn't read.

He took his cup to the table and glanced down at the open page. The seventy-fourth Psalm.

She sat quietly studying the page, ignoring him. The little vixen showed no fear whatever. So it wasn't his presence that caused the look of tension about her mouth.

He sat opposite her. Silent minutes passed. He'd make the damn water last all morning if he had to. As he watched her bowed head, one of her fingers reached out and began to move slowly across the text a single word at a time. Was she actually reading or carrying on a charade? There was only one way to find out.

"The seventy-fourth," he said. "One of my favorites. Would you read it aloud so we can pray together?"

A quick flash of eyes. God, the girl had wit. Nothing of his intent escaped her.

"I will," she said. She began haltingly, her voice unsure at first until the poetry gathered momentum and swept her into its terror.

*"Determined to destroy us once and for all, They burned down every shrine of God in the country, Deprived of signs, with no prophets left, Who can say how long this will last?"*

Her body tensed over the page, her finger moving more and more rapidly, almost unnecessary now.

*"By Your power You split the sea in two, And smashed the heads of monsters on the waters."*

She wasn't merely parroting the words. He could see how they caught at her and set her on fire.

*"Rise, God, say something on Your own behalf... Remember the shouting of Your enemies, This everrising clamour of Your...Your ad..."*

Puzzled by the word, she frowned at the page.

"Adversaries," he said.

"Aye," she acknowledged. "Adversaries."

He caught his breath as she sounded out the word and then lifted her gaze from the page to his face. He cleared his throat. "Thank you. That was like being in church. An Irish one," he added. "Your Gaelic lilt added much to the reading."

She shook her head. "The Psalms are not read at Mass. Not in the English. Not much in Latin, either."

"I see."

She closed the Bible. "I'll find out what's keeping Kath."

"No, don't bother. I'm leaving." He held up the empty cup. "You gave me what I came for."

Before getting to his feet, he pointed to the gilding on the book's leather cover. "That's the Rheims Douay version. You prefer that one?"

"'Tis the only book I know. Young Con has me read it with him."

*Young Con.*

He must have his cap set for her. And why not? Any man would want her. Any man. But what of her own desires? Most likely they would be a luxury she couldn't indulge. No doubt Mann offered the best chance in life she'd ever have.

Or did he?

"You have never read English poetry, then, or a play?"

She stroked the leather cover. "This only. I do not know the meaning of 'a play'."

He realized her expression hadn't changed since he walked into the room, except for that sardonic suggestion of a smile when he begged for the water, but just then, for an instant, he saw a spark of longing flare up in her eyes. Yes, he would tempt her. Offer her the golden apple. Make her smile at him.

He stood. "I must go. My horse will think I've deserted him. But should I remember it, I'll have Connor bring a play book to you."

She stood as well. "Thank you, but I can accept nothing from you."

She had the gall of ten men. And as he suspected, she hated him, at least for now.

"I'm not *giving* the book to you. It's a loan. I'll expect you to return it to me after you've read it. Nothing will be given, nothing will be taken, except a smattering of language—"

"Good glory, your lordship, I didn't know." Connor's wife hurried into the room, her quick curtsy made clumsy by the eggs in her upturned apron. "The hens are hiding their eggs more cleverly each day. I've had a terrible time finding them."

Her glance moved from him to Grace. "Did you offer refreshment to his lordship, Grace? There's ale in the cupboard."

"My needs have been nicely cared for," he said amused by his own lie.

The woman took the eggs from her apron and set them one by one into a wooden bowl on the cupboard. "'Twould only take a minute to have the kettle boiling."

"I must get back. Lady Anne is much alone."

"May I ask how her ladyship fares?"

"Not well, I'm afraid. But she'll soon be better."

"God willing."

Far gone in pregnancy, Anne faced her coming ordeal by resting in bed much of the time. As he did most days, he'd see that she dressed, swollen belly or not, and come to his study for tea. Without his insistence, she'd remain isolated until her lying-in. Poor Anne. 'To hell or Connaught' must have been uttered with her in mind. How she hated it here.

But as the second son of a man with impeccable bloodlines and dwindling purse strings, he considered himself fortunate to have inherited the unencumbered, if rundown, estate of his childless uncle. Without General Rushmount's bequest where would he be?

Not here on the western edge of Europe, on the least fertile land in all of Ireland, that was certain. But unlike Anne, he enjoyed this untamed place, its freedom from constraints, and the heady experience of ruling his own fiefdom with no one to say 'nay' to his wishes—not even Anne—as she'd learned. And not the locals who feared him even more than she. All except this O'Malley girl who stared at him now with questions in her eyes.

"Good day, ladies."

He tried to keep the irony out of his voice as he spoke the word 'ladies.' From the sudden color that leaped into Grace's cheeks, he hadn't tried hard enough. Yes, he'd be certain to inquire about her from Connor.

She's a mere peasant, he reminded himself. No more than that. Did she realize the favor he conferred by conversing with her as if she were an equal? By offering her a folio of Shakespeare?

Why bother, he wondered? He could take what he wanted, and no one could stop him. What would the Manns do if he had her, made her his own possession? Nothing. Young Connor would smolder with silent oaths, but he wouldn't defy him openly.

So why not topple her the next time she roamed the woods and fields alone? It might come to that yet, but first he'd try enticing her. The pleasure would be sweeter that way.

He strode out to the meadow and whistled for the chestnut. It cantered toward him eager for its run. "We both need a good ride, boy," he said as he swung into the saddle. "But you're getting yours first."

# CHAPTER NINETEEN

The library study table, usually bare during Connor's meetings with his lordship, groaned under an array of food. A ham showing more meat than bone sat on a platter. The fat clinging to it made his mouth water. Beside the ham, he spied a loaf of dark bread and a wee tub of mustard sauce. Resting on the cloth was a silver-handled knife sharp enough by the look of it to slice open his very throat.

Next to the meat, a tiered tray piled with artfully arranged bits of pastry caught his eye—each pastry small enough to scoop up with one hand. Preserved fruit covered some of the goodies. Glazed nutmeats sat atop others, and still others had the sticky look of honey buns.

A round tray held a silver pot of tea, a rare treat, and made from unused leaves he would wager. Beside it was a smaller silver pot with cream and several porcelain cups.

As always, on the edge of the desk, a decanter of port surrounded by crystal goblets awaited his lordship's arrival.

*He must be expecting a visitor. There's never a feast laid out when I'm due here.*

He hadn't long to wait. Rushmount swept in with his usual air of impatient hurry. Connor sighed. The man would never learn the Irish way of things. Hurry had no purpose in life except to rush a man to his grave, and why be in a hurry for that?

"Connor."

"Your lordship."

Rushmount rubbed his hands together over the

laden tabletop. "Lady Anne will not be down to join me, so I thought you and I might have this repast instead. What say you?"

"A mighty fine collation, my lord. I've been admiring it."

"Help yourself, man. Help yourself. Take up a plate. Fill it."

Connor carved a thick slice of ham, laid it on a slab of the dark bread and picked up two of the wee pastries. The honey buns.

Ignoring the tea, Rushmount poured two glasses of port wine and placed one on the desk near Connor's chair.

Although not really hungry, Connor ate. The bread had been baked so soft it fairly melted in the mouth, and the cakes, gorgeous they were. If Kath could taste the like of them, she wouldn't believe the sweetness.

With Rushmount's attention focused on him, he finished the last of his food, washing it down with a short swallow of the port. This he'd imbibed before on the rare occasions when his lordship, pleased with his accounts, had offered him a glass. It tasted sweet as well, without the power to quench a man's thirst like ale or to burn with whiskey's clean fire.

An overly refined drink, this port, not suited to the Irish palate. He twirled the half-empty glass in his fingers and held it up to the light, admiring the wine's rich, red color.

Rushmount pointed to the decanter. "More?"

Con couldn't believe his ears. He was being treated like a guest of the house. Why? Suddenly alert, he put down the glass. Port, for all its sweetness, pooled in the gut like other strong drink. He'd have no more today.

"Thank you kindly. 'Tis rich for me."

Rushmount picked up his own glass. "You prefer the local whiskey."

"Some of it. Some *uisce beatha* is better than others. But in the end, thanks be to God, they all have the same effect."

Ross laughed. "I'd like to try a superior sample sometime. What I've had so far tasted like piss and set my insides on fire."

"'Tis not smooth like port, your lordship, even the best of the best. But I'll see what I can do."

"Excellent. Now to business. If you've had your fill, let's begin."

Dusk darkened the corners of the wood-lined study before Connor's accounting ended.

All tenant farms had been plowed, the larger holdings of five acres or more with the use of Rushmount's team of oxen. And again, for a second year at Rushmount's insistence, an experimental field at Con's own farm had been put to potatoes. From what he'd observed of the *praities* last year, Connor had to admit the yield was higher than any of the staple grains. His lordship's pigs had grown fat on the tubers, but so far no man or woman in the village could be persuaded to taste one. Poison they termed them and shuddered at the thought of boiling them up for a meal. A shame, really. If the pigs thrived on them, then perhaps humans would as well. When the crop came in, he'd insist Kath cook a few for him, and he'd take the chance. No one lived forever. And perhaps as his lordship predicted, potatoes *were* the crop of the future.

The rest of the fields had been planted in oats, rye and barley with smaller plots given over to perishable vegetables: cabbage, onions, turnips, carrots. A few of the larger holdings, his own included, had put in a few acres of flax.

By week's end, Connor's older son, Hugh, and his wife and lads would be off *boolying* for the summer. On the green grass of the open uplands, Rushmount's dairy cattle would grow heavy and yield the rich milk that produced the butter and cheese he exported to English markets.

"What a word," Rushmount said, "*boolying*. Only the Irish could make cattle grazing sound like a wild game."

"True," Connor agreed, "the Gaelic is a language like no other." His report over, he quaffed down the last of the wine. 'Twould not do to leave it neglected in the glass. "Overall, given reasonable weather, the season should produce well."

*And God help them, the people need a good crop.*

Rushmount snapped the account ledger closed with a grunt of satisfaction and gave it over to Connor before leaning back in his chair. "There's another matter."

"My lord?"

"I visited your home the other day looking to slake my thirst and encountered that same girl, the one who helped Lady Anne the night of the accident."

"Grace O'Malley."

"Yes, I believe that's her name. She can read."

*Oh Christ, I knew that would cause trouble.* "She means no harm—"

"No, of course not. I was rather amused by her, as a matter of fact. She seems an intelligent girl. The daughter of that poacher?"

Connor nodded. Rushmount knew damned well she was Red Liam's lass. He wanted something, and with a sinking feeling in his belly, Connor feared he knew what that might be.

"Tell me what you know of her and her people."

So that's what the cakes were for. He'd been sweetened up for the telling. He cleared his throat. "We have a name for Grace hereabouts."

"Oh?"

"We call her the Queen of Ballybanree."

"Queen? Indeed." Rushmount's eyebrows quirked up in amused disbelief. "Queen Katherine in London should know she has a rival here in Ireland."

Connor studied Rushmount's face for a telltale sign of anger but saw none. Instead the hint of a smile hovering about his lips grew broader. The sight did little to relieve Connor's fear. The mere idea of an Irish queen should have angered the man. He suspected the less said about the O'Malleys the better. But as he glanced across the polished desk and into Rushmount's waiting eyes, he knew he had little choice except to plunge on.

"She is descended from the most famous woman who ever lived on this shore, Granuaile O'Malley of Clew Bay and Castle Rockfleet. Surely you've heard of her, my lord. She's known in the English as Grace O'Malley. The lass bears her name."

"A rumor of some sort, about a woman sea captain who plied these waters years ago. Spurious, of course. Just another Irish fantasy."

"Not at all, if you'll pardon my saying so. Granuaile lived a full, long life. She was as real as the earth we stand on. Why she met with Elizabeth herself in London at Greenwich Castle. They were both old women then—"

"Nonsense."

Connor clutched the estate ledger to his chest. "There must be a recording of the audience somewhere —in the royal archives, perhaps. 'Twas in 1593 that they met—"

"For what purpose?"

"Granuaile's lands had been seized by the queen's governor, Sir Richard Bingham. She wanted them back. And her fleet of ships. And her son Tibbot released from prison."

Rushmount leaned back in his chair. He raised his arms, elbows out, and cupped the back of his head. "You mean to tell me that a peasant woman, not a *queen,* Connor, a *peasant,* walked into Greenwich Castle and made demands like that of the most powerful woman on earth?"

"As the Lord is my judge."

"Ha! And escaped with her life?"

"'Twas said the queen found Granuaile fascinating." Connor leaned forward feeling the excitement rise as it always did with the telling of this tale. "Think of it, sir, the queen recognizing that this woman matched her in courage and derring-do."

"Hardly that." Rushmount's expression changed from mild amusement to annoyance. He dropped his hands to the desktop and drummed his fingers on the polished mahogany surface. "Not that I believe any of this, you understand, but does rumor say whether the demands of this Granuaile were met?"

"Some were. Her fleet was restored to her. That couldn't have been easy for Her Majesty to grant. You see,"—how he loved recalling this bit—"Granuaile had savaged the British ships over the years and seized much in the way of booty. But she'd also fought and sank Spanish warships, and Elizabeth knew that. So with the promise that Granuaile would no longer attack English vessels, her ships were returned and her home on Clew Bay restored. But not her ancestral lands."

"Which were?"

Con felt sweat break out under his arms. Would he come out of this encounter intact? "Your holding is one, sir."

Lord Rushmount flung himself back in his chair. "You're lying, Connor. This is all Irish blarney. God, you people are insane. My lands belonged to a female pirate? You want me to swallow that."

"The tale that's told is that Bingham, with Elizabeth's blessing, regranted the land"—he was careful not to say 'stole'—"to English loyalists. And so it has remained, but you know the history better than I."

*God, he could do with a drop of the uisce beatha this very minute.*

"What I know and what I have proof for, is that this estate was given over to my ancestors for service to the Crown. Never forget that, Connor. Never. You hear me? I have the support of the English government for what I own. Nothing else amounts to a boil on a horse's arse."

Rushmount's voice had taken on menace. Connor recognized it well. "I do, indeed, sir. Forgive me. My tale got away from me. 'Tis the Irish way when we're excited from the talk."

Connor looked down at the floor covered in a Turkey carpet wondrous with color and interlocked figures. Kath should see this, he thought. As a weaver, she would marvel at the skill it took to create such a rarity.

He dared not look up. He'd gone too far. Revealed himself too openly. Yes, he'd embraced the Protestant faith. Yes, he'd done so out of expediency. But in his heart of hearts, he remained Irish. There was no changing that or the thrill that rose in him with the retelling of Granuaile's defiance.

"What happened to the pirate's son?" Rushmount asked, his voice calm once more. "The one in the British gaol?"

"He was released unharmed and came to love all things English."

"Aha! So the story has a happy ending." Rushmount uttered a short bark of laughter and got to his feet.

*A happy ending.* Now that's the part of the tale that is untrue, Connor thought, but he squeezed out a smile and stood as well. The meeting had ended. As always after one of these sessions, he felt drained of energy, even more so today than usual. He'd been treading dangerous water in revealing these ancient truths to his lordship. No good could come of it.

"Just a minute," Rushmount said. He walked over to the bookcases lining an entire wall of the room and plucked out a thin volume. He handed it over to Connor. "Here, take this with you. It's for the O'Malley girl."

The title *Richard III* had been tooled into the red leather binding. He had to take it. Refusing was not a possibility.

"She knows I'm lending this to her," Rushmount said. "You can return it when she's through."

Connor tried to keep his face impassive, to let no glimmer of apprehension or curiosity show as he tucked the book under his arm. "Very good, sir."

"It might be amusing to learn her opinion of this," Rushmount said almost as an afterthought.

*Her opinion.* The man's smile set Connor's hackles rising.

"I'll see she gets it, my lord."

\* \* \*

Connor threw the book onto the trestle table where it banged against the empty wooden bowls Kath had set out and sent them rocking. She rushed to take the book from harm's way. "If I had the food served, you would have beslopped this." She took the book over to the safety of the cupboard.

"To hell with the book."

"'Tis valuable!"

"Jesus, Mary and Joseph, woman, Rushmount's after Grace."

Kath sank onto the bench by the table. Picking up the hem of her apron, she wrung her hands on it. "I know. I saw it in his eyes the day he came here. He couldn't keep himself from staring at her—everywhere. What can we do, Con?"

"We can do nothing. Nothing! He'll take what he wants and none to stop him."

"'Tis a difficult time for a man. With his wife in the family way, he's feeling the need—"

"Say no more, Kath. That's not the truth of it. His appetite's been whetted, and not by that timid creature he calls wife."

Kath's mouth sagged open. "You've never spoken of a man's need that way before, Con."

"Well, I have now." He sat on the stool opposite her and, resting his elbows on the table, sank his head in his hands.

Kath kept twisting the end of her apron. "I fear for the lass, too."

Connor raised his head, his plump cheeks suddenly feeling haggard as if he'd not eaten his full over and over again these past years.

"I fear for all of us, Kath. Young Con is so taken with Grace there's no telling how he'll react if Rushmount uses her ill. He could ruin us over this if he's not careful."

Kath began smoothing the apron with the flat of her hand. "The lad wants her. I know that full well."

Connor nodded. "And who could blame him? It's all

my fault, Kath."

"'Tis not—"

Con waved a hand, cutting off her protest. "'Tis! I encouraged him with the reading and the courting. She's a rare prize. I wanted him to have her. But is she worth starving for?"

Her apron forgotten, Kath stared across at her husband. "Is that what will become of us?"

"Think, woman, think. We've taken the English faith as our own. Who would have us as friends after that except a loyalist? Where would we go and be welcomed? To another lord's estate with no recommendation from Rushmount?"

"You own your acres outright. His lordship can't take them away."

"Look at our neighbors, Kath, tenants all. The English can do as they will. The laws can be changed. What court would I appeal to if my land were seized? The old Brehon Laws that guided us for centuries are useless now."

Ignoring his fatigue, Connor rose to pace the room. "No matter how accurate I may be in toting up Rushmount's figures, my greatest value is obedience. Without that, I'm dirt under his nails."

Kath came over to him and took his arm. "Hush now. That's enough. Your imagination is running away with you, and all over a wee book. Give me a minute or two and I'll have the meal ready."

"Not tonight, Kath. I've had all I can stomach."

"But—"

"Give the food to Young Con. He'll be in shortly. After he has his fill I'll talk to him."

# CHAPTER TWENTY

Grace slipped the shawl, heavy with spring mist, from her shoulders and laid it on the seat by Kath's loom. Her hair had kept dry, but her ankles and the hem of her skirt were wet from the damp.

Young Con, on his knees by the fireplace, smiled as she entered. The fresh peat he'd laid on the coals hissed and gave off its musky, earthen odor. They would need the light to read by. No sign of Kath and Con. They must be abed. She and Young Con had the main room to themselves more and more often lately, but since the night she'd fled from him, he'd not touched her in any way.

The fire caught and flared up bright and strong. Young Con got up from the hearth. "Mam left food to have while we read." He lifted a linen cloth from a wooden plate. Kath had split oat cakes and lathered them with soft pot cheese. Grace's mouth watered at the sight. Summer food and so early in the season.

"Fresh made," he said. "Mam wants you to try it."

She needed no second invitation. The cows from Rushmount's herd had begun to calve. There would be milk aplenty for those who were fortunate. Then the thought of Mary Burke's hungry children flooded her mind.

Her hand, poised to take up an oat cake, fell to her side without touching one. "Thank you, but I'm not hungry."

"Whatever you say." He replaced the cloth over the plate.

She'd be less tempted, Grace thought, without the sight of the cakes sitting in front of her while they read. Or, as most often happened, while she read and young

Con sat by listening and giving her the meaning of words she didn't know. His da had taught him well. He stumbled over very few words, and there were even fewer he didn't understand the meaning of at all.

She took her place on the bench by the table near the rush light, and he sat by her side. When she went to open the Bible, he placed his hand on the cover, staying her. She caught a whiff of sweat from him, he was that close.

"Not yet," he said.

His usually placid face, the cheeks tending toward plumpness like his father's, wore an anxious crease between the brows.

"There's something else." He went to the wall cupboard and came back with a slim volume bound in red leather. "'Tis for you."

She gasped. "Oh my God, where did you get this?"

"From his lordship. He's loaning it to you. He wants your opinion of it."

"My op—" Grace's mouth opened into a round 'o' of disbelief, then catching her lower lip in her teeth, she bit down to make certain she wasn't dreaming.

He held it out. "Take it. It's yours. At least for a while."

"'Tis unbelievable. He did what he promised he would do."

Young Con nodded, frowning.

She took the book from his hands. Unlike the Bible, it was small and light enough to hold up off the table. Carefully, as if it were the door to a secret treasure vault, she opened a page. The printing looked different from the Bible with names running down the left side of each sheet.

"What are these names, Con? King Richard, Lady Anne, the Prince of Wales? Why are they here?"

He sat beside her again, close enough to let his leg rub against hers. "See this," he pointed to the word Richard. "Until you come to the next name, everything you read is spoken by Richard. The same with each one."

"Then it's a book of talk."

"Exactly. A play it's called. Da saw one once when he was a lad. A troop of players came to Galway. 'Twas magical, he said."

Grace couldn't tear her gaze from the book. She held it up to the light and slowly began to read, stumbling only at the most difficult words.

*"Now is the winter of our discontent*
*Made glorious summer by this sun of York;*
*And all the clouds that lour'd upon our house*
*In the deep bosom of the ocean buried."*

"'Tis beautiful sounding," she said.

"You are right to begin at the beginning. To understand the tale, you must start there. 'Tis different from the Bible in that as well."

"I see." She looked back at the page eager to go on, but the weight of Young Con's hand came down on her own.

"Not now. We need to talk first."

Her heart sank, and she closed the play book. From his serious expression, whatever he had to say would be serious as well, and she feared it as she'd never feared anything.

"All these many weeks you've been coming here for the reading, I've hardly been able to keep my hands from you, or my mouth...or anything else...except the one time I failed."

His face turned red as he spoke. Ah, the night she ran from his hand on her thigh straight into Owen's path.

"You know how I feel. You have to. Mam tells me she can see it clear in my eyes every time you come near."

She slipped her hand out from under his. But what escape would there be from the noose he was about to slip around her neck? She waited for the rope to tighten.

"Marry me, Grace. I want you so much."

She stared straight ahead at the half-filled loom,

then at the fire, then back to the books on the table, then back to the loom. Everywhere, anywhere, but at Young Con's anxious, questioning face.

How could she marry him loving Owen as she did?

How could she not with no room for her in Liam's home?

The truth then. She would have to tell him the truth. "I love another," she began. "My heart is not mine to give."

Before she could continue, he picked up her hand and held it to his hot cheek. "I have heart enough for two. I'll take whatever you have to give as long as you agree. Once we're man and wife you'll change. You'll have our sons to raise. They'll fill your heart."

She stared at him. He would settle for so little, the crumbs of her affection, just as his father scurried for the crumbs that fell from Rushmount's table. Once more, she pulled her hand free. No! She couldn't marry into this family, and then her gaze fell on the linen-covered plate. Hadn't she nearly stuffed the whole of the plate's contents into her mouth? Didn't she still want to? And wasn't she thrilled, *thrilled,* to be reading the wee play book? She was no different from the Manns. Maybe Owen had the right of it when he said to marry Young Con.

She laid her arms on the table and lowered her head to them. Hesitant at first, Young Con began to stroke her hair, smoothing it over her shoulders and back.

"Grace, look at me."

She knew what would come and didn't move.

"Grace."

Why deny him? The reality of her days from now on was about to unfold. She lifted her head. His lips, so thin in such a full face, seized hers. A clumsy kiss he gave, the first in a long parade of such kisses.

An eternity of moments passed before he paused to catch his breath. "We'll have Father Joyce marry us. He can announce the banns beginning this Sunday. We can be wed within the month."

*Within the month.* Like a moth beating against a wall that had no opening, her mind darted about looking for an escape. "But you're not of the faith. He cannot marry us."

"I'll promise to convert. He can instruct me in the faith."

"There's time yet, Con. 'Tis true Liam would like to see me married and out of the cottage, but after the harvest will be soon enough. When the work is easier."

"After the harvest is not soon enough."

"We've made no plans. You've had no instruction—"

"You're in danger."

*Someone knows of the poaching!* Her heart froze at the thought.

"Your face just went white, Grace. Don't be afraid. He won't harm you, not if we're married."

"Con, what are you speaking of?"

"Da says Lord Rushmount has taken a fancy to you."

"Ha! That's all!" The tight band around her chest eased. "For that I am in danger? Not at all."

"Da says what if Rushmount tries to claim you? What then?"

"If he does, I will refuse." Even to her own ears, the boast sounded hollow. She slumped against the table. What Young Con said must be taken seriously.

By royal decree, Rushmount owned virtually all of Ballybanree and, if truth were told, all of the people who inhabited it. Lord and master, he could do as he wished, when he wished, with any one of them. What defense would she have if he came after her?

"Why me?"

"God, woman, you need a clearer mirror to see yourself in."

"Thank you. 'Tis lovely of you say that. But it doesn't make me happy. It tells me I'm no more than a slave, as we all are, every man, woman and child of us." Her fist pounded the table. "'Tis unjust. Evil!"

"Shhhh. You'll wake Mam and Da. We don't need them here with us, do we?" He began to caress her. His hands, emboldened, explored her shoulders and arms and went to curve around the mounds of her breasts. At that, she pulled away from him and stood.

"Grace, we'll soon be married. It's all right for us to—"

"We're not wed yet, Con."

"Soon we will be. It's the only way to protect you. I told Da, Rushmount won't tamper with a married woman. Not even he would do that. It goes against all the laws of man."

Grace's eyes narrowed. "What does your da say?"

He hesitated.

"Tell me or I shall leave for home."

"There's no need to repeat—"

"I want to know."

He studied his hands as if they were a page from the Bible. "Da said to forget you. You're a danger to yourself and to all of us."

Grace nodded and smiled despite herself at Con's self-serving wisdom. "Your father is a practical man."

"I will have you, Grace. I'm determined on that. Marriage is your greatest safeguard. And besides, Rushmount has made no attempt to...to—"

"Indeed, he has not."

"So perhaps Da exaggerates. But whether he does or not, I want us to meet with Father Joyce tomorrow evening."

One more day only and then betrothal to a man she didn't love. That was a great wrong, like so much in life. Yet she nodded. As Mistress Mann, she could be of help to the villagers. And she would be, she vowed—to every man, woman and child of them, so help her God.

"It's settled then," he said with a smile that split his face in two. "Tomorrow evening we'll tell the priest of our plan to wed."

*Not our plan, Con. Yours. Your plan and Owen O'Donnell's.*

# CHAPTER TWENTY ONE

"Damn this road!"
Ross cursed again as the chestnut's hooves barely missed a second rut. He sat deep in the saddle and pulled back on the reins. He'd have to watch the blasted lane like a hawk all the way to the village.

Couldn't the Irish do anything right? Not even fill in the holes in their roads? Road, ha! This one was little more than a pockmarked disaster. And the only approach to his estate.

The moment the field work eased, he'd order some of the tenants out here with spades. Without a direct order, they'd keep on ignoring the damn holes, let them turn into lakes each time it rained...now if the ruts were lined with stone to prevent further eroding and then topped off with clay, they might be less likely to wash out.

God, he'd love a good run. As soon as the blacksmith shoed the chestnut, he'd drive him hard, put him through some jumps. The low stone walls edging the fields were a good height for the sport. Jumping shook off a foul mood like nothing else except a woman, but Anne in her present state was useless.

The birth should be any day now her old nurse had said. He couldn't endure the sight of Gertrude with her prim, holier-than-thou airs. Yet the thought of the local midwife, an ancient hag, pulling his son into the world made him shudder. Hell, he wanted the whole ordeal over and done with. Maybe then Anne would smile more, and talk more, and...

With his feet in the stirrups, Ross leaned forward to stroke the chestnut's throat. He rewarded him with a quickened gait. "You like my touch, boy?" He eased back into the saddle with a frown. "You're the only one who does."

The stretch ahead appeared smooth enough. "Shall we chance it?" Ross flicked the reins. They picked up speed and cantered into the village, a plume of dust like the tail of a comet following in their wake.

He slowed for the urchins who played a rowdy stick game in the center of the lane. It wouldn't do to harm one. The wailing from the women would never cease, though they seemed to breed constant replacements.

Smoke furled from a few of the cottage vent holes, and the door to the one-room hut the villagers used as a public house stood open. A quick glance as he rode by showed no one lounging at the bar, a splintered board supported on two hogsheads. The men would all be in the fields at this hour. Nor was the slattern who served up the pints anywhere in sight.

A worn looking woman with a baby clutched to her bosom turned as he rode by, but not before he caught a glimpse of her bare breast and felt a familiar rise at the sight. He must be needy, indeed, to respond to *that,* but there were no easy women hereabouts except the slattern, perhaps.

In front of the blacksmith's forge at the far end of the village, he spotted the cripple, Owen O'Donnell, deep in conversation with one of the locals. The second man looked strangely familiar. That red hair flecked with gold he'd seen before. Ah, of course, he must be the girl's brother, Red Liam's son.

He reined in and dismounted. The redhead ceased talking and sent a darting glance toward the blacksmith.

What had they been hatching between them?

The redhead doffed his hat. "Good morning, Your Grace."

Ross nodded. The fool doesn't know I'm not a duke, he thought. Why bother to correct him? The blacksmith said nothing but returned his nod. That would do, he supposed. "My horse needs reshoeing."

The man eyed the chestnut his glance sliding over him missing nothing—mane, withers, rump, tail, and finally, the four long, surprisingly delicate legs. "He's a fair beast."

"Yes, Arabian stock. He's a fine specimen, but you should have seen his sire. Now there was a stallion. Unfortunately, the mare's bloodline proved a little disappointing. I've had this boy gelded." Ross reached up to stroke the chestnut's nose. "He's easier to ride now."

"Owen, I'll be leaving you to your work then," the redhead said tipping his hat again before he walked away.

No response from the blacksmith, Ross noted. God, he was a dour son of a bitch, but gifted with his hands. "I'll stroll back to Rushmount Manor. My steward, Connor Mann, will come by for him later in the day."

A curt dip of the man's head, no more. He'd ignore it, Ross decided, for the sake of a good shoeing.

\* \* \*

*So she's betrothed to Young Connor Mann. And Liam so happy to tell the news.*

Dear God, where would he find the will to live now that he'd truly lost her forever? An endless stretch of days flashed before Owen's eyes, each one as flat and dry as the other. A desert of days without the love of his life raising the hours into mountaintops.

He'd earned this fate, sought it out, forced her away, denied his deepest desires, and all for a reason that remained irrefutable. How could he ask her to share this existence of his? To live behind a rough curtain in back of the shop, on land he didn't own, tied to a cripple with a withered leg? Watching her fade as the babes began to come into the world and not enough food for all. No, these pictures his mind painted of a life with Grace or, God help him, without her, were too bleak to be endured. And yet, oh, Christ, how he longed for her.

Enough! He picked up the bellows and began fanning the embers in the forge. A cloud of smoke rose up fast and as quickly disappeared into the open air. Soon heated, he stripped off his tunic and tossed it on the ground out of his way.

Tethered to the hitching post outside his hut, the handsome chestnut stood placidly cropping at the grass by his hooves. Owen eyed him as he worked the bellows. A well-fed beast, he thought, better tended to than the village children.

In a fury, he worked the bellows with all his strength, forcing the air in and out like the breath from a mad creature. As soon as the fire burned blue-white, he would lay the first shoe on and heat it for shaping.

While he waited he examined the horse's hooves. When he lifted the chestnut's left foreleg he saw that the iron had been worn down nearly to the horn. Holding the leg between his thighs, he released the shoe. The hoof would need trimming before he could apply the new iron.

The shoe on the right foreleg looked no better. Rushmount must have been riding him hard lately. If the rear hooves showed the same wear, he had a day's work ahead of him. Good. The task kept his mind filled whenever it tried to dart to the image of Grace...Grace in the cave...Grace in his arms...

"Top of the day to you, Owen."

At the sound of the child's voice, he looked between the hooves and spotted two dirty little feet, legs like sticks, and a shift's ragged hem.

"How are you, Eileen?" She didn't answer. He glanced up from the chestnut. The lass had her finger in her mouth, sucking on it, like a babe at a tit. "Aren't you too old for that?" he asked.

She shook her head.

He released the last nail and the old shoe fell to the ground.

Owen straightened. "One more to go."

With her finger never leaving her mouth, Eileen picked up the fallen shoe in one hand and gave it over to him. It was unlike her not to speak. Words tumbled

from her every time they met, but today her shadowed
eyes looked troubled and ill.

"What's the matter, lass?" he asked.

Reluctantly, she freed her mouth to answer. "Mam
said I was not to tell anyone."

Owen studied her thin form. How old could she be,
he wondered, nine maybe, or ten? Of all the children in
the village, she touched his heart the most, and he
feared he knew what troubled her.

"So Mam said that, hmm? Well, I'm not anyone, I'm
Owen. But before you say a single word, love, let me ask
you something. Does this secret have to do with food?"

Astonishment widened her eyes. She nodded.

"You haven't said a thing, have you now?"

She shook her head.

"That's right. Come inside. The chestnut can wait a
while. I think I might have something for you."

She hurried after him. The kettle of soup he'd
simmered over the forge fire last night stood cooling on
his table. It was just as well Rushmount had stayed
outside earlier. The meat odor still clung to the air.

"Sit yourself, Eileen. I have a broth made from the
last of the venison bones, with barley boiled in. Would
that do?"

Without waiting for an answer, he filled a wooden
bowl with the soup not knowing how it tasted, but
knowing that hardly mattered. As soon as he set the
bowl in front of her, Eileen lifted it to her lips and began
to drink.

"Here's a spoon for the barley bits."

She put down the bowl and seized the spoon, taking
only a second to say, "Don't tell Mam, Owen."

"This is between you and me and the chestnut. Just
we three."

She laughed and went back to the soup.

He wished he had more to give her. "I must finish
the work, Eileen." He knew she heard him, but the
spoon in her mouth kept her from answering.

He returned to the shoeing. God, thinking of himself

he'd been, awash with self-pity for what could never be, and the little ones in such deep need. As soon as he finished the job, he'd call on Father Joyce. He hoped to God he hadn't waited too long.

*          *          *

Swish, swish. Swish, swish. The sound, like the scratching of mice in a wall, echoed in the silence of the church.

"Should you be doing that, Father?" Owen asked. "Is there no one to help you?"

Broom in hand, the priest kept on with his sweeping. He'd cleaned the mud from the chancel and had made his way toward the nave, the pile of dirt in front of his twig broom growing larger as he worked it forward.

"Father?"

"I know you're there, Owen. And you've not come to see me sweeping up the dirt from men's feet. Or have you?" Slightly breathless, Father Joyce leaned on the broom handle but said nothing more.

*Why should he welcome me warmly?* Owen thought. *I've hurt him with my indifference, and now I'm seeking his counsel.* Embarrassed, he wanted to turn away and leave the man to his task, but he'd not come for himself alone. "There is a matter I need to speak of, if you will."

"Why is it, Owen, that after all these years of silence, I've been expecting you for weeks now?"

"I know not, Father."

"Hmmph." His eyes lidded to mere slits, the priest appraised him. "Very well, come, we will sit. Meditating with a broom in one's hand is one thing, conversing with a friend is another."

"Father," Owen said, staying the man with a touch to his arm, "forgive me."

"Forgive yourself, lad, for falling on the rocks years ago. And forgive Him." He pointed to the crucifix above the altar. "As for me, I have nothing to forgive."

He led Owen to a bench near the altar. "We'll sit

next to the tabernacle." His eyes twinkled of a sudden. "It can't hurt if He hears."

Owen grinned at Father Joyce's little game. Christ would hear their words, or not—as he sometimes believed—no matter where they sat. "You're after treating me like you do the old grannies," Owen said, enjoying it.

"And what would that be like?"

"Like the smartest man in Ballybanree."

The priest threw back his head and laughed but quickly recovered himself in this sacred place. Sobering, he bent forward his face a serious mask. "'Tis grand to exchange a word with you, Owen. To be honest, I have missed the talk."

"I, too. I hope we will talk together again, many times, and of whatever fascinates us, but for today I have come with a problem."

"Ah." All the sympathy in the world showed in the priest's face.

*Does he know of how Grace and....has she spoken to him? She must have.* The possibility comforted him. Father Joyce would have been kind to her.

The priest sat on the opposite bench with no sense of hurry about him, one strong, square hand planted on each knee.

"It's about the people that I've come," Owen said. "Every year at this season they go hungry, the children especially, and the women with babes to feed. The men too—out in the fields all day with little in their bellies." He raised his hands in the air then let them drop to his lap. "Each and every one. Every person."

"This is not new to me, Owen."

"Nor to me, but it must stop. 'Tis a goddamn outrage."

The priest held up a warning hand. "Remember where you are, lad."

"Sorry, Father, but the injustice galls me, robs me of all peace. I watch the hunger grow day after day. And it's not the lack of food only. The children go about in rags and their parents no better. How many have warm blankets for the winter nights? And their tools and pots! I've patched most of them so many times 'tis the patches holding them together." Owen glanced around him, his arms sweeping wide. "And look at this church. Little more than a hollow shell—"

"Stop!" Father Joyce's voice rang to the rafters. "You're wrong. This is a haven for all who enter it. Just a few short years ago, I had to hide from Cromwell's men, say Mass in secret by the hedges and in the fields. Now the people have a church again. They can worship their God openly."

"They can't eat their religion."

"Only His body. It feeds their souls."

"That's not enough!"

"That has to be enough!" Father Joyce rose to his feet. "Have you forgotten when Cromwell paid five pounds for the head of a wolf or the head of a priest? It didn't matter which. I am alive today for one reason only. To help my people endure what must be endured."

"You're telling me their misery is God's will?"

The priest shook his head. "Not at all. I find His will a great mystery." He dropped back to the bench, his voice falling to a whisper. "I cannot fathom it." For a brief moment, Owen had the strange conviction that it was he who was hearing a confession. Then Father Joyce smiled. "But I don't need to fathom His will, only to accept it. And that is what He asks of you as well."

"Impossible! Accept this hell the English have created. Never!"

"You'll get yourself hanged, son, if you persist in this thinking."

"Then I'll die a man. Like Red Liam."

"You'd hurry your own death? Abandon your soul to the devil?"

Owen smiled. The possibility was not at all remote, and yet... "I have no wish to shed blood, mine or any man's. Our island's been awash in blood many times over and to what avail? No, we must work within the law, the English law we all hate. And in Ballybanree one man is the law. Rushmount."

"Go on."

"Any change will have to come through him. We must make him see the people are in pain. Make him understand he must take less profit from the land." Owen slammed a clenched fist into his palm. "He *has* to take less. The rents *must* be reduced."

"Let me take the devil's side for a bit, lad. Why must he take less? What incentive can you offer him?"

Owen's lips curled in derision. "His love of humanity?"

The priest shook his head.

"His reputation as a compassionate human being?"

"Not that."

"Greater profit?"

"Aha!"

"Then you agree. 'Tis true well-fed men and women work harder, produce more, raise healthy offspring to carry on the work!" Owen's thoughts caught fire as he spoke. "In the end, a rent reduction would bring greater wealth to his lordship."

"There's a flaw in your logic."

"And what would that be?" Owen asked abruptly.

"Lord Rushmount isn't known for his patience. You must bring him something he can sink his teeth into *now* and let the future take the hindmost."

"Bring him what?" Owen scoffed. "We have nothing. Not one of us in Ballybanree. We live on the land, we work on the land, but we do not *possess* it. It flowers for strangers, not for our own people, as it should."

"You're speaking treason."

"Treason? Ha! What loyalty do I owe to a sovereign not my own? To laws I hate?" Owen got to his feet and clumped back and forth, ignoring the noise of his wooden boot on the stone floor. "We've nothing but our bare hands and a meager crop for all our toil." Mid-step, he swiveled back to the priest. "<u>Part</u> of a meager crop."

"Sit, lad, sit."

He did, sinking back onto the bench, elbows on thighs, hands clasped together between his knees. "We have no rights, none at all. No monetary power. No political power." He raised dark, hollowed eyes to the priest. "We're an enslaved people."

"Careful, son, in what you say. This is dangerous talk."

Owen shrugged. "I'm losing hope, Father. We had a glimmer of it after Cromwell was axed, but no more. What does it matter if this Charles II is a Catholic sympathizer? He's restored none of the land to the Old Irish families. The Protestant loyalists are as firmly in place as in Henry's time or Elizabeth's. So what has the Restoration done for the people except to tolerate their religion?"

"Is that so little? 'Tis their only solace."

"Aye, that and the occasional drop of *uisce beatha*." Owen's head snapped up. "The *uisce beatha*!" He leaped to his feet. "That's it, the *uisce beatha*! I knew you would help me, Father!

"*Uisce beatha,* you say? I don't like the sound of my help."

"You need have no fear. Dear Christ, if I could dance, I would do so now! Rushmount will not refuse the whiskey!"

The smile that had come to Father Joyce's face disappeared. "I have no idea what you're shouting about in God's house."

"You have given me an idea Rushmount will love."

"And if he does not?"

"We'll turn every man in the village into a poacher."

Owen grinned to give the lie to his words, but alarm leaped into the priest's face. "You don't mean that?"

"I do not. Without weapons we're no match for Rushmount's men. But there is a poacher at work. A deer was taken a short while ago. It's a damned dangerous game someone's playing. But if Rushmount agrees to be more lenient, there'll be no further need to steal food."

The priest frowned. "I'm aware of the poaching. Some meat was laid at my doorstep."

Owen grinned across at him. "Did you eat it, Father?"

"I did not!"

Owen laughed. "You should have. 'Twould have done you good." Then the old scowl clouded his face, and he slumped back onto the bench. "My English is as rusty as an unused hinge, but I'll think on what needs to be said. When I do will you join me, Father, in speaking to his lordship? Should my English falter you could aid my argument."

The priest shook his head. "Please understand I cannot, Owen. I serve my people at the pleasure of God in heaven and at the pleasure of Lord Rushmount in Ballybanree. I can do nothing that might jeopardize that privilege."

Owen nodded. "All right. But when I collect my thoughts together, will you listen to them before I approach Rushmount?"

"I will that." Before Owen could take his leave, the priest pierced him with a keen glance. "Is there anything more you wish to discuss today?"

*Grace!*

"Nothing, Father. Nothing at all."

"Or to confess?"

Owen shook his head. Lying with Grace had been a sacrament, not a sin. How could he speak of losing her without sobbing? How could he live without loving her?

Aye, he would approach Rushmount, and soon. He had nothing to lose.

# CHAPTER TWENTY TWO

"**I** felt the baby move, Grace!" Brigit rested her hands on the mound of her belly and sat stark still, waiting. "There it goes again! He's alive!" she said, her face glowing with the wonder of it.

"Of course, he is."

"Come, put your hand on me and feel for yourself."

Grace rested her hands on Brigit's stomach. Faint flutterings like birds' wings reached her fingertips. "I felt it, too! 'Tis a miracle!"

They stared at each other, their mouths rounding into o's of delighted awe. Brigit got down from the stone wall. "Liam's out cutting turf. I must find him and have him feel his son move."

"Or his daughter."

Brigit nodded, too excited to banter about the difference, and went off to look for Liam. Looking for her lover, Grace thought. Maybe that was the true miracle, having the one you love create the new life within you.

Six months or a year from now she could be feeling the stirrings of life, but her joy would not be all consuming like Brigit's. 'Twould be a duty only. With a smile, she watched Brigit climbing over the stone wall at the edge of the field, the baby no hindrance to her.

She caught a sigh before it escaped her lips. Strong people did what they had to do without whining, and she would not be weak. In the matter of men, Granuaile hadn't been weak, either. She'd knocked on Richard Burke's castle door and proposed marriage. For one year only, she'd told him. After that, if he wished, she would set him free.

Grace let the sigh escape her. If only she could go to Owen in that way, but Richard had had a stronghold, Castle Rockfleet, to offer in marriage, while Owen was convinced he had nothing. He'd made his wishes clearly known, and she would respect that if it killed her.

She'd spent the whole morning weeding between the turnip rows, their new green leaves peeping through the soil. They would be ready for harvesting by the end of August. The time left in the day was her own for the reading. She washed her hands in a bucket by the well and went in to fetch the red book. She would read by the doorway in the clear light.

*Richard III.* A strange tale it wove of a twisted, evil man bent on seizing power no matter the cost. Were all Englishmen the same, then? Or had this king's deformity twisted his soul to match his body? She had no way of knowing. Maybe Rushmount would have the answer, although if what Young Con said was true, she'd best stay out of his way.

Richard was a man who'd truly lived, like Jesus. Like Owen. But Owen had been born without a flaw. He knew what it meant to be whole and perfect. Richard had never had a single day of such knowing. That must be the difference. With no one to blame but himself, Owen had not sought to punish the world, just his own self. Even in not wedding his life to hers, he meant well.

"But 'tis a cold consolation," she said aloud.

"What is?"

The book slipped from her fingers to the ground. Startled, she looked up and into the troubled face of Mary Burke. "Mary! You took the heart out of me!" She stooped to pick up the book. It would be a shame to soil it.

Holding Deirdre in her arms, Mary stood uncertainly in the path.

"Come in, come in, Mary, and sit for a spell." Grace kissed Mary and the top of the baby's fuzzy head while her mind raced. Was there anything in the cupboard she could give them? "'Tis a long walk from the village.

What brings you this way?"

"Eileen's ill."

"Oh, dear." A simple ague would not bring Mary so far from home.

"She's coughing blood."

"Dear God. How can I help?"

"Do you have anything to spare? I wouldn't ask for myself, but—"

"Of course, let me see." The wall cupboard held a bowl of boiled turnip Brigit planned to mash with an egg and fry in the spider for Liam's meal. She did not dare give that away. But she could check under the hens for eggs. There might be one or two more.

If only she had some milk to give, but against her wishes Liam had sent the milk cow and her calf to the uplands with Young Con's brother, Hugh, and his wife. "We have to keep the calf healthy," he'd said. "I plan to use it and hams from the pig for a goodly part of the rent, and *boolying* is best for the cattle. They thrive in the open fields."

"But Brigit needs—"

"Brigit will be fine, like her mother before her. We have to meet the rent. That comes first."

She'd kept silent after that. Liam couldn't risk debt, or worse, eviction.

"Do sit, Mary. I'll pour you a mug of ale and look for hens' eggs. That's all I can spare from here, but I'll go to Kath Mann and tell her Eileen's ill. She'll not refuse me some food."

With the baby asleep on her shoulder, Mary sank onto the bench at the table and sipped at her ale. "My thanks to you, Grace, and to Kath. 'Tis a fine mother-in-law you'll be having soon."

Grace stiffened. Owen's mother had gone to God years before.

*I shouldn't be gaining a mother-in-law at all, at all.*

She managed a smile. "Rest a bit, Mary. I'll be back in a trice with eggs if I'm lucky."

She found three and put them in a clean rag along

with a handful of barley. She could do without her share.

"I'll go to Kath after you leave and come by your cabin later with her food. I'll ask for milk and some soft bread for Eileen. But what of the boys, and you and your man?"

"Donal brings the boys with him now when he has a job of work. Sometimes they're fed. But we all have to hang on for another month at least."

"And the babe?"

"As you see. She's quiet like this most of the time. She's a good darling, hardly cries at all."

"What Kath will give me won't last long. 'Twill be stopgap at best. I can't ask for the whole village."

"No."

"What of Gram O'Neill? How is she faring? Brigit's going to need her."

"The same as all of us, hanging on 'til harvest for her payment. She helped birth the O'Flaherty child two nights ago. A boy for them."

Grace's face turned serious as the wisp of a smile she gave the baby disappeared. "I'll have to go out again some night soon." She glanced toward the open door and dropped her voice though she saw no one about. "One more kill will take us through the next few weeks."

Mary let go of her mug to lean across the table and grasp Grace's hand. "Don't. 'Tis too dangerous. What if you're caught?"

"I'll have a tale ready should that happen. Besides, Rushmount's men will never suspect a peasant lass of felling a deer. They won't touch me."

"You can't be certain of that. There's no telling—"

"If we die by degrees or all at once, Mary, what's the difference?"

*What is life to me? My heart is a stone in my breast.*

The baby whimpered. "I must go," Mary said.

"Until later, then."

\* \* \*

The July dawn would soon cut through the scudding

clouds and make the woods dangerous with light.

Now! Grace urged. Come towards me now!

The deer moved through the undergrowth gracefully, quietly making its way without hurry. He hadn't caught her scent. With luck, he wouldn't until he came within range, and then she'd have him.

Of a sudden, without a warning, he bolted, leaping through the brush, crashing against the branches maddened with fear. But fear of what? She was downwind of him. He hadn't been aware of her. Something else had alerted him to danger.

And then she knew. Voices whispering in English came to her as clear as the bell that rang at Mass. Rushmount's men on patrol!

"This is a damn fool job of work, Jacko. Sitting here half the night waiting for another strike. I say let the poor bastards take a deer or two, what harm in that?"

"Let his lordship hear you spouting, it'll be worth your neck."

*Dear God, if they find me with this bow, my tale will be useless.*

From the sound of their talk, they were only a few feet away. What if she'd taken the deer? They'd be on her now, and she their prisoner. Fear pulsed up and flooded through her. She didn't want to die after all, not with the first light ready to finger the leaves and bring along the summer morning.

She laid the bow and the sheaf of arrows on the ground next to an oak trunk. Working silently, she scooped up handfuls of rotted leaves to cover them. She glanced about marking the spot well in her mind. She could not lose the yew wood bow fashioned by her da's own hand. Holding it was like having him back with her once more. After the danger passed, she'd return for it. But now she'd best get away before the men spotted her. She'd caught nothing. Why risk having them find her alone and defenseless?

She picked her way through the underbrush, her bare feet inching along the thick ground cover. A dry branch snapped under her instep, the sound like a musket shot in the still air.

"Come on, Jacko, someone's here. No animal made that noise."

His voice sounded closer. Crouched behind a tree, she caught a glimpse of his uniform, the Rushmount green and orange livery, and the musket poised in his hand ready to shoot.

Hide or run? A few steps closer and they would have her. She backed away from the oak and slid silently behind its neighbor and the one behind that. Then, with a bit of distance between herself and the patrol, she ran like a forest creature between the trees, fleet on her bare feet, risking the sounds of flight in her hurry to get away.

"This way! After him!"

She knew these woods better than any English hireling, but she'd best be fast of foot. If they caught her now, all would be over! But where could she run to? Not home and lead them to Liam and Brigit, not to the village. *Where?*

Behind her, the snapping of branches kept on. They'd not give up their prize easily. She slowed a minute, listening over the pounding of her heart but heard nothing. Were they playing the same game? Keeping still, making ready to pounce? She stood quiet as a deer being stalked until the English voices sounded farther away, but still she dared not risk going home.

Once out of the copse, she'd hide somewhere till they gave up the search. And they would soon. No fool would go poaching in daylight. An hour of hiding is all she'd need. After that, she could stroll back to the cottage as innocent as a lamb.

But for that hour? Only one place—the cave. They'd never find her there, and she'd put no one in danger.

She slipped from the woods and ran. If they spied her in the distance, they'd have a difficult time catching her, burdened as they were with their heavy, clumsy weapons.

No shout of alarm rose in the air as she fled the covering of the trees. She'd be down the path to the shore and out of eyeshot before they spotted her. After that, just a short run along the pebbled beach and up the slope to the cave.

Panting, breathless, taking in gulps of salt air, she ran along the water's edge, climbed the slope, slid behind the gorse bushes, and slipped into the cave.

The cool, dry air smelled the same as she remembered, of sea and earth, but the early morning rays lit the vaulted space more clearly than the fading light of gloaming. It revealed a sleeping figure wrapped in a blanket. She gasped, and at the sound, Owen threw off the cover and scrambled to his feet.

"'Tis you!" Grace said, delighted surprise flooding her face.

"And you."

"What are you doing here?"

He scowled. "That's my question."

"I'm out for a stroll."

"That's a lie I'm thinking."

"Think what you wish, you always have."

His lips quirked up. "I have many thoughts I don't wish to have."

"And some that you do?"

His mouth tightened. "Some." He stood facing her, one hand braced against a stone outcropping.

She stepped closer to him. "You've been well?"

"What do you want, Grace?"

The sun had risen high enough to send its rays into every crevice. The lines his face was too young to bear were clear to her, as well as the stubble on his chin, and the lower lip caught in his white teeth, and the hollows around his eyes, and the leg he favored as he leaned against the cave wall. All of him the new day revealed, and all of him she loved.

"I want you," she said.

He didn't answer.

"I shouldn't have to beg for a man who looks as

dreadful as you do."

He gave out a short bark of a laugh. "My heart is at your feet, Grace. It kneels there and always will. But I have nothing else to give." He reached into a breeches' pocket and pulled out the square of embroidered linen left in his Bible the summer last. "Your gift. I've never given you one in return. I've nothing to give." He tucked the linen back into his pocket. His hand fell to his side. "And there you have it."

"In that you're wrong." She came closer. "You gave me hours of gold. I'll have them all my life...when I'm lying with Young Con, they'll be with me."

"No more!"

"Does that hurt? Every night, Owen, every night I'll be in his arms and under him, and I'll be—"

He grasped her shoulders, moving so fast she drew in a quick, shocked breath as he gripped her.

"Do you want me to shake you 'til you stop?" His fingers dug into her flesh.

"I do. At least I'll have your hands on me. I love the feel of them. I love *you*."

"Christ, you make it hard for a man."

She smiled.

His hands still locked on her shoulders, he looked down at her upturned face without returning her smile. She tried to move in nearer, to nestle herself against his chest, but his iron grip held her at arm's length.

"I heard the banns read on Sunday," he said. "You belong to him now."

"I belong to you."

"Try to understand." He let her go and moved farther into the cave, lowering his head where the wall slanted down to meet the floor. "You will have a better life with Young Con."

"How could that ever be? There is more to life than a full belly. The soul needs food as well."

He'd reached the back of the cave and had no where else to go.

She moved in closer. "You are the world to me. My

east and my west, my north and my south. Without you, I'm lost."

Shyly, as if she would be rebuffed, she put a finger on his mouth and began to trace it, carving its shape into her memory. She ran her finger from the left corner of his top lip to the dip in its center and up again following the curve to the right, along the wide fullness of the lower lip, then one long sweep across the center of his mouth.

"Ahhhhhhh!" The growl coiled up from deep in his throat. He brushed her hand away, and with his fingers entangled in her hair, pulled her face to his. The mouth she'd toyed with opened, and he kissed her with a hunger that tenderness had no part in. All the need he'd denied his kiss contained, and she met it with her own need. They devoured each other, feeding lip to lip, their hunger too great, finally, for mere kisses.

"Come," he urged, moving away from the wall to the blanket on the floor. "Take off everything. Be quick before I turn sane again."

Her hands trembling with haste, she untied her skirt and let it fall, and he unlaced the front of his breeches. In moments their clothes littered the cave floor. She held out her arms to him, but he shook his head.

"Get down," he said, his voice hoarse.

She lay on the blanket. He lowered himself to her. She opened her thighs and wrapped her legs around his hips. With his mouth on hers, his tongue entered her in the same instant he entered her below. Her entire body had been claimed by him. And then he began to move.

Afterward he withdrew and lay by her side, his breath coming in ragged gulps before settling into a deep, calm rhythm. It was then he said, "Forgive me, *mavourneen.*"

"Whatever for?"

"For my haste. For my selfishness. I should have worshipped you slowly." He raised himself on one elbow and gazed down at her, at the curtain of her hair spread wide about her, at her smile, at her white flesh. "I found

I could not stop myself. The need maddened me."

"There was no—"

"Shhh." Kneeling over her, he straddled her body and began the kisses softly. He started with her hair, stroking the strands, putting the golden tips to his mouth, and then he kissed the lids of her eyes and her lips and her breasts. He moved down, his mouth adoring her, his tongue licking the slight salt taste from her skin. He kept on and on, stopping only when she cried out and after one prolonged, shuddering move lay still beneath him.

He raised himself up beside her and pulled her into his arms. "Sleep, love," he said, "and I will, too."

When she awoke, the sun was pouring a brilliant light into the cave, and she was alone.

# CHAPTER TWENTY THREE

No time would be truly safe. Yet Grace gambled that Rushmount's men wouldn't be on the prowl a second night running, that they would believe the poacher too fearful to strike again so soon. Hoping to God her guess was right, the next night she retrieved her bow and quiver of arrows from their hiding place and stood watch by the ravine.

In the three raids since she'd taken up Da's mission, her luck had been poor. The first kill had been discovered before she could make use of it. Although the second had succeeded, last night's had been a dismal failure. Ah, no! It had led her directly into Owen's arms. His words and his touch had been her meat, her bread and wine, but not so for the others she loved, and not so for her ever again. She knew that with certainty when she awoke midmorning without his arms about her.

She'd trapped him into making love to her. Though wrong as hail at harvest time, he wanted more for her life than he believed he could give. She wouldn't keep pursuing him lest they come to hate each other, and she would stay away from the cave altogether. If caught this dawn, she'd lay down the bow and arrow and step forward to meet her fate.

She took her poacher's place behind a thick oak and waited, determined to keep to the hunt even into the broad light of day if need be. One sight of Eileen's fevered face, and the thin sticks of boys and the eerily silent baby had set her blood boiling.

Mary could make a broth and simmer bits of meat in it until they were tender enough for Eileen to swallow. She'd bring her a dish of salt for flavoring and give her the rest of their tea leaves as well.

She sat down by the tree. No need to stand, for hours perhaps, with the weariness threatening to over-come her. She'd had no sleep the night before, only the short rest in the cave. That had carried her through the day and into the dark, but she would have to fight now to stay awake and watch.

The deer had almost breached her hiding place when the slight slap of a branch against his hide woke her. Without a sound, she groped for the bow and slid the arrow's notch into position against the bowstring. In the dawn's light, she could see he was a young hart, just what she'd hoped for, and so far unaware of her presence. Using the oak for a shield, she eased upward against the trunk until she stood with her weapon poised at the ready.

She'd aim for his throat, always a difficult shot, but if successful, it would drop him where he stood. The last thing she wanted was to wound him and be forced to give chase between the trees, crashing through the undergrowth, alerting anyone within earshot.

He came a few paces closer, his movements stately and without fear. A shame to bring him down, but—

He'd caught her scent! Close enough to see his brown eyes, she leapt from behind the oak and fired. Spurred on by terror, he bounded, wild eyed, for safety, but the arrow flew faster and struck him, felling him like a stone.

She ran over to where he lay and stared down at him. Unaccountably, tears sprang into her eyes and a prayer to her lips. But precious time was fleeting, and while whispering words of atonement for taking his life, she hurried to the hollow tree, dropped in her weapons and carefully removed the sharpened carving knife.

Now for the hellish part—cutting the beast, separating it limb from limb, drenching herself in its gore—but she had no choice. The meat might carry the village through until harvest.

She plunged the knife into the hart's belly and began.

# CHAPTER TWENTY FOUR

"What do you mean the wet nurse has failed?" Rushmount asked.

"Her milk's dried up, your lordship. It happens without warning sometimes."

"Good God, woman, what now?"

Nurse Gertrude shrugged. "Lady Anne has no choice. She must be persuaded to nurse baby Elizabeth. At least until a local woman can be found."

"A local!" Rushmount's shout awakened the infant who began to howl. "Do something," he said. "I can't stand that din."

"She's hungry, my lord. She can't wait."

"Do what you must." He had to get away from the squalling, but paused at the nursery door. "Is Lady Anne aware of this problem?"

"Not yet, my lord. I wished to inform you first."

"I see." He sighed. His lady wife would view this latest demand as an insult, an infringement on her person, yet another reason to hate what she considered an isolated outpost of hell. "Convince her of the necessity," he said, and went down the center stairs to his office where Connor Mann waited.

Each time he strode the stairs, he silently acknowledged his great-uncle's superb taste. The double staircase rose to the second story like stone arms reaching for the sky. Despite their solidity, the open-work balustrades kept the mood of the great hall light and airy.

He disliked the ponderous Norman architecture, more fortress than manor house, so typical of Irish estates. Ireland's future lay with England. Let English dreams prevail.

After Connor Mann calculated the year's profits, Rushmount would decide whether or not to repave the great hall floor. He fancied black and white marble and some life-sized statuary in the center of the stairwell. A white marble figure, female, carelessly draped, perhaps a single breast exposed. A focal point he'd heard such called. The cynosure of all eyes. He liked the idea. Anne had no reason to be so discontented, none at all.

He flung open the study door. "Con, what brings you here today? I recall no appointment."

Connor, hat in hand, cleared his throat. "I beg your pardon, my lord, but I've come with a special request."

"Oh? What now?"

"Not for myself am I asking. For Owen O'Donnell."

"For whom?"

"The blacksmith, sir."

"What about him?"

"He requests leave to speak to you. He has a proposal to present."

Rushmount lounged in the chair behind his desk. His lips curled. He could use a good laugh. "A proposal, you say? How ridiculous."

"I think you'll find it interesting, sir."

"I doubt that. Where is he?"

"Outside, by the scullery door."

Why not hear this? It might prove amusing on a dull, irritating day. "Bring him in, Con. Bring him in, by all means. You've piqued my curiosity."

"I'll fetch him, sir."

\* \* \*

Connor hurried through the great hall to the carved mahogany door behind the grand staircase and down the dark, back corridor that led to the service area of the house. Clever, he had to admit, to conceal hallways and narrow, hidden stairs that gave the servants access to the whole of the mansion without being in view or interfering with the lives of the nobles.

He knew the villagers who worked here from sunup

to sundown considered themselves fortunate. They were fed and clothed for the privilege, housed under the attic roof, and given a few pence at Christmas time. When the housemaids left to marry, they brought those pence to their own households, and their clothes, and a few useful discards they had either filched or been granted.

Thomas, who served as butler and jack-of-all-trades about the place, and Margaret, the English cook who'd gone fat sampling her own dishes, had come from London with his lordship, as had Gertrude, Lady Anne's personal woman, and Frazer, the head gamekeeper. Only the lower order of servants were Irish, the lasses who helped Margaret prepare the elaborate meals, the scullery maid, the laundress, the lad who laid the fires and kept them burning. An army it took to keep the estate going. No wonder Rushmount squeezed every penny from the farms and the dairy.

How his lordship would receive Owen's bold offer, he had no way of knowing. The uncertainty, as it always did, caused him to sweat. Damp slicked the palms of his hands, and wet circles would soon be springing out on his woolen shirt. No help for it although in the old days he would have said an *Ave* as he hurried to fetch Owen.

Agnes, the oldest of the O'Flaherty lasses, stood bent over the stone sink scrubbing a stew caldron with a wet rag dipped in sand. He nodded to her as he passed by. The poor soul, her left eye wandered, seeking its own path to the light. Ugly it made her. She'd never rise above a scullery, or find a mate for that matter.

Owen sat outside on the top step by the door, a small ironstone jug at his feet. Christ, this had better go well, Connor thought. What a chance he was taking bringing Owen in here with his wild scheme.

"He'll see you. Hurry now. We don't want to keep him waiting."

"He'll wait. Bad enough you insisted I use the back door, but I won't rush, nor will I scrape," Owen said.

"Jesus, man, you need him. He doesn't need you."

"Don't be so sure."

Owen picked up the jug and followed Connor into the scullery, through the vast, busy kitchen, and down the chill, dark corridor to the great hall door.

"We're almost there. Be careful how you act," Con said. He knocked on the study door. At the muffled response, they walked in.

\* \* \*

"You asked to see me?" Ross said.

"I did that," Owen replied. "I have a bit of a proposition for you."

As a flash of stunned amusement came over Rushmount's face, Owen held up the jug. "It concerns this."

"Which is?"

"The finest *uisce beatha* in all of Ireland."

"Distilled illegally, of course."

Owen shrugged.

Ross glanced over at Connor. "Nevertheless, I've wanted to sample the local whiskey. You remembered."

Connor managed a smile.

"It's early in the day for spirits. Leave the jug. I'll try it later," Ross said.

"'Tis not for the pleasure of the drink alone that I've come," Owen said.

"Oh, really?" The man had gall, all right. The way he spoke without any deference in his tone reminded him of someone else, but of whom? Most people, his bailiff included, tended to grovel at the mere sight of him. Ah, yes! The beautiful girl, the redhead. She took liberties, but somehow that aroused him. This surly blacksmith was a different matter altogether.

"Exactly why have you come?"

"On business," Owen said. He turned to Connor. "I think that's the correct term in English."

"What could you possibly—"

"Before I share what's in my mind, you need to taste what's in the jug here. Otherwise, there's no use in further talk between us."

Rushmount regarded the man. His clothes, a canvas shirt and faded blue breeches, were clean, and he could see where a comb had been raked through his thick, black hair. He was like midnight without a moon in the sky.

Standing still, he carried himself well, his broad blacksmith's shoulders and chest filled out his shirt. Then he moved, and his shoulders dipped up and down, awkward with effort. But strangely the strength of the man did not disappear with his clumsy gait. Strange, too, that he'd missed that quality about him the time they held him for questioning. Regardless, he'd never be able to chase a buck through the trees. He'd been right to dismiss him that day.

The question now was should an English lord share a drink with one of the peasants? Violate every social code? Well, this was Connaught not England, and he did want to sample the local, ah, *uisce beatha.*

"Very well. Con, three glasses."

Connor hurried over to a tiered table covered with crystal glasses and several decanters of port and brandy.

Unlike most landlords, Ross kept liquor out in the open. He had the eye of an eagle when it came to the levels in the bottles, but so far none had been trifled with. The household help wouldn't dare tipple.

Connor brought three glasses to the desk. Incised with diagonal lines that caught the light, they were as delicate as spun air.

Ross indicated the jug with a lift of his chin. "Pour it," he said.

Owen uncorked the jug and poured a stiff measure for Rushmount, less for Connor, and a mere taste for himself.

Rushmount raised his glass and held it to the light. "Not as dark as I expected. And it hasn't eaten a hole in the glass yet." He laughed at his own jest and sniffed at the drink. "Rye, of course."

"Aye."

"And something else. Is there a scent of wild flowers?" He sniffed again. "No, there couldn't be."

Owen shrugged and let a few drops fall on his

tongue.

Rushmount took a tentative sip. He paused and rolled the liquid around in his mouth before swallowing. Then he held the glass up to the light once more. "I detected a hint of brine in the back of the throat. Do they make the cut with sea water?"

"Only the brewmaster knows the exact recipe," Owen said.

"The brewmaster! How you Irish do glorify your-selves."

Owen's gaze pinned him where he sat. "We do, indeed. Who else will do so for us?"

Rushmount laughed and took another sip. "I will admit, this *uisce beatha*, as you call it, is excellent." He held the glass to his nose and sniffed. "As good as some of the better Scots whiskies I've tasted. I've rarely had a rye I liked as well."

Owen shifted his weight. "We thought that might be your opinion."

"You and Con both?"

"Con and me and the entire village of Ballybanree."

His entire holding was in on this? Was it a plot of some kind? Ross looked across his desk at Connor who had gulped his small tot in silence and now avoided meeting his glance. He swung his attention back to the blacksmith. "Explain yourself, man."

"I would do better sitting."

Ross heard Connor groan out loud at the audacity, as well he should. They'd have a few words together when this meeting ended, but for now he wanted to know more. His interest had been aroused after all. "Very well. Pull up chairs, both of you."

Once they were seated, Owen plunged ahead. "We are well aware of the high quality of our whiskey. In our opinion, it is too grand a drink for Ballybanree alone. We think men everywhere, Englishmen like yourself, would love a drop of it from time to time."

"Get to the point."

"Up to now, the brewmaster has produced only

limited amounts, a few demijohns at a time. After his day's work was done, of course—by the light of the moon." Clearly enjoying himself, the blacksmith grinned. "The grain is too precious to distill much from any one harvest. And his still is small as well. But if the amount of grain were increased and we built a bigger still, or more than one, we could produce a quantity sufficient for export. Legally."

Rushmount's eyebrows arched up. He couldn't believe his ears. Did this local really think he would enter into any such enterprise with the likes of him? "Did I hear you say 'we'?" he asked.

"Aye. That's the rub, your lordship," Owen said.

Had he heard a sardonic note in the man's voice? With the Irish lilt coloring his English speech, he couldn't be certain.

The blacksmith glanced over at Connor. "What's the word in English for an undertaking that benefits all?"

"An association."

"Aye, that's it. We work with you to produce the *uisce beatha*, and we all share in the profits. And the profits I predict will be great."

"*You* predict?" Ross remained at his ease behind the desk although it took all of his training to maintain the pose and not leap up and grasp this O'Donnell by the throat. "Who do you think you are?" he said, drawling out the words, refusing to let his outrage show.

"I am an Irishman, God help me," Owen said.

"And as such you are in thrall to me. You and every man, woman and child on my land. Mistake that not."

"You're not interested then?"

"Owen," Connor said. "You'd best leave off. His lordship—"

Rushmount's glance snapped over to Connor. "I'll be the one to dismiss him, not you."

"Yes, milord."

"Go on, O'Donnell. I'll hear it all."

"The people are perpetually in need. Their children go hungry. Their women are in rags. But if part of the acreage were devoted to rye and turned over to a distillery," he paused, and Ross guessed that here was the crux of the matter, "and that acreage released from rent, the people could live as befits human beings. If in addition, of course, they were paid a part of the profits each year." O'Donnell paused again no doubt to let his effrontery sink in. "With this arrangement you, for your part, would become wealthy. Ah, *wealthier*," he amended.

Through a clenched jaw, Ross said, "So that's it. Do you realize, *Mister* O'Donnell, that I can force the people to make whiskey, and claim the profits, all of the profits, as my own."

"Not so."

"This is outrageous."

"I agree with you there." Owen rose to his feet. "But I'll finish what I started now that I'm here. You claimed the hour too early for spirits. Spirits is the word. The making of Irish whiskey is a mystical joining of elements. It cannot be forced." He picked up the jug and waved it in the air. "This is a labor of love. To force it is like forcing a woman. The result is not the same as when she comes to you willingly. You will never achieve this same quality without respect for the people who make it."

"Who did make this? I can easily find out if you refuse to tell me."

"Aye, I'm sure Con here would enlighten you. But what will you gain from that knowledge?"

"You go too far."

O'Donnell inhaled and then let the air leave his body in one expelled breath. "I have nothing left to lose, and the whole village is approaching that same state. Their children have gone hungry too long."

For a second, Rushmount listened for the sound of Elizabeth's cries, but he could hear nothing so far from the nursery.

"If you make life worth living for the people of Ballybanree, they will produce more for you, not less.

'Tis only common sense."

Had he been away from the seat of power too long? Ross asked himself. Consorting with peasants, hearing their outrageous demands and actually stooping to consider them? Perhaps he had, and yet whiskey like this would bring far more on the London market than butter and cheese.

"Your nerve intrigues me, O'Donnell. Enough so that I'll think over your, ah, outrageous proposition." He allowed himself a smile and got to his feet. "For now, feel free to go, but leave the jug."

# CHAPTER TWENTY FIVE

" Christ, I thought we were done for in there. You took a terrible chance." Sweat beaded on Connor's forehead as he and Owen made their way across the great lawn to his cottage. "I could ring your bloody neck for you."

Owen laughed and gave Connor a hearty clap on the back that sent him staggering. "Buck up, man. Nothing good's won without a risk."

"Risk yourself. Not me and mine. He could have dismissed me on the spot. And then what?" Connor stopped in his tracks. "He still could, by God. I should never have let you talk me into this crazed scheme."

"Your old Catholic conscience took hold of you. You had no choice in the matter."

"Don't toy with me, Owen. I'm beyond jesting. Jesus, I wish you still had the jug. I could use a taste. A bigger one than you doled out in Rushmount's study."

"Let him nurse that jug to his heart's delight. 'Twill convince him to take up our plan. Besides," Owen grinned over at him. "I left another one with Kath. I knew we'd have a cause for celebration."

"You know a pile more than I do then. He said he'd give me his answer when he was ready. That could be anytime. Or never."

"The greed fairly jumped out of his eyes. We'll hear, and soon."

"Well, I'm parched to a fare-thee-well. Let's go faster," Connor said. He had no sooner spoken then he slowed his steps. "I'm sorry, Owen. I forgot about your-"

Owen smiled. "I wish I could as well."

"Forgive me. I'm clumsy with my words."

"Nothing can steal my good humor today, laddy. I think we've got him. In my heart I do." For good measure, he clapped Connor on the back, again sending him staggering forward from the strength of it.

"Your arms make up for that leg of yours, I'll vow to that."

Owen laughed. A taste of the whiskey would put a good seal on this good day. One drink only would do them. No sense in addling their brains before he and Con calculated the percentages each farm could commit to the plan. And the size of the new copper still they would need. He'd have to see the McElroy brothers about that, and he had to inform the people of what he'd done.

Letting Rushmount think all of Ballybanree was in on his plan had been bold of him. Some were bound to say wrong, but wrangling with the villagers ahead of time would have weakened his strategy. Tomorrow, he'd ask Father Joyce to let him speak after the Mass. That would be the quickest way to spread the news and to answer the questions that were sure to arise.

He turned to Connor trudging along at his side. "How would you like to do something you haven't done in years?"

"The look on your face tells me it's devilment you're thinking of."

"No such luck. It's the opposite in true fact. We have to let the village know what we've proposed to his lordship. After Mass would be the best time. We could lay it all out then."

"Owen, you'll be the death of me yet," Connor said. "I can't go public with this until his lordship gives his approval. Even then, the less I say the better. Nor will I pass through the doors of St. Mary's."

Once again, he stopped walking and caught Owen by the shirt sleeve. "Understand me, man. I made my bed a long time ago, and I'm content to lie in it. I agreed to speak for you back there"—he cocked his thumb at the manor house—"because I know what the rents are doing to the people. And you were right—from time to time my conscience flogs me, but further than this I'll not go. You be the one to speak to them, and when you do, no mention of my name is to leave your lips."

"They should know of your help in this."

"Not a word. Rushmount may agree for the gain that will come to him, but he won't like being manipulated, outfoxed so to speak. So be warned, Owen, from here on in, he'll see you as an instigator, Ballybanree's trouble-maker, and he'll hate you for it."

Connor shivered in his sweat-dampened clothes although the mists had dried up and the afternoon sun shone warm.

"Hate is a good clean emotion," Owen said. "I'd rather deal with hatred than with hungry children. Come on, I can walk faster than this. That jug is calling to us."

"Aye." Connor grinned. "I can hear it singing from here."

As soon as he left Con, Owen planned to hike over to the McElroy brothers' farm. Had he told them of his intent before approaching Rushmount their fear of reprisals would have prevented him, but he'd spend the night, if need be, telling them of what he'd done and why, and laying their fears to rest. They had a gift, the two of them. He had to convince them of that and of the necessity to keep their distilling methods secret, no matter what pressure Rushmount brought to bear.

A prick of anxiety stabbed at him. If Rushmount demanded to know their recipe, would the McElroys crumple? At that possibility, Owen gritted his teeth so hard his jaw ached. If they did, would he kill them himself? Not before learning their distillation secrets, and then, God help him, he didn't know what he would do.

As they approached the Manns' cottage, he wondered if Grace would be inside and, if she were, how he could bear to be so close to her yet so far away.

When they walked in, Kath alone greeted them, and

his heart sank in his chest. Despite all his resolves, his disappointment told him the pleasure of seeing Grace would have been worth any pain.

* * *

Sean McElroy's long, narrow face turned white at Owen's news. "Jesus, Mary, and Joseph, we've always kept the still a secret, Owen. 'Tis the only safe way."

"A well-kept secret that everyone knows?"

"The villagers don't count. 'Tis Lord Rushmount who—"

"The people do count," Owen said. "That's my point entirely. I thought long and hard before I met with the Englishman. 'Twas the only solution that made sense. We have nothing else to bargain with. And he's fascinated with what the whiskey can do for him."

"He knows of us?" Tim McElroy asked.

"Not yet. Con and I mentioned no names. But he soon will. He'll make it his business to find out."

Anger replaced fear in Sean's eyes. "You should have told us first before you spoke to him."

"And what would the outcome of that have been?"

The McElroys exchanged a telling glance. "We would have refused," Tim said.

"As I guessed." Owen shifted his weight on the stone wall seeking a comfortable spot. The brothers' small holding had more than its fair share of neatly piled walls. They'd been farming the rockiest soil in the county for years and their father and grandfathers before them. Not by accident did they become masters of fermenting rye. Unlike barley and oats that needed richer land, the rye thrived on poor soil.

It would be nothing short of poetic justice if their enforced poverty, and the knowledge that came of it, aided the whole village. It was an idea he would enjoy tossing about in his mind, but before he did he had to be certain of them.

"For my plan to work, Rushmount has to know everything with one exception, and that he can never know."

"The recipe?" Sean asked.

"Exactly. If he learns that, he'll think he doesn't need us. Make no mistake, Rushmount has the resources to make spirits without our help, but not of the same quality. Superb, he called it. Without your skill, the best he'd likely get is rotgut. That won't fetch the price in London he'll be after."

The whiteness behind his beard stubble had not left Sean's pinched face. "He can force the method out of us. He has ways. Look at what he did to Red Liam."

"You think he'd kill the goose that can lay a golden egg? I doubt that. But he well may threaten you despite what I said to him."

Sean beat at the air with clenched hands. "You said more? God help us."

Owen smiled a little. "I said making *uisce beatha* is like making love to a woman. If you force her, the result is not as sweet."

Tim guffawed. "Jesus, what a fanciful concept. And how would you be after knowing all that?"

"Call it my Irish imagination. But he took my meaning, I'd place a wager on it."

"Then you think he won't come after us?"

"Maybe. Maybe not. So two things you must swear to do if you want to live like men on this rocky scrap of land. One, if he threatens you, and you sense you're in danger, change the recipe before you give it to him."

"He'd kill us for that alone."

"Not so. Not until he perfects the method. As soon as he learns he can't do so without your skill, he'll relent." Owen hoped his words were true. It was a dangerous chance they were taking. For now, Rushmount undoubtedly believed they were all drunk on their own stupidity and that he would outsmart them in the end. When he discovered otherwise, no telling how he would react.

"What's the second thing we must do?" Tim asked.

"Tell the true recipe to Father Joyce. To him alone. He'll write it in English, seal the paper, and keep it safe should anything go awry."

"You mean if he kills us. You ask too much," Sean said.

"Not for myself. For the people. This could be their salvation." Owen grinned. "Although the priest might argue with me there."

Tim turned to his brother. "What say you to this?"

"You want to take the risk," Sean said. "I can see it in your face."

Tim nodded. "I do. It's that or struggle forever. We're already a year behind on our rent, a step away from eviction. This gives us a chance. We've never had one before. I say yes to Owen's plan."

"What if Rushmount comes after us?"

Tim waved his arms about, at their pitiful one-room hut, the rocky ground, the general desolation of their farm. "He already has." He got up off the wall and stood in front of Owen, his hand outstretched. Owen grasped it.

"Count me in," Tim said. Then to Sean, "Shake the man's hand. Go on now."

Sean scuffed his toes in the dirt for a bit, but in the end, he held out a reluctant hand. Owen took it and shook it hard. "You've got a powerful touch, Owen," Sean said, forcing a bit of a smile.

"I hope to God that's true," Owen said. "And now let's plan our future. Con thinks that this planting season we can turn an acre of rye grain over to you from each ten-acre farm in the village. A half acre or less from the smaller holdings. And once Rushmount gains a taste of the possibilities, a good portion of the Manns' fields. If so, how much whiskey is that likely to produce? And how large a still will you need?"

Tim looked into the distance as he began calculating. "With twenty-four farms contributing, we could have as much as fifteen acres of grain to start. If we have a good year, that's ten bushels an acre, so roughly one hundred and fifty, possibly two hundred bushels." His eyes took on a dreaming glow. "You're talking more than we've ever distilled in our lifetime or our da's either."

"And for that you'll need a new still. Rushmount will have to provide the funds for it and the oak for the barrels. But how many barrels? You'll need to estimate the number," Owen said.

Warming to the subject, Sean said, "Not one large still. Small ones like we're used to. That's the key to controlling the quality of each batch."

"All right, you decide."

Agitated by the talk, Tim got up off the stone wall and paced, stooping every few moments to pick up a stone and toss it into the next field.

"A futile game that," Owen said watching him. "The rocks are growing out of your ground, man."

"As well we know," Tim said, a smile lighting his face. "I don't remember feeling this fine my entire life long."

"It's called hope," Owen said. "A thing as rare as gold in these parts. Who knows, maybe soon we'll all have a wee bit of both."

Later, as he walked back to the forge, the gloaming had gone by and full dark ruled the sky. No matter that his leg ached from a day of tramping the fields, no matter that his own life was a misery, a glimmer of the same hope that had excited Tim McElroy shone for him and for everyone he knew.

He went into the forge and closed the door behind him glad to be home. He'd remove the wooden boot and seek some rest although sleep might not come weary as he was. And then he saw it. Another bundle wrapped carefully like an infant in swaddling.

*Christ, no! Not the poacher again. Not now and endanger everything!* He hurried to the bundle and flung open the blood-soaked canvas.

# CHAPTER TWENTY SIX

Good God, listen to that, Ross thought, as fresh from his morning ride about the estate, he walked into the great hall and straight into the sound of baby Elizabeth's screams. Her cries filled the air destroying his relaxed humor and his conviction that all was well in his life and about to become better. On his ride, he'd decided that with his daughter a month old, Anne could not continue to protest his presence in their bed. He intended to resume his marital rights that very night. He would prefer to be made welcome, but if not—

*How could such a little thing create so much havoc?*

To think in peace, he went into his study and shut the door.

This bizarre idea of the blacksmith's had him fascinated. He'd pondered it the whole week long and overall was tempted to let it proceed. True, it had its flaws. Most notably that he would stoop to dabble in trade with the lowest of the low. How his peers would scoff. But this was Connaught not London.

He picked up the demijohn O'Donnell had left, poured a dram and sniffed it. What was that intriguing hint? Something he couldn't quite name...something Scots whiskey lacked. Before sipping, he held the glass to the window. The liquid in its bottom caught the light like melted gold.

On the other hand, no one in England need learn the truth. At the risk of falling into disfavor, his London agent could be given strict orders not to bandy his name about. And if the truth did escape, what then? Could he afford to worry? He needed all the funding he could get hold of. Once the estate became magnificent, no one would dare scoff.

Yes, upon reflection, the blacksmith's plan for distilling their *uisce beatha*—what a confounded word— had all the hallmarks of success. So let them begin, and for the time being let the louts believe they were in charge. After production got underway, he would take over and teach the natives, once and for all, who controlled Ballybanree.

But if he flaunted his authority at the onset, they would refuse to cooperate. He'd seen defiance in the blacksmith's eyes and in the insolent way he spoke, but he could be dealt with later. Yes, whether this were a gentleman's pursuit or not, at his next meeting with Connor he would have him send for the blacksmith. There were details to work out.

The idea caught fire in his mind. Why wait? He'd have Connor alert O'Donnell immediately. He got up from his desk and opened the study door. The baby still wailed. Where the devil were the women? He took the stone stairs two at a time and flung open the nursery door.

Nurse Gertrude gasped at the sight of him looming in the doorway, her lined face flushing as red as the wailing infant in her arms.

"Calm her," Ross ordered, "this is outrageous."

Tears started up in the old woman's eyes. "She won't be satisfied, my lord, no matter what I do."

"Why not?"

"She's hungry, sir."

"Isn't Lady Anne taking care of that?"

Fear of him and loyalty to her lady warred in Gertrude's face. "She is trying my lord. She did not expect to have to—"

He'd heard enough. "Give the child to me," he said. "Have someone bring her cradle to Lady Anne's bedchamber."

He stormed out, carrying baby Elizabeth in his arms, her long, lace-edged gown trailing over his jacket sleeves, her cries filling the upper gallery. Tonight, he vowed, the whole family would sleep together in the same room, and Anne would fill all their needs or be damned.

No doubt Anne would be abed at this late hour hiding from every distasteful duty. Well, by God, this angry bundle of humanity was his flesh and blood. No one, not even the woman who birthed her, had the right to place her in jeopardy.

He burst into Anne's chamber. As he'd suspected, the crewel hangings were closed around the bedstead and the window draperies were drawn as well. He jerked open the bed curtains, and holding the baby against one shoulder, he reached out with his free hand and shook Anne out of her feigned sleep.

"She's hungry," he said. "How could you listen to her screaming and not respond?"

"No, Ross, no," Anne said, burrowing deeper into the pillows. "I fed her just a few hours ago. It hurts to—"

"Sit up."

"I can't, not again so soon."

"Anne, listen well. I have never struck a woman in my life, but if you don't sit up and put my daughter to your breast, I swear I'll beat you black and blue."

"I hate you," she said. "I hate this place." Her chin quivered. "I want my mother."

"So does *she*. Here, take her and open your bed gown or I'll rip it open."

Slowly, reluctantly, Anne sat up against the pillows and unbuttoned her gown with trembling fingers. Her breasts, though still not large, had changed he noted. Blue veins stood out against the white flesh. Gone were the virgin rosebuds; the nipples now were brown and swollen.

"We need a wet nurse, Ross. No lady—"

"There is none. The two village women with infants can't keep Elizabeth alive and their own as well. And from the haggard look of them, I won't have my daughter pressed to their bodies."

He kissed Elizabeth's forehead. How smooth her

baby skin felt against his mouth. He placed her gently in Anne's arms. The baby quieted instantly and rooted around on her mother's breast searching for the nipple.

"Help her," he said. "Guide her mouth."

Her face set, Anne did as he ordered. He sat on the foot of the bed and watched. The sight was both beautiful and arousing. Yes, tonight would be the night, and if the baby whimpered in the dark, he would bring her in with them and see that Anne took care of her.

If all went well, at this time next year they would have a son, and Elizabeth would be growing fat and sturdy on cow's milk. But for now, watching her suckle at Anne's breast, the happy mood of early morning came back in full, and for added measure another thought occurred to him. The beautiful redhead still had the Shakespeare folio. He hadn't yet plumbed the depths that situation offered, but with a certainty he would. He'd been patient long enough.

The baby suckled noisily. Yes, life was good, very good, indeed. And then he heard a knock on the door. The cradle, no doubt.

"Not now, Ross," Anne demurred.

"Cover yourself. It's Elizabeth's bed. She's staying in here with us."

"Us?" Dismay flooded Anne's face.

"Beginning tonight." Ignoring her dismay and the stab of irritation that pricked him at the sight of it, he got up off the bed. "We both thank you for the warm welcome, darling."

"It's too soon."

"Not at all. You only think it is."

The tap sounded again.

"Come in," he shouted.

Thomas, his major-domo, stood hesitantly in the doorway.

"Pardon, my lord, but your gamekeeper would have a word with you. He says it's important."

"Send him to my study. I'll be down shortly."

After Thomas bowed his way out, Ross lifted the

sheet Anne had covered herself with and bent to kiss the crown of Elizabeth's head and to stroke the long hair that fell in a straight, pale curtain on either side of Anne's delicate face. She winced as he touched her.

"When they come with the cradle, tell Gertrude to bring in the baby's napery and whatever else is needed for her welfare."

"In *here*?"

"Exactly. Your duty from this day forward is to keep Elizabeth happy. Do you hear me?" He put a finger under Anne's chin raising her face, forcing her eyes to meet his. "And to do the same for me in the way you know I prefer."

She didn't answer him. When he took his finger away, her gaze fell, unseeing, to the baby at her breast. He stepped from the bed and without looking back strode out of the room.

Yes, he'd seek out the redhead without delay or go mad. He was certain she wouldn't merely flinch at his touch. She'd fight him tooth and claw. He smiled at the thought. A good tussle is what he ached for. And a wild resolution. He'd have both, by damn, and soon. In the meanwhile, there was tonight.

He jogged down the stone stairs. Frazer, the gamekeeper, hadn't disturbed his day without reason. He wasn't in the mood for bad news, so it had better be good.

He flung open the study door. The gamekeeper, wearing a worried look, snapped to attention.

"What is it, Frazer?"

"Sorry to tell you, sir, but I've found evidence of poaching."

"What! Where?"

"In a gully near the northwest boundary."

"Fresh killed?"

"One was, milord."

"More than one, by God!"

Frazer nodded. "We recovered two racks of antlers and the hide of a red hart. From the jagged cuts on the hide, the poacher knows little of butchering. He did a clumsy job of it."

"You found no one, of course."

The gamekeeper shook his head. "It's thanks to the dogs that we found anything at all. The ravine is well hidden with a treacherous slope. Jones damn near—sorry, sir—Jones nearly broke his neck scrambling down the bank to see what the dogs were tearing at."

"The poacher left only the offal and the hide?"

"Yes, sir."

The natives would never learn. Not even the hanging had taught them that these forests were his by God and by royal decree. His to pass on to his daughter and to the son he would some day have. His and his family's forever. Nothing could be allowed to undermine that fact. To think he'd seriously contemplated a partnership with these stupid fools.

He paced the room forcing Frazer out of his way against the bookcase. What to do? He couldn't hang every man in the village. He needed them to work the farms. Yet this act of insubordination could not go unpunished.

*Think. Think.*

There had to be a way to bring them under control. Ignoring the gamekeeper waiting against the wall for orders, he continued to pace the rug, his boots grinding into the pile as if he were trudging through his twice-raped woodland. The colors swirled together as he moved, their interlocking pattern of reds and blues a blurred jumble. And then he had it!

"Take some men, as many as you need, and bring Owen O'Donnell, the blacksmith, here. Don't waste a minute."

"No, sir. Right away."

"And send for my bailiff. I want Connor Mann as well."

\* \* \*

For this meeting, no comb had tamed the blacksmith's hair. His shirt sleeves, dotted with spark holes and scorch marks, were rolled to the elbow, and the thighs of his breeches were blackened with soot. And this time he had the gall to scowl. "I was taken from my work," he said. "Why? What is this about?"

"I ask the questions," Rushmount replied. "You give the answers. Is that understood?"

Still scowling, the man said nothing, but shifted his weight from one leg to the other.

Was standing difficult for him? If so, good. Let him stand and hasten this proceeding. Rushmount jerked his head at Connor. "Tell him."

Connor cleared his throat. His forehead shone with sweat.

"Two more deer have been taken."

No surprise appeared on the blacksmith's face. "Poached, you mean?"

"Don't act the fool. Of course, that's what we mean," Rushmount said.

"The people are hungry. Once they have enough food, the poaching will stop."

"By God, you're correct in that. The poaching will stop, and you"—he riveted O'Donnell with his gray English eyes—"will see that it does."

The blacksmith snorted in protest. "I'm not responsible for the actions of every man in Bally-banree."

Rushmount leaped to his feet and leaned over the desk, his face a mere hand span from O'Donnell's. "I do not intend to dignify this session by pleading with you to name the man. But know this. I want that poacher. I will have him, and you will bring him to me."

The blacksmith shook his head, his eyes glittering with refusal. "I'm to bring a man to his death for the sake of a poached deer? I think not."

Rushmount slumped back into his chair. Despite himself, a glimmer of respect flickered through his anger. He let himself smile. "I like your plan for making whiskey. I'm prepared to proceed along the lines we discussed, but on one condition only. Bring me the poacher. Until that happens, nothing changes."

"Clever, Lord Rushmount." Now the blacksmith leaned over the expanse of the desk, trapping him, Ross realized with a tad of unease, between the desk and the wall. "But hear me well. I do not know who took your deer. And if I did, I could not lead the man to his death. Not for any plan on earth."

Rushmount nodded. "What if I tell you this poacher will not meet the same fate as the last one?"

O'Donnell straightened and shifted his weight to his sound leg. "Death can come in many forms."

"I won't execute the poacher. You have my word as a gentleman. But he must repay the value of what he stole." Rushmount's clenched fist came down on the desk top. "Stole, do you hear me? A poacher is a thief, and thieving cannot go unpunished."

"If I might speak, my lord," Connor ventured.

"Go ahead," Rushmount snarled.

"Owen, as you know, there is much at stake here. What if you present his lordship's request to the people? Perhaps after the Mass Sunday next, and leave it to the poacher himself to come forth. For the sake of the village, he might be willing to confess his transgression. His lordship has given his word that all he wants is a fair repayment."

O'Donnell's attention swiveled from Connor's sweating face back to Rushmount. "You give your word that you will be just with the man?"

"You heard me."

"A man's word must count more than his life, or his life's not worth much."

"Are you threatening me?"

"Not at all. I'm after giving you the belief of an Irish gentleman."

Damn the man. He had the balls of an ox. Go easy, Ross, Rushmount said to himself. Get what you want first. Revenge can wait for later when it's convenient. He cocked an eyebrow. "A gentlemen's agreement, then?"

"Since the matter is put that way, I'll inform the

villagers of your demand. In conscience, I can do no more than that. The rest will be up to them. Unless, of course, you care to relent and excuse what happened as the act of a hungry man."

"Impossible and you know it."

Rushmount got to his feet. To his own surprise, he extended his hand, the first time he'd done so to one of the natives. "Shall we seal our bargain?" For a moment, he thought O'Donnell would refuse, but after staring at the extended palm as if it were a strange, alien sight, the blacksmith took it gripping him with a hand of iron.

# CHAPTER TWENTY SEVEN

Owen genuflected awkwardly before St. Mary's tabernacle then stood in front of the altar rail facing the congregation. For years he'd left church early, but on this day, and on Sunday last when he gave his exciting news to the villagers, he hadn't seemed to care what anyone might say about his clumsy gait.

A born leader he is, Grace thought, as he began to speak. She hadn't expected him to talk to the people again so soon, but there he was, hair neatly combed back and wearing his best breeches and shirt. He'd shaved, she noted, so that if he were to kiss her, he would leave no red marks on her skin as he had the morning she'd surprised him in the cave. The last time. Aye, the last.

For if he had the strength to deny their love, to live in loneliness and pain instead of in joy with her, she would match his strength and anger with her own. She, too, would exist with nothing she cared for, nothing that made her heart leap up, nothing that made living worth the while. Like him, she would have her blasted pride to sustain her, not his kisses, not his arms about her. As much as she adored him, her resolve remained strong. She'd not beg him for what he could not, or would not, freely give.

Pride would be her lover. Pride and Young Connor Mann.

She glanced over at Young Con standing beside her. He wanted to be with her constantly now that the banns had been read for the second week. Her life with him loomed ahead, only a short while away, and forever afterward no escape.

Then Owen began to deliver his news and all else
fled her mind. As he related Lord Rushmount's
demands, she stiffened, as rigid in place as a woman of
stone.

*Oh my God in heaven, I have destroyed us all.*

Father Joyce had warned her about pride, but she
hadn't listened. She *would* defy the English as Da had
done, as Granuaile had done, regardless of the
consequences. Not true, her mind protested, wild for an
excuse. 'Twas food for the village only. But the lie
refused to be buried. She'd *enjoyed* the defiance for its
own sake. It had made her feel whole, had fulfilled a
need in her to lash out, to reclaim a measure of justice.
Yet as revenge for what had been taken away from all of
them, her retaliation had been a small, unimportant
gesture. Small but big enough to kill Owen's dream.

"Owen's wasting his time," Young Con whispered in
her ear. "No one will risk the noose over this mad
whiskey plan."

Her eyes took him in, Con, her betrothed, with his
blond hair receding at the temples—in a few years he
would be bald like his da—his stocky, well-fed frame, his
thick hands that tended to dampness.

"Sure and you're wrong, Con. I think the poacher
will come forward," she replied.

*And if Rushmount goes back on his word, I will
escape from a life without Owen in it.*

* * *

The next morning, Grace washed her hair using
water from the rain barrel for the shine it gave. When
her tresses dried, she held them back from her face with
the two high copper combs that had been her mam's.
Cunningly formed with intricate knots and piercing,
they were a marvel to behold, by far her finest
possession.

In the years when Da struggled to meet the rent,
Mam had offered to sell the combs. But Da never would
allow it. They had belonged to his ancestress, the
famous Granuaile O'Malley, the pirate queen. Grace had

loved hearing how even in her old age Granuaile had sailed from Clew Bay into the great Atlantic and from there around Ireland into the Irish Sea, leading ships full of men to adventure, letting the world know an Irish woman had the courage to defy crowned heads.

Today, she would wear Granuaile's combs proudly, glad that Da had saved them for her. They would give her courage of her own this day. With her hair at the ready, she dressed in the new waist Kath had stitched for her, the neck and wrists edged in open work. With it, she donned the black skirt she'd made from Rush-mount's wool. For her feet, the moleskin brogues would have to do. She would carry them along with the red play book until she got to the manor house lawn. Then she'd sit on the green and tie them on. Fine leather shoes with heels and buckles would be grand, but she put the wish aside as another prideful thought.

"How beautiful you look. More so than ever," Brigit said when Grace finished dressing. "Young Con is a fortunate man, indeed."

As Grace gave her a farewell kiss on the cheek, the mound of Brigit's belly bumped against her. "Your son is growing large," she said with a smile.

"As is his mother."

Happy she looks, Grace thought, and rosy with health, thank God. "His mother is the one who's beautiful. More so than ever," Grace teased. She took the book from the wall shelf and picked up her brogues. "I may be late returning from my errand. Don't worry if I am."

"Indeed not. You'll be in Young Con's hands."

God Almighty, I hope not, Grace prayed as she left the cottage. 'Tis better this way. Feeling as I do, I would not make a fit wife for Young Con, and he'll not want me once the truth is told.

The sky shone bright, promising a day of sunshine, a rare happening in Connaught. The salt air blowing in from the west lacked its usual force. Filled with birdsong, it caressed her skin softly lifting strands of her hair one by one before releasing them gently to settle back about her shoulders.

At the edge of the long drive leading to Rushmount Manor, she paused and looked about. If she didn't know better, she'd believe the place deserted. Nothing stirred. Even the sheep that kept the grass cropped around the great house were nowhere in sight. She sat on the edge of the drive, tied on the brogues, then picked up the Richard play and walked on toward the manor house.

When the villagers came here for any reason, she knew they went to a back door somewhere off the kitchen wing. But for what she had to say, only the huge double front doors would do. She would not skulk in as if the land this pile of stone stood on did not by right belong to her family. As did the deer she'd taken.

But to dwell on that would do Owen's plan no good at all. 'Twould turn her around on this gravel path and lead her straight back into the woodland for her bow and more revenge. If confessing to Lord Rushmount was all she could do to make Owen happy, then so be it.

At the formidable doors, she paused again. Each one held a huge brass knocker. She'd never seen the like of them before. Two ugly, grimacing faces they were with rings in their noses.

She grasped one of the rings and banged it against the clapper. The sound, fierce enough to raise the dead, echoed in the air. Nothing happened. She waited a bit, annoyed with the heart in her breast for quickening its beat. Still no response. Again she slammed the nose ring against the mighty door. This time the door swung wide, and a small man in green livery piped with orange stood there glowering—his eyes, as they swept over her, rested overly long on her brogues.

"It's the back door for you," he said through stiff, English lips.

Before he could shut her out, she held up the red play book. "This belongs to Lord Rushmount."

"How did you get that?" he demanded, jerking his chin at the book.

She returned his glance, letting her eyes linger on his livery, letting him see her own contempt for such a rig.

"Well?" he asked.

"I came to speak to Lord Rushmount."

"You upstart baggage! Be gone before I sic the dogs on you."

"I think not. I have news of the poacher."

"That had better be the truth."

She stared at him, but said nothing. The weight of her silence brought a frown to his face and finally a muttered, "Wait here," before he slammed the door shut.

She stood outside in the warm sunlight, her eyes riveted on the brass gargoyle. No matter how long it took, she would wait. Someone would come back seeking news of the poacher. Someone eager for punishment would seize her. She was ready, but long before she despaired, the door swung open again.

"You're to come in," the little man said.

Sniffing his disapproval, he led her into the largest room she'd ever entered. So large it was, all the cottages in Ballybanree could fit into it easily. Made entirely of stone, the massive space had a ceiling that near reached the sky and a curving double row of what must be stairs. She'd heard of flights of stairs, but had never seen any. Instead of rungs like a ladder, there were platforms, a score of them at least, each one wide enough to receive an entire foot, and they spiraled up, up toward the ceiling making a body dizzy just looking at them.

Pierced stone railings like the altar rail at St. Mary's bordered both sets of stairs. *To keep a climber from falling, no doubt. Climbing up might be easy enough, but how did one get down? Backwards, like on a ladder?*

"This way," the man in livery ordered.

She followed him into a smaller, wood-paneled room off the grand entrance. At the sight of it, her jaw dropped open. Surely she'd entered the most beautiful place in the entire world.

"Wait here," he said again.

After he left she twirled around, setting her skirt awhirl as she gazed from one marvel to another, to another. An enormous, many-paned window filled the room with sunlight revealing a huge kind of table adorned with candlesticks and pens and paper. Chairs there were with backs to them and seats cushioned for ease with beautiful, embroidered cloth.

In the stone fireplace, a fire burned despite the warmth of the day—just for the cheer of it. Feeling softness under her feet, she looked down at a glorious floor cloth all in reds and blues. Then wonder of wonders, behind the big table, books covered the whole wall, shelf after shelf of them, a hundred maybe. The sight of so many took her breath away.

Footsteps! She peeked out the open door to the vast entrance room and saw Lord Rushmount running— there was no other word for it—down the stairs toward her. *Ah, so that was how to do it. One faced outward coming down. 'Twas not like using a ladder at all!*

At the foot of the staircase, he caught sight of her, his look of stunned surprise quickly giving way to a smile. "Grace O'Malley," he said. "Thomas told me a village woman had news of the poacher, but I had no idea..."

He put a hand on her shoulder and drew her back into the wood-paneled room. She felt his hand's heat through the linen of her waist before he let her go and closed the door behind them.

"Have a seat, Grace." He pointed her to one of the cushioned chairs and took a seat himself behind the big table. Placing his elbows on the polished wood surface, he tented his hands and peered at her over them. "You have something to tell me?"

She nodded. "Yes, but first, I have your play book. Thank you for the loan of it." She placed the slim, red volume on the tabletop.

He made no move to pick it up, but kept studying

her with his heated gaze. "Tell me what you think of the play."

She glanced over at the wall of books. Had he read all of them? If so, what need did he have of her thoughts on the only play she'd ever read in her whole life. "My thoughts won't interest you, Lord Rushmount."

"Let me decide what interests me. My payment for loaning the book is that you tell what you think of it."

She eyed him carefully. Tall, and narrow in the shoulders and chest, he had a hawk like profile and luminous gray eyes. The gray at his temples would spread someday to all of his hair, but that day was still far off. For now, he had the same gleam in his eye as the village lads. So book learning didn't change everything.

"Well?" he said.

She took a deep breath. Why hesitate? Once he learned the truth about her nothing else would matter anyway. "Richard is a dangerous man. An evil man. An evil king."

He nodded and smiled. "I agree."

"Only an evil man would rule as he did."

Rushmount waved a hand urging her on. "Tell me more."

"Anne was a good woman. She understood what was in his heart. She hated him for it."

"Oh?" Rushmount looked amused. "I don't recall that passage. Does she say so?"

"I'll have to find the place."

"Go ahead. I'll wait."

She picked up the book and opened it. The page she sought was near to the beginning. She almost had no need to read the passage. It had etched itself into her brain. But she would read aloud, to prove to his lordship that she could do so...her pride again pulling her into harm's way.

She cleared her throat. "These are Anne's words,"
*Foul devil, for God's sake, hence, and*
*Trouble us not.*
*For thou hast made the happy earth thy hell,*

*Fill'd it with cursing cries and deep exclaims.*
*If thou delight to view thy heinous deed,*
*Behold this pattern of thy butcheries.*

"That will be enough," Rushmount said, shifting in his seat, his voice no longer warm and playful.

She looked up from the book. A frown replaced his smile of earlier.

"Plays are dangerous things," he said.

"They make a person think. They make injustice come alive."

"But by play's end, justice triumphs. The laws of England prevail."

"English justice is for English people only."

A red stain mounted his cheeks.

*Dear Mother, I've annoyed him entirely.*

"I loaned you the first play that came to hand," he said. "I should have chosen a different one. *Romeo and Juliet*, perhaps. It's a love story."

"Between a man and a woman? People talk of such things out loud?"

He laughed. "Indeed, and no one better than Will Shakespeare. You may take that one next. But now, what is it you came to tell me?"

"First I must ask a question."

"Ask it."

"Once you have the poacher, is it true you will allow the villagers to carry out Owen O'Donnell's plan?"

"Ah, for the *uisce beatha*, as you call it?"

She nodded and waited, her eyes intent on him, searching for the lie or the truth in his answer, hoping she would know the difference.

He got up from behind the table and sat on its edge, his legs in their high, leather boots planted in front of her chair, his long, slim hands gripping his knees, his face so close to her own she could feel his breath on her cheek. He bent even closer and, reaching out, wound a tendril of her hair around one of his fingers. "You are a brave girl," he said, "and a beauty to boot. You must know that."

Careful not to touch his finger, she pulled the curl free and tossed her hair back over her shoulders. "I know I cannot speak, Lord Rushmount, until you answer me."

"Marvelous! You are marvelous! You want *me* to answer *you?* Very well, then." He began to laugh.

He was not taking her seriously. He acted like a lad teasing for a kiss. She should have expected it. Young Con had warned her.

"I give you my word that once I know the identity of the poacher and am repaid for what he stole, the villagers will be allowed to carry out their plan." His teeth showing between smiling lips, he added, "Is that fair enough for you?"

"Yes, sir." She took a deep breath. But before she could say a word, he stood, and placing his hands on both arms of her chair, locking her in place, he leaned forward and caught her mouth in a hard, open kiss.

*Like the lads! No better!*

She had no chance to escape, no breath to protest. Without taking his mouth away, he grasped her shoulders and pulled her to her feet, pressing himself against her from his polished boots to his chest. She felt his hardness.

*So soon!*

His lips softened and opened wider. His tongue, his English tongue, entered her mouth.

She struggled to wrench free, but he wouldn't release her. His mouth ground on and on. She went to lift a knee to his groin, but he held her imprisoned so tight against him, she couldn't move.

*Only one thing to do!*

As his tongue darted forward again, she bit down and tasted his blood.

His hands dropped away, and he stepped back. A testing finger went into his mouth and came away red. "You will never do that again, do you hear me?" he said, his breath coming in shallow gasps.

"And neither will you."

"You think not? We've only just begun you and I. Make no mistake about that."

For the space of a moment, she thought he would strike her, but he laughed again and began to walk about the room. Is he trying to calm himself? she wondered, eyeing him as he moved, turning to face him each time his pacing brought him behind her. She couldn't keep her back to the likes of him. He was not to be trusted. Yet she must put her life in his hands.

As abruptly as he'd begun trodding the wondrous floor covering, he stopped and stood in front of her. Before she could move away, he put his hands on her shoulders. "I'll hear what you came to tell me."

She tried to free herself, but he held her fast.

"Speak," he demanded.

"I know the poacher," she replied.

"I'm pleased someone does. Who is he?"

"Grace O'Malley is her name."

His grip tightened, his long, bruising fingers pressing into her flesh. "Don't play games with me, girl. I want the truth."

"You have it. I don't lie."

He let her go so swiftly she fell back a step.

"You actually expect me to believe you? You take me for a fool?"

At the menace in his face, Grace felt a stab of fear. Dear God, he had to believe her or she would fail Owen utterly.

"I'll take you to the very spot where I downed the red hart. I'll show you where I hide my bow. I'll—"

"You'll listen to me!"

She moved away, putting the cushioned chair between them. But he stalked her, yanking the chair out of his path so hard it teetered on its slender legs. She rounded the giant table. He followed her. She had nowhere to go except to press against the wall of books. Seizing her hands, he held them up, spreading her arms wide apart, forcing her to the wall.

"Who sent you? The blacksmith? Was this his idea? Send a girl with a preposterous story to throw me off scent? You go back and tell him his trick didn't work. I want the poacher or nothing."

"You *have* the poacher!"

"Who are you hiding?"

"No one!"

"I don't believe you. Nor will I be made a fool of. Not by the likes of you and this Owen O'Donnell." With fury reddening his face, he released her hands. "Or Connor Mann either, by God. He must know of this plot. Sit down," he commanded and, striding across the floor, he flung open the door. "Thomas!" he bellowed into the grand stone entrance. "Thomas!"

Was Thomas the little man in livery, she wondered?

"Thomas!" Still no response.

"Is everyone deaf?" No one answered.

"Stay there," he ordered before stomping off in a rage.

Grace peered out into the vast room. As she watched, he went through a door hidden behind the staircase and disappeared from sight.

She'd done what she came to do. No need to stay longer. Neither Owen nor Connor would have anything to tell Rushmount, so why wait and listen to their denials and watch the anger at what she'd said climb into their eyes?

Her soft brogues made no sound on the stone floor as she walked over to the tall entrance doors and, after fumbling with the unfamiliar latch for a few seconds, managed to open one and slip out into the sunshine.

If Lord Rushmount wanted to question her further, he would know where to find her. When Owen and Connor denied any knowledge of the poacher, he would come after her, of that she felt certain. But as to the outcome of this day, for that she had only a deep, black foreboding.

# CHAPTER TWENTY EIGHT

"Thomas! Where the devil are you?" Rushmount called out as he navigated the dark servants' passage. Getting no answer, he shouted his way to the kitchen wing.

Margaret, the cook, startled by her master's sudden presence, looked up from the spit where a goose had begun to brown, filling the air with a succulent aroma. "He's answering the call of nature, sir," she said not missing a turn of the spit handle.

"Good Lord. When he comes in, send him to me immediately."

"Very good, sir."

She turned back to the spit, and Ross left her to her work. She was one of the estate's treasures. After he tasted the goose, he'd be sure to send her his compliments. Imagine depending on the locals to prepare their meals! It would be boiled turnip and gruel.

He hurried back to the study. If need be, the girl had to be forced to tell the truth. He'd leave that chore to Connor Mann. It wouldn't do to become an ogre in her eyes any more than necessary, not over this. He had other plans for her, and she'd gotten a hint of them today.

God, the way she'd fought him, writhing in his arms, making him struggle to hold her fired his blood. She'd even tried to knee him. That spoke of experience. Good. Virgins were a bore as Anne had proven.

He hurried back through the servants' passage. He'd ordered her to wait. Well, they would wait together. Once he dispatched Thomas, there would be ample time before Connor could be found and brought to him—

ample time.

The door to the study stood open. Hadn't he closed it? His heart pounding like a boy's, he hurried across the great hall, but his prize had eluded him. Damn it to hell and back. She hadn't obeyed his orders. Hot for her though he was, her defiance pleased him. It held so much promise.

Thomas came up behind him, his step silent as always. "Beg pardon, my lord. I was indisposed when you called."

"So I heard. Get Connor Mann here and be quick about it."

"Yes sir. Right away, sir."

Ross waited with growing impatience. Pacing helped and a glass of sherry, but not enough. She'd slipped through his fingers, and they still tingled with the urge to stroke her. He should never have left her alone, not before taking what he wanted then forcing the truth out of her. He was in the act of pouring a third drink when Connor knocked.

"Come in," he shouted.

Connor's shiny forehead had the look of hurry. He must have run across the grounds.

"I've just had an unbelievable conversation with one of your local women."

"One of the women, my lord?"

"Yes, a young woman. She claims she's the poacher."

"A lass?" Connor snorted. "That is pure rubbish, plain and simple."

Ross peered at him. "I agree. She had to be lying, covering up for someone, some man, no doubt. Trying to make a fool out of me."

"I doubt that, my—"

"I don't trust any of them. And this one's a vixen."

"Who is the lass, my lord?"

"That O'Malley girl. Grace, the one with the red hair."

"Oh my God, not Grace! Young Con's intended?"

"What!"

The sweat began to collect on Connor's cheeks. He swiped at the drops with the sleeve of his shirt to little avail. In an instant, more beads appeared in their place. "The banns have been read for them," he said, reaching into his breeches' pocket for a linen square. "They're to be married in a few weeks. The lad's smitten with her, but I can assure you, my lord, he had nothing to do with the poaching. Why the lass would come to you with such a wild tale I can't imagine. But my son knows nothing of it. Nor do I. I swear to that." His speech ended, he mopped his entire face with the linen.

Ross took the sherry in one long swallow. He believed Connor. The Manns would not jeopardize what they had with an act of open defiance. No, the girl was covering for someone. But who? The natives were such a clannish lot, it had to be someone close to her, most likely a family member.

Yes, it had to be someone close. The crippled blacksmith? She'd claimed he was but a friend. An unlikely candidate for a poacher, but the possibility couldn't be dismissed out of hand, not a second time. She'd come searching for O'Donnell when they seized him for questioning last spring.

He remembered the relief that had swept her face when she learned O'Donnell had been set free. And the stab of envy he'd felt at the sight of it. He'd send for him.

She had a brother, as he recalled. Newly married with a family on the way already, or so rumor had it. She might well want to protect him. He'd have the brother brought in as well.

"All right, Mann, don't just stand there. Get the blacksmith in here. We'll question him first." Ross waved the back of his hand at Connor sending him on his way.

He brought the sherry decanter to the desk and poured another. So she was to be married. He should have expected it, a beauty like that. But Christ, to the Mann lout! Of all the families in the county, the Manns were the ones he relied on the most.

Dallying with Young Con's woman would create havoc. No question about that. The natives prized female virtue above food. He expelled a lungful of air. Fools!

So what next? Take her at the first opportunity? Hell, create an opportunity. The sooner the better.

Was she worth the trouble?

*At the first opportunity.*

His mind was made up, but even a short wait was too long. He had to have relief. Any man who called himself a man would vow the same. No doubt, Anne would still be abed. She'd spend all of her days there hiding from life if he allowed it. The habit annoyed him to madness, but today he'd make use of it.

He gulped down his drink then took the stairs two at a time. For once, he didn't fling open the curtains in her darkened bed chamber, but began to strip off his clothes in the gloom.

"Anne," he said, "wake up if you're asleep in there. Your husband wants you."

A soft mewl of protest came from behind the crewel-worked curtains. God, she hated his very touch. What a welcome for a passionate man. Never any enthusiasm, only an ordeal to be lived through. A duty. Well, so be it. He'd take what he had to have and to hell with her reluctance.

The redhead wouldn't give in with a little feeble cry and lay there enduring him. She would meet him like a tigress and give as much as she got. But for today, Anne would have to do.

He sat to pull off a boot letting it thud to the floor. Then he clawed at the other one and flung it across the room where it banged against the wall and fell with a crash.

"Did you hear that?" he shouted. "It's my breeches next!"

No answer. If he'd frightened her, good, maybe that would cause her to react. Something, anything except a lifeless surrender.

The kitten-like mewling began again.

"You do hear me," he said, "I thought so."

"Ross, please, the baby."

Elizabeth! He'd forgotten about her.

From the cradle on the other side of the bedstead, a shrill cry rose in the air. Quickly, without a pause between sleeping and waking, Elizabeth began to scream, her cries growing louder and stronger with every second she remained hungry and wet and ignored.

The crewel work curtains parted. Anne peered out, her silver-blonde plaits falling across her bosom. "See what you've done."

"Christ, woman, my problem is I haven't done anything. But by God, I damn well will. Let her cry. This won't take long."

The curtains closed, and Anne disappeared behind them. So she couldn't stand the sight of her naked husband? Would that never change?

He fumbled with the brass buttons holding his breeches closed. Damn the fool things! Clumsy with haste, he was ready to tear them loose when the last one yielded. He pulled off the garment, tossed it on the floor, and threw his smallclothes on top. The shirt wouldn't be in his way. He'd take no more time.

*God, the child had a powerful set of lungs.*

He parted the curtains and put one knee on the mattress. In the half-light amidst Elizabeth's screams, he felt for Anne's softness.

Nothing.

The bed was empty. She must have slipped out the other side and fled the room while he stripped. She couldn't have gone far in her bed gown. Why not chase her about the house? Find her and take her wherever that might be—in the nursery, in Gertrude's room, in the scullery—wherever. He didn't give a fig for what the servants might think.

No?

Yes. He'd better or become the laughing stock of

Ballybanree.

He could hear the natives now. "Chasing his woman about the house he was, his mast on high for all to see...frantic for her and she not to be had...and, ooh, the screaming when he caught her...pure terror to the ears...the maids had never heard the like...he tumbled her like a common slut right on the stones of the floor."

He couldn't allow that. Trying to ignore the baby's cries, he parted the draperies and flung open the windows to the bright, sunlit day. He took in deep gulps of salt air. From this vantage point, he had a clear, unobstructed view of his estate with its palette of green fields and woodlands, the crystal blue sky above, and off in the distance the iron gray Atlantic. But to his eyes, everything appeared washed in the red tint of blood.

# CHAPTER TWENTY NINE

The stream below the cottage sparkled in the morning light, the sun today as strong as yesterday when she'd gone to Rushmount Manor. For sure, 'twould be a shame not to take advantage of the sunshine and wash their clothes. They'd dry easily spread out on the grass with no need to hang them about the cottage waiting for the dampness to disappear from the folds.

Besides, Grace thought, she would like to be alone for a while to think about what had happened and to keep her hands busy while she waited for Rushmount to strike. For strike he would. It was only a question of when and of how. Still, nearly a full day had passed, and she'd heard nothing.

She'd half expected Young Con to stop by last evening full of questions and anger. But he hadn't come near her. No one had. Nor had she spoken of her actions to Liam and Brigit. No need to worry them or to see the fear leap into Liam's eyes. That above all, she couldn't bear.

She sighed and clubbed her hair up off her nape with a length of blue ribbon she took from her pocket. The sun shining on her neck felt good. Much better than the tug of a rope. Liam's clothes were the heaviest and too much these days for Brigit to struggle over. She knelt by the bank on a flat stone and dropped a pair of breeches into the water. Years ago, Da had set the stone there for Mam to use, or maybe Grandda had done so. After the breeches soaked for a few minutes, she'd beat out the dirt with the stick saved for that purpose.

The water flowed cool against her hands. If she lifted

her skirt to her knees and waded in the stream, 'twould be like the time she'd been in the ocean with Owen. After a moment of happy reflection, she shook her head. No, not like that. Nothing would ever be like that again.

She splashed a handful of water over her cheeks to cool them. All little streams like this one flowed to the oceans, Da had said. What would it be like to sail those deep waters as Granuaile had done? Thrilling, no doubt, battling Elizabeth's ships, and bringing booty home to her people. What a warrior she must have been! 'Twas grand to bear her name, but in nothing else were they alike at all, at all. Not with her own poor acts of defiance ending in disaster for herself and the villagers and, most of all, for Owen.

"Grace."

*Him!*

Although the sound of his deep voice thrummed in her like music, she didn't look up, but seized the stick and began pounding the breeches.

"Grace, stop and look at me," Owen said.

"I have nothing to say to you."

"But I do to you."

"Did you come to beg my hand in marriage? You're too late for that." The bitterness in her heart had spilled out after all, poisoning the air between them.

"Rushmount doesn't believe you are the poacher, but I do," he said.

From her knees, she turned and looked up at him. "'Tis not your opinion that counts, only his."

"I agree. He won't harm you. I saw that clear enough in his eyes. But he's half crazed with anger. He will have his man, or all is lost."

She lifted the sodden breeches onto the stone by her knees. It would not do to have them float away. "I'm sorry, Owen, for many things, but for this above all. Had I known of your plan, and 'tis a magnificent one, I might not have gone out for the deer. I tried—"

"No need to explain. Not to me, Grace. You tried to help the people. And you did." He looked across the narrow stream to Liam's north pasture now full-leaved and deep green with the coming barley crop. "The harvest will be a good one this year, the Lord willing, but until then the meat is tiding us over. Best of all, you've helped little Eileen. She still ails, but at least Donal has not had to dig up his half-grown fields to feed her and her brothers."

"There's comfort in that, but if I destroyed your plan, I beg your forgiveness."

"No one needs to be forgiven for courage."

"'Twas my pride as well."

"I, too, have pride."

She nodded. "I know that full well, Owen O'Donnell."

The water from Liam's breeches had seeped along the stone wetting the skirt bundled about her knees. She had no more to say and turned to her work.

Before she could drop the wet garment back into the stream, Owen said, "Grace, I have a message for you."

She looked up. "From his lordship?"

He shook his head. "From Connor. The Manns will not contact you in any way until this matter with Rushmount is settled. Until then, they don't want you to visit their cottage."

"What of Young Con?"

"He agrees. Their livelihood depends on the Englishman's good will. They're frantic with worry."

At the thought of kindly Kath made heavy-hearted, she sat back on her heels and hid her face in her hands. "What have I done? Oh God, what have I done?"

On the bare nape of her neck, she felt the warmth of his breath as he leaned over her to whisper, "You defied the world, Grace. You alone of all the villagers like your da before you."

Not willing to be comforted, she said, "But look at the evil I've caused."

"Not so! You fought it. For that I adore you." He drew in a deep breath. "There's more. Rushmount wants to question Liam. I've come to fetch him."

"Not that! 'Twill kill him." She scrambled to her feet. "You can't take him, Owen. I must warn him."

As she went to rush past him, he caught her arm, staying her. "Rushmount has given his word, no hanging, but he's convinced you're protecting someone. A man. He says no lass could do what you claim." Owen frowned. "He won't accuse the Manns, not even Young Con...or me." He clapped his palm against his injured leg. "That leaves Liam as the one you'd most likely protect."

"Oh dear Jesus, no!"

"Grace, it will be better for all of us if Liam walks over to the main house willingly and tells Rushmount what he wants to hear. Once he's satisfied that he has his man, we'll offer to pay him back out of the harvest. Spread out amongst the villagers, the price should amount to just a few shillings for each family."

"Ah! No!" Grace threw herself at Owen, her fists beating on his chest, her head tossing back and forth whipping her hair about her face until the ribbon loosened and the freed tresses cascaded about her like an unruly curtain of gold.

Owen grasped her flailing hands. "Stop it, Grace. Stop."

At his tone, she did and slumped against him. He smoothed her loosened hair away from her face with hands that were all tenderness.

"They can spare no shillings, not one, for meat that's nearly gone," she said.

"They'll have to. Don't blame yourself. You fed them during these hungry weeks. No one else did as much. But we must get our plan underway. 'Tis the villagers' only hope. If need be, we'll spare a few shillings today to gain far more tomorrow."

He eased her back onto the stone slab where she sat with her skirt crumpled about her and her hair lifting in the breeze.

"Stay and finish your washing. I'll find Liam and send Brigit to you." He went to walk away, then hesitated, and turned back to her. "Be careful of Rush-mount. Stay clear of him. The look in his eyes when he spoke of you—"

"I'm aware."

"Ah, you know then," he said giving her a sharp glance of inquiry, but asking no question.

After he left, Grace wrung out the breeches puddling at her knees and spread them on the grass, then washed the other clothes—her shift and one of Brigit's and their linen waists.

In a short while, she saw Brigit crossing the fields toward her, her expression serious but calm enough. "Owen sent me," she said.

"He told you?"

Brigit nodded, uncertainty beginning to cloud her face. "'Tis hard to believe...a lass like you..."

"Owen believes me."

Clumsy with the child so big inside her, Brigit managed, nonetheless, to sit on the grass next to Grace. She arranged her skirt and lifted her face to the sun. "Nothing will happen to him, will it?"

"They've gone?"

"Liam didn't want to, but if he refused Owen said his lordship would send his men. 'Tis better this way, he said."

With her fingertips, Brigit began making pleats in the wool of her skirt, pinching line after line into the fabric. If she felt anger, nothing about her betrayed that, but she could not keep the worry from her face, and for that Grace wanted to die.

With a sigh, she bent to her work. One last shirt to pound clean and she'd be finished. Liam would need a clean shirt for Mass Sunday next. She lowered it into the stream.

"I should be doing the washing," Brigit said. "'Tis my duty."

"You have a lifetime to wash Liam's clothes. No need to strain yourself. Or him," Grace said with a smile and a glance at Brigit's rounded form.

Brigit stroked her belly mound. "I know 'tis a him. I had a dream."

"Tell me."

"He has red-gold hair like yours and his da's, broad shoulders and a smiling face. He's a happy lad, and he grows up tall and strong. I saw his whole life. 'Twill be a good one." Tears had started up in Brigit's eyes. She sniffled them away and smiled.

Grace plucked the shirt from the water and picked up the stick. "Of a certainty, his life will be good. How could it not be with the parents he'll have?"

Brigit's chin quivered. "I'm so frightened, Grace. If his lordship harms Liam—"

"He won't. He doesn't want revenge. He wants repayment, that's all. I thought Rushmount would believe me. I've never been taken for a liar." She brought the stick down on the linen garment, pounding it over and over. "Killing the deer was not so hard...the English Elizabeth did as much...of course, she did not have to sully herself with the butchering."

Brigit stretched out on the grass. "You're right, of course. It's foolish of me to worry. The Lord has made this day so beautiful; He will allow nothing bad to happen in it."

With the shirt beaten clean, Grace wrung out the water and shook out the creases before laying it flat in the sunshine. "Let's stay outside the whole day," she said. "'Tis far too lovely to be doing chores inside. We'll wait here by the stream until Liam returns. It won't be long, you'll see."

\* \* \*

As Rushmount looked on, annoyed, the blacksmith walked into the stable as if the building and everything in it belonged to him. He gestured toward the prisoner huddled in a corner on a pile of straw. "I wish to speak to him."

"You'll do no such thing," Rushmount retorted. "Leave us."

The man made no move to go.

"Leave or my men here will see to it."

Frazer and the others stood straight, fists at the ready.

"Five against one, is it? My da raised no idiot. I'll wait outside," O'Donnell said to the prisoner's bowed head then clumped out of the stable.

When he and his men were again alone with their prisoner, Ross continued his interrogation. "Wasn't it enough to see your father hanged? You escaped that time for one reason only. English law is just. You weren't caught skulking about the woods, so you weren't punished. But this is an outrage."

He smashed a clenched fist into his open palm. "Sending your sister to me! A young girl! What were you trying to do? Make a fool out of me? Who do you think you're playing games with?"

"My lord—"

"Quiet! You're her next of kin. It's you she's protecting, not your crippled friend and not young Mann. He's not that stupid! You! Hiding behind a woman's skirts!"

"I swear I did not send her to you."

The man's face had turned white as milk, Ross noted. So he had him frightened? Excellent. Frightened men told the truth. But it would not do to terrify him— that might clamp his mouth shut for good.

The chestnut, already saddled and ready for a run, pawed at the floor of his stall.

"Ready for a ride, boy?" Ross asked him.

At the sound of Rushmount's voice, the horse stopped pawing and quieted. Gelding him had made him a peaceable beast, far less likely to throw his rider.

Rushmount looked down at his prisoner. The man trembled in place.

He was like a woman. No stomach. No staying power. No wonder he sent the girl in his stead. Bold enough in the dark with an arrow in his hand, but not in the world of men where it mattered.

"There's still time. I'm going for a ride. When I

return, I'll expect the truth from you."

His voice trembling like the rest of him, the man said, "I've told you what I know. My sister is a fine marksman. I have no reason to doubt her word."

The stupid oaf, expecting him to swallow that ridiculous tale. "A disgusting lie. One hour."

Ross led the chestnut out of the stable into the sunlit morning. For a second day, the perpetual mists had held off. The sky was glorious, perfect for a canter about the property.

He swung into the saddle. Suppose the girl actually did what she claimed? Clearly, she possessed a courage her brother lacked. But no, he dismissed the possibility. Even if true, to accept a mere girl as an adversary was out of the question.

Damn the complication! He'd begun to warm to the O'Donnell plan. Distilling whiskey for sale had captured his imagination. Now this annoying problem stood in the way. Nevertheless, it couldn't be ignored. Let the natives think they were in control and his authority in this isolated place would crumple. Too bad Anne hated it so. She should consider herself fortunate to be here. Disease, he'd heard, was raging through London. Surely plague was worse than being forced back into his bed in the middle of the day.

Leaning forward in the saddle, he patted the chestnut's neck then dug his heels into his flank. "Come on, boy. Let's move out. Maybe we'll find someone exciting in the fields."

\* \* \*

Owen saw the chestnut and its rider canter up the slope and disappear down the other side. So Rushmount had left. Did that mean Liam was free to go? He came back into the stable. Liam had collapsed deep into the straw, his knees bent, his head in his hands. Not the picture of a man about to be set free. A short distance from him, Rushmount's men were taking their ease.

Owen lifted his chin in Liam's direction. "I might persuade him to confess. All right?"

"Go to it, man."

Owen crouched down in front of Liam ignoring the strain to his injured leg. "Liam," he whispered, "there's only one way out of this. Tell Rushmount you're the poacher. He'll exact his payment, then we'll both go home."

Liam raised lifeless eyes. "Why should I tell a pack of lies? I never stole a thing belonging to him. I'm innocent."

"That doesn't matter." Owen looked over his shoulder at the two guards. They sat against a stall, their eyes closed, grateful for the chance to sleep, or more likely to feign it. He turned back to Liam. "He won't accept a lass as an adversary. I know she did it, and you know the same, but that isn't important now. He wants a man to blame, so he can salvage his pride."

Liam shook his head. "I can't take the chance. He murdered my da for the sake of a deer. He'll do the same to me."

"He swore he wouldn't."

"If only Grace hadn't—"

"She has more strength than all of Ballybanree put together. Don't fault her, Liam. Give Rushmount what he wants to hear and be done with it."

"I can't. And that's the truth of it. I can't."

Owen grasped a fistful of Liam's shirt jerking his head upright, forcing his eyes to look into his own. "I'd say I was the one in a heartbeat. But he'll only laugh. He knows I'm not fleet enough to follow a deer. It has to be you."

Liam shook his head.

"I'm after telling you, man, he will not accept a lass as his foe. Give him a way out he can take and still save face."

"I won't do it. It makes no sense to me."

Owen released his shirt. "Then God help us all," he said and walked out of the stable.

# CHAPTER THIRTY

The day passed with agonizing slowness. When night fell, still Liam had not come home. On the second day, gloaming had nearly turned into dark before Grace and Brigit heard him approach the cottage. He came along the path with slow steps, his face an unreadable mask.

"Thank God you're home," Brigit said running to him and flinging her arms about his neck. "What happened, love?"

He groaned and with an effort took her hands away. "I need the bed," he said, his voice flat and toneless.

"No food before you sleep? They fed you, then?" Brigit asked.

"No. They fed me not. I fed them and their blood lust."

Brigit looked past Liam to Grace and shrugged. Grace shook her head. The bitterness in Liam's tone puzzled her, sent a chill down her spine, but she couldn't name the reason why.

"I don't know what you mean, love, but if it is the bed you want, come," Brigit said and led him into the cottage.

Grace stayed in the main room. She had no call to invade their private space and would have to wait until morning to hear Liam's news. But as long as he didn't want his food, she'd take the cook pot off the spit. The last of the stew could cool for the morrow.

Brigit's scream tore her from the fire. She ran, her heart in her mouth, into the bedroom.

"His breeches," Brigit said. "They're all over blood."

Her pulse racing, Grace took the rush lamp from

Brigit's trembling hand and held it over Liam. He lay on his back, one hand covering his face. A large, bloody stain had oozed from between his legs and soaked into the front of his breeches.

"What happened to you, Liam?" Grace asked.

"Leave us, Grace," he said.

Frightened for him, she backed away from the bed, handed the lamp to Brigit, and closed the door behind her. In the main room, she laid a peat brick on the fire, and when it burned down, another, and then another until she lost count and gave up, letting the flames die into embers while she sat through the black hours with terror in her soul.

Before dawn, Brigit slipped out of the bedroom. Without saying a word, she knelt down, heavy and awkward, on the floor before the embers.

"Brigit, what's wrong?" Grace asked. "Speak to me for God's sake. I'm half mad with worry."

"He's sleeping now. I thought he never would again." Brigit looked over at Grace, but her eyes remained unfocused as if she saw no one and nothing. "They've gelded him," she said.

Grace gasped, shock bringing her to her feet, readying her to flee from what she'd heard. But the awful truth could not be outrun. "They took his manhood?"

With a darkness coming into her eyes, Brigit nodded. "Rushmount had his men tie him down and cut him. He wouldn't show me, and that's all he'll say of it." Her hands went down to caress her belly. "This son is the only one we'll ever have. Liam will never love me again, not in the same way." Her voice trailed off into the nothingness of silence.

Oh God. Everything had gone horribly wrong. *And it's my fault. My fault. My fault.*

"He wants no one to know," Brigit said. "He's that ashamed." Her chin jutted up. "He needn't be. He's done no wrong."

"None," Grace agreed. *I am the one.*

"He won't have my mam or Gram O'Neill or anyone tend him," Brigit said. "Only me." She looked up at Grace, her face as bleak as a starless night. "I should put the kettle on and wash him when he wakes. He wouldn't let me earlier." Her voice shattered into sobs.

Grace crouched by her side and went to take her in her arms, but Brigit shrugged her off. "There's no comfort in your touch, Grace. Leave me be."

"I will if you wish," Grace said and got up from her knees. "I'll be outside if you need me."

"I won't need you," Brigit said.

Though morning came and went, the cottage door didn't open or Brigit's gentle voice call to her. Grace sat on the doorstep, and paced in the yard, and wandered in the front meadow. Still the door remained shut. From time to time, she went up to listen but heard only faint stirrings from inside, once the low murmur of voices, then silence. Most of all, silence.

They hated her. Both of them. As long as they lived, they would blame her for what had happened. How could she have been so willful, so wrong, so intent on revenge that she would endanger those she loved most on earth?

For hours on end, she tormented herself with questions that had no perfect answers.

*Is it wrong to feed the hungry in any way possible?*
*Is it wrong to have pride?*
*Is it wrong to tax a people until they bleed?*

To that question, the answer did come swift and clear. To tax a man without his consent made him a slave. And what else were the rents that kept Ireland on the verge of starvation? Taxes with a different name, taxes that had forced her out into the night.

But to her brother and Brigit none of that would mean a tinker's damn on this evil day with its bright and cheerful sun. Had the mists deserted them forever now, like Liam's hopes for his life?

By noon, she could stand her isolation no longer and opened the cottage door. She walked in, her bare feet

silent on the hard dirt floor. The main room was empty.
She risked looking into the open bedroom. Brigit lay
curled against Liam, her swollen body slack, her eyes
closed in sleep.

Liam lay on his back. With his eyes wide open, he
stared up at the thatch. If he heard Grace come in, he
made no attempt to glance her way, but kept his eyes
intent on what loomed over his head.

She watched the two of them lying together for a
long, bitter moment before taking her leave.

\* \* \*

She stayed away two days wandering the fields
aimlessly, hiding behind an oak when she spied Lord
Rushmount riding in the distance, cooling her face from
time to time with water from the stream, picking wild
flowers and mindlessly weaving them into chains,
dozing for brief periods in the woods, fitfully waking out
of nightmare into nightmare, sobbing until her eyes
went dry, then maddened with thirst seeking the stream
again, but seeking no solace from anyone, not Mary
Burke, not Gram O'Neill, not Father Joyce...not Owen...
not anyone, though a question pounding in her mind
demanded an answer.

What was she to do with herself?

She couldn't stay in the open forever with no roof
overhead, no food, and no clothes but those she wore.
The cave beckoned, but she refused its call. She
wouldn't go there as if looking for Owen to rescue her
from a fate she'd brought on herself, and worse, on
those she loved. She didn't deserve his solace or his love.
On the second night of near despair, when she could
think of no other solution, she finally sought out Gram
O'Neill's hut, coming to it in desperation at the
midnight hour when all the villagers had their doors
closed. Even Owen, she noted, as she passed by the
smithy.

Gram would shelter her and be wise enough not to
ask questions she couldn't answer. Without being told,
she would recognize that a great evil had driven Grace

to her. Ah, if only Gram had a poultice to heal her grief and restore Liam to whole manhood, but that could never be.

Grace scratched at Gram's cabin door. Used to being wakened in the night to deliver Ballybanree's babes, she would hear the slight noise.

As Grace expected, in no time at all, the door cracked open to reveal Gram, her thin wisps of white hair hanging down on either side of her face, her small form, not much bigger than a half-grown child's, wrapped in a shawl despite the warm night air.

"Grace, is it? You're not here about Brigit, I hope. 'Tis not her time yet."

"'Tis not about Brigit...help me, Gram," Grace whispered. "I need to come in."

The door opened wide. "Come in then, child, come in. Sit. Ease yourself."

The firepit gave off a soft glow. Like the rest of the village, Gram's home contained but a few simple furnishings. What made it different were the dried herbs and berries and grasses she'd tied together in neat bunches and hung upside down on pegs from every available drying space—the roof trusses, the low rafters, the walls. Mysterious roots and gnarled tubers filled baskets piled up in the corners of the room.

Confined together in the small cabin, the medicinals gave off a pungent, exotic odor, a combination of rosemary, thyme, wild garlic and other herbals Grace couldn't recognize, but loved to inhale. A remedy Gram had for every ailment except the one for which nobody in the whole wide world had a cure.

Gram peered at her. "Whatever brings you here at this hour will keep. You look done in, child, even in this poor light. When have you slept last?"

Grace shook her head. "I can't. I dream."

"Bad dreams, eh? They're fearsome things." She peered closer. "When have you eaten last?"

Grace shrugged. "I'm not hungry."

"I have just the thing. Sit by the table. This will only

take a minute."

Grace sank onto a stool, laid her arms on the tabletop and rested her head on them. The sounds of movement faded in and out of her consciousness.

A mug came down on the table by her elbow. "Drink up, Grace. 'Twill put you to sleep without the dreaming. Go on, go on, try it."

Grace raised a head almost too heavy to lift and picked up the cup of steaming liquid. She took a tentative sip. A taste alien, yet somehow familiar, filled her mouth. "*Uisce beatha*?"

Gram nodded. "Aye, and some soothing herbs. I'll spread straw in the far corner, and here's an extra blanket to cover you. After you finish what's in the mug, you must lie down. For as long as you want to," she added.

"I knew you wouldn't seek answers. You're a wise woman."

"I'm a woman who's lived a long life and seen much sorrow. 'Tis sorrow that brings the wisdom. Now drink. Drink."

Grace did, grateful for the kindness. Too tired to speak of it, she squeezed the old woman's hand.

"I know," Gram said. "I know. You'll tell me when you're able."

The warmth of the drink trailed its way to Grace's stomach, soothing her into drowsiness.

"Come, take off your skirt and waist. They're covered with leaves and grass. You'll sleep better without them about you."

Grace stood and let herself be undressed to her shift and led like a child to the rough bed. When she lay down on the straw, sleep came so fast and so deep she knew nothing of it until high noon the next day when she awakened, and the nightmare returned.

Gram heard her stir about on the straw. "Ah, you're awake. You've had a good rest, I warrant."

"Indeed. That potion works magic."

Gram chortled. "Many's the time I've been told that

over the years, but it's effective only if used sparingly."
She eyed Grace's pale face. "You'll eat now?"

"I can't take your food."

"From what I hear tell from Mary Burke and some
others, you've brought me my food these past several
weeks."

Grace didn't answer.

Gram pulled a stool up to the straw and sat. "The
whole tale of your doings has been told to me, and I
heard Lord Rushmount thinks you lied to him. Men can
be such fools. Of course, you had the spirit to defy him.
Why is it men believe women lack courage? To see them
in childbirth gives the lie to that. But I rant like an old
woman." She stopped talking to cackle and slap her
knees with the palms of her hands. "No wonder. In
truth, that's what I am."

"You are the soul of kindness, and I am grateful to
you."

"Pish. Now you'll eat. I have an egg for you and a
piece of oat bread. I might even find a pinch of salt for
the egg."

"I can't—"

"You can and you will. It's all ready. And then have a
quick wash. I brushed your clothes as best I could."
Gram hauled herself to her feet. "Father Joyce will be
here soon to have a word with you."

"But—"

"Come, come!"

\* \* \*

Under the seal of Confession, she knew she could
tell what had happened to Liam. Father Joyce would go
to his death before revealing a word. Besides, Brigit, but
Liam most of all, would need the priest's aid and all the
power of God as well.

In her freshened clothes, her face pale but shining
from the washcloth, and her hair tamed and neat once
she combed it with the aid of Gram's coarse, wide-
toothed comb, she sat and waited for him.

He would come by after the noon meal he'd told

Gram, and shortly after the sun reached its zenith, he ducked through the hut's open door. Despite her stiff knees, Gram attempted a clumsy curtsy.

At the sight, he said, "None of that, *mavourneen*. We're two old rascals who need not kneel to each other." He put his hand under her elbow and lifted her upright. "A blessing might do instead."

"Indeed, Father." She lowered her head as his hand passed before her in the sign of the cross—north, south, east, west.

"Amen," they chimed in unison.

"Now I'll go to see how the Burke child is faring," Gram said.

Father Joyce followed her to the door and closed it behind her. From his pocket, he took a folded length of purple silk, the confessional stole as Grace well knew. He placed the silk band over his shoulders and sat across the table from her. "I'm here to listen to what troubles you, child."

She poured it all out. She told him everything, every last detail, hesitating only when she came to Liam's secret. But there was no holding that back, and in halting words she managed the telling of it.

As he understood the full nature of Liam's wound, the priest caught his breath in a sudden, convulsed gasp. It was then she knew beyond any shadow of a doubt the full horror of what had been done. Liam's punishment was worse than death to any man—any man. Even to this man of God and his lifelong struggle for sanctity.

With that insight came the foreboding of an evil so black it shook her to the soul.

"I must go to him, Father. I have a fear—"

"Follow your heart, child. It speaks the truth. But first, your absolution."

She bowed her head sure that Father Joyce's healing hands could feel her blood pounding through her scalp.

*Liam! Wait for me!*

Shriven of her sins, she ran—newly forgiven, reborn,

and terrified—all the way back to the farm.

The cottage door stood wide open. She darted in. Brigit sat alone at the table. The fire had gone out, and one of the hens wandered about pecking at crumbs on the floor.

"Where is he, Brigit," Grace asked.

Brigit raised her head, but no words came from her lips.

Grace darted to the open bedroom. The bed, a tousled mass of coverlets lay empty. She ran back to Brigit. "Where is he?"

No answer.

"Brigit, you must talk to me. Where is Liam?"

She raised a haggard face. "I don't know. He's not been here for a whole day. I've searched the entire farm. I can't find him."

"He's all right. You'll see. Come now, I'll straighten out your bed. You can lie down for a bit while I go search for him.

"I can't rest."

"The baby needs you to. Please."

At that, Brigit allowed Grace to guide her to the bed where she lay on her back as Liam had, with a hand over her eyes, blocking out the sun and the truth.

"I'll come back with him," Grace vowed. "Now sleep for a while."

If Brigit had searched the farm, he wouldn't be close by. But where? *Where?*

Her mind darted from one place to another—the woods, the fields, the village, and dear God, not the sea.

She had to think.

What would he be drawn to in his despair? Who would he turn to? The person he'd relied on his whole life long!

Da! He would go to Da.

# CHAPTER THIRTY ONE

But where was Da? Owen had kept his secret well. Of a certainty, Liam possessed no more knowledge of where their father lay than she did. All they both knew was where they had last seen him alive. Her throat constricted. *Ah no. Not there.*

For the second time that day, Grace yanked her skirt up to her knees and began running. Leaving the path outside the cottage, she raced over the fields, through the copse and along the back road, the one the villagers avoided, Hangman's Lane.

The hanging tree stood on the edge of the lane, tall and proud, its stout branches alive with the full, dark green leaves of high summer.

To her relief, she spied nothing untoward hanging among the foliage, no creaking rope, no swinging limbs, no arms gone slack, no head awry...no one. Nothing.

*Thank you, God.*

She breathed easier, slowing her step, letting the salt air fill her straining lungs. She studied the oak as she approached. 'Twas beautiful, Da's shrine, after all. Perhaps the ancient druids had been right. Trees were the eternal God made visible. Like men, they possessed immortal souls.

Such pagan thoughts she was after having. 'Twould not do. And then she saw him. She stopped where she stood, unwilling to come nearer, unwilling to prove what her eyes were seeing.

He lay flat on his back under the oak as unmoving as when he'd lain in his own bed. Could he be asleep, lulled by the music of the branches rustling in the wind? He must be worn out from his ordeal. A good sleep would restore him. Ah, but no, it would not. Yet she approached softly so as not to waken him from his dreaming.

As she drew nearer and then nearer, a few inches at a time, she heard the buzzing drum of a thousand feasting flies. The odor came to her next, a sickly sweet scent somewhat like the smell of deer when she plunged a knife into its belly, or the odor of pig in the leaf falling time when Da would slaughter a sow to help pay his land rent.

Her feet slowed even more the closer she came to him, but in the end she could not escape what awaited. *What she knew.*

Still, when she stood nigh to him at last and looked down, a scream burst out of her throat that sent the birds scattering into the sky, wrens and daws alike, their wings beating madly as they flew away, away, from the terrifying sound.

His field knife lay at his side. A black crust of flies covered the slash wound and the thick scum of blood that had not yet soaked into the earth, their excited humming making an obscene music in the quiet lane.

*He must have lain here like this for hours.*

She had to cover him. That alone would keep the horde away.

*The shift would have to do.*

Stifling her sobs, she stripped off her skirt and linen waist and then the shift, for a moment standing naked in the lane. Working fast, she shrugged her waist back on over her bare skin and tied the skirt in place. She picked up the shift, flapping it again and again over Liam's dear face forcing the flies away from his eyes and mouth and the deep cut in his left wrist.

Once cleared of the insects, the gash gaped wide like a mouth with lips but no teeth. She covered his head and arm with the garment, then sank to the ground at his feet.

Of all the horrors she could imagine, or the English had enacted, this by far was the worst. As well as his life here on earth, in his anguish, Liam had cast away his immortal soul. He would lie unshriven, unblessed—a suicide—the sin of sins for which God had no forgiveness. Why should He? Liam had taken His sacred gift of life and thrown it back in His face.

For a man with no stomach for violence, how had he found the will to destroy himself like this? Had his fear of living been greater than his fear of death? She would never know the answer, nor did she need to. What she needed most was courage. The hardest part lay ahead. Brigit had to be told. Dear God in heaven. A sob tore free and then another and another, their mingled sound finally reaching her own ears and wrenching her out of her black thoughts of eternal damnation. She had a present hell that must be dealt with—the buzzing had returned as the flies settled back around Liam's body and the bloody ground she had no way to cover.

He had to be moved, but she couldn't lift him, and where to take him? Home to Brigit first, then where thereafter? Father Joyce would refuse him burial in the churchyard. No suicide had ever been put to rest there.

So where could he lie? On the farm, in one of the fields where he'd struggled his whole life long? Or with Da? They would be together that way, forever. It must have been what Liam wanted. Why else pick the Hanging Oak as his place to die? But Brigit must be the one to decide. *Brigit!* She had to get Liam home to Brigit. To carry him, she would need a cart or a barrow, at the least, and a strong pair of arms. For that, she would go to Owen and once again seek his help.

\* \* \*

Using one of his heavy mallets, Owen pounded the legs from his tabletop and with the help of Donal Burke and the McElroy brothers carried Liam home on its smooth boards. They lay him, boards and all, on the table in the middle of his cottage.

The door to the bedroom remained closed. Brigit was worn out from the worry, Grace thought, sleeping the sleep of the exhausted.

"Before I go into her, I'll wash him a little," Grace told the men.

From the bucket by the door, she dipped up a bowl of water and brought it back to the table. She lifted away the shift that covered him, stained now with his dried sweat and traces of his blood, and dropped it to the floor.

As if he could feel her touch and be disturbed by it, she wiped his face gently, drawing a wet cloth over his forehead and down the sweep of his nose and cheeks. She rinsed the cloth, stained now like the shift, in the clean water before wringing it out and touching it to Liam's open mouth and chin. With tears blinding her eyes, she dropped the cloth onto the soiled shift and bent over to kiss his cheek.

At the last, she closed the lids of his eyes and brushed smooth the mustache he'd once taken such pride in, hoping he would be called Red Liam some day as his da had been, but that day would never come.

She folded his arms over his chest, the wounded one first, positioning the intact arm over it to hide the lips of the gash.

Finished with the little she could do, she picked up the fouled cloths and tossed the wash water out of the cottage door conscious that Owen had watched her every move. "I dare take no longer," she said. "I'm afraid Brigit will hear and come out before I can tell her."

He nodded. "I'll wait in the yard with Donal and the McElroys. You'll be needing us for a grave."

"We will." She met his eyes then looked away quickly from the pity she saw in them.

She should lift the latch to the other room and go in with her news, but somehow she couldn't make her feet move in that direction and stood rooted to her spot. "This is so hard, Owen. How can I walk in there and destroy her life?"

"You can do what you must." He came up to her, putting the strong hands she remembered so well on her shoulders, pulling her in to him, holding her against his breast, kissing her forehead, his lips anointing her flesh, giving her his absolution. "You have never lacked courage, *mavourneen*. God will give it to you now." He released her. "I'll be close by."

Grace cracked open the bedroom door. Brigit had hardly moved. She still lay on her back, her belly raising the coverlet into a rounded hillock.

She looks so lovely, Grace thought, with her hair fanned out on the pillow, the high pink color back in her cheeks, at peace, warm and relaxed, oblivious to what lay ahead.

An errant breeze caught at the door, squeaking it toward a close. *Oh, dear!* Grace whirled to catch it before it slammed, but too late.

At the sound, Brigit opened heavy eyes. "Grace," she murmured suspended between the worlds of dreaming and truth, but for an instant only. "You're back!" She raised herself on her elbows. "You found him?"

Grace nodded. "I did."

Brigit swung her feet to the floor and sat up. "Where is he?"

"In the other room, love."

Before Brigit could pull her distended body to her feet, Grace hurried across the room and sat beside her on the bed. She took her in her arms.

Brigit wriggled free. "I want him. I want to go to him."

"In a moment. But first, there is something you must know."

"What?" Brigit pushed her lank hair from her face, impatient with the strands falling into her eyes, and went to brace herself to stand.

With her hands on Brigit's shoulders, Grace tried to hold her in place. "He's not here on earth, Brigit. He's gone from us."

"But you said..." Brigit's hand flew to her mouth. "Oh no! No, no, no, no, no!"

Nothing could hold her now. She leaped up, the child within her no hindrance in her awful haste to know.

She flung open the bedroom door to the sight of Liam lying spread out on the table like an animal sacrificed on a terrible high altar, no longer hers, no longer anyone's.

Her keening cries brought the waiting men running to the cottage door. Over and over, she called out Liam's name imploring him to answer, screaming her disbelief that he would not. Her hands, tender with him at the first touch of his cold flesh, grew fierce. When he wouldn't warm to her caresses, she began pounding him about the chest and shoulders, pulling at his hair, slapping his cheeks, demanding a response that didn't come. In one of her lunges, she dislodged his right arm. It fell free, dangling away from the gashed left wrist it had hidden.

At the sight of the deep, blood-drained slash, her keening took on a fresh wildness as the true cause of Liam's death came over her. Her eyes, great with a hideous knowledge, flared wide. After that, there was no stopping her madness. She beat him with her fists pounding his body everywhere—the chest, the shoulders, the face, the gut. "You did this! You did this! You're in hell, Goddamn you, Liam O'Malley. In hell. And I'm in hell with you. In hell! In hell!"

Her belly with its once precious burden, she struck again and again against the boards of the table ignoring its need for protection, punishing what lay in her flesh, what Liam had caused to be.

"Help me, Sean," Owen shouted above her wails. "She's hurting herself."

She fought them. As soon as they put their strong arms on hers and went to move her back from harm, she wrenched free. The fists that had flailed at Liam found new targets, the force of her frenzied blows as powerful as those of a work-hardened man.

"Use your strength, for God's sake, Sean. She's out of her mind," Owen said.

Together, they wrenched her away from the table

and held her hands to her sides. Frenzied, she began to strike out with her feet. They lifted her under her elbows, raising her off the floor so she had only air as a butt for her kicking heels.

"We can't hold her," Sean said as she writhed in their grasp.

"Put her down," Grace said.

Not loosening their grip, they did as she asked. Once Brigit's feet gained a purchase on the floor, she reared up, bucking her head back and forth, whipping her hair about her face, incoherent words streaming from her mouth as she struggled to break free, to fling herself on the corpse and beat it into life.

Grace stood in front of her, out of range of her kicking feet, and waited until Brigit's grief-crazed eyes met her own. "Stop!" she said.

The command caught Brigit's attention, and for a fleeting instant, she obeyed. In that moment, Grace darted forward. With a flat palm, she slapped Brigit's cheek, leaving the imprint of her open hand on her face.

Like a bundle of rags with nothing to give it form, Brigit collapsed, sagging in the men's grasp. Gently, they lowered her to the floor where she sat in a crumpled heap.

Grace knelt before her. "I am so sorry, but we had no way to stop you."

If Brigit heard, she gave no answer. The fire had left her as surely as flames leave the peat and burn into ash.

Grace raised a trembling hand. She stroked Brigit's hair, smoothing the damp strands from her face, massaging the tight muscles of her back. Her touch brought no response. Brigit sat rigid in an eerie, unnatural calm.

"Give her this, Grace." Owen stood over her, a mug in his hand. "'Twill soothe her."

"*Uisce beatha?*"

"Aye."

"She needs her mam, as well."

"I'll fetch her," Sean said.

He hurried from the cottage, glad no doubt, Grace

thought, to be away from them and the madness that had entered their lives.

# CHAPTER THIRTY TWO

Before the complete turn of an hourglass, Brigit's mam came hurrying along the path with Sean McElroy at her heels.

Grace went to the door to greet her. From the harried expression on Widow Fallon's care-lined face, and the work smock she hadn't bothered to remove, Grace knew she'd learned what had befallen them.

"I can't rouse her, Mistress Fallon," Grace said. "She's been like a stone since we calmed her."

Widow Fallon brushed past without speaking and hurried into the cottage. At the sight of Brigit huddled on the floor near the table, she wrung her hands for a helpless moment before getting down on her knees and taking her daughter in her arms. "Love, I'm here now. I'm here," she soothed.

Grace knew all the words of comfort a mother might use to aid a beloved child in agony could not be uttered. Mistress Fallon could not say Liam was happy in heaven, waiting for Brigit to join him when her own life came to an end. She could not say he dwelled in a better place, enjoying the presence of God in the company of the heavenly host. Nor could she say he'd descended into hell and sat at the right hand of Lucifer.

She could only murmur incomprehensible syllables, turning her own keening into a lullaby.

In her mother's arms, Brigit lay motionless without a murmur of her own, without a gesture of recognition, without the stirring of a limb or the flutter of an eyelash.

The sight drove Grace out of the cottage into the yard where the men had settled on the stone wall waiting to learn where they should dig Liam's grave.

Knowing this burial wouldn't have the blessing of the church, no one had gone for the priest.

"Have you instruction for us?" Owen asked when Grace approached.

She shook her head. "Brigit's as if dead herself. I've never seen a living person go rigid that way. Even her mam can't rouse her."

"Liam can't wait much longer. It will be a full day soon, I warrant."

Grace glanced at him, full of unspoken realization. The body was already rigid. With an effort of will, she forced her mind away from the direction it had taken.

"If Brigit cannot decide in time, then I will have to."

"I see no other way," Owen said.

In his face she read his sympathy, his understanding. He didn't blame her for being the instrument of this terrible outcome.

*He must love me very much.*

"I think he wanted to be with Da," she said. "Could we do that for him, Owen? Only you know of his grave."

He smiled a little. "My thought has taken the same path. That is what we will do if that is what you wish."

"First, let me see if Brigit will agree."

On quiet feet, Grace went back inside. Nothing had changed. Brigit and her mam still knelt huddled together near the table with Owen's body lying high above them. Then, with a gasp of awareness, she realized there had been a change after all.

Seeping out from under Brigit's skirt a large, wet patch was soaking into the floor.

"Mistress Fallon," she said. "Look."

Startled, the woman glanced over at where Grace pointed. As they gazed at it, the wet stain kept growing, puddling on the floor in places where the hard-packed earth couldn't easily absorb it.

"Oh, dear Mother," Mistress Fallon said. "'Tis beginning too soon. She has another month to go."

She shook Brigit gently. "You must get up, love. Come now. Your babe's on the way. We have to care for you."

Brigit sat unmoving as the water continued to trickle out of her body.

"She threw herself against the table edge," Grace whispered. "Do you think she ruptured something?"

"Either that or the shock of him." Mistress Fallon's chin jutted up toward the burdened table, then back down to the wet floor. "Her water broke in any case. We must get her away from here."

In a coaxing murmur as if Brigit were a wee child, she pleaded, "Come colleen mine, show your face to me. I want to help you. But you must help me, too. You can't stay here in your wet clothes. We'll get you to bed where you can rest for a while. Your babe's coming. Do you hear me?"

Slowly, as if emerging from a nightmare, her eyes still bleak with its ghastly visions, Brigit raised her head and nodded.

She understands, Grace thought, thank the Lord.

With Mistress Fallon on one side and Grace on the other, Brigit managed to get to her feet. As they helped her away from the table one slow step at a time, she didn't turn back or try to look down at Liam's body. It was as if he weren't there at all.

As indeed he is not, Grace thought. In that same instant, she resolved not to add to Brigit's agony. Liam should be with Da in the secret place Owen had devised. She could do nothing better for her brother than that. When Brigit came to herself again, she would explain and hope for understanding.

In the bedroom, Brigit leaned against Grace as Mistress Fallon quickly stripped off the sodden black skirt and linen bodice. But at the sight of Brigit's white shift, she drew in a shocked breath. "Blood," she whispered. "She's covered in blood. 'Twas not her water alone. Hold her, Grace, while I get the shift off her. Then I'll need clean cloths, as many as you have. I'll try to pack her to staunch the bleeding."

As they went to ease Brigit onto the bed, the first of

the pains caught her, and she screamed when they laid her down.

* * *

Within the space of an hour, everything had come to an end.

Strange, Grace thought, the sun shone as brightly as ever, the fields bloomed with summer richness, the birds rode the breeze cawing their delight to the four winds. Undaunted by what lay within the cottage, the natural world kept on as usual.

And outside, the men waited. She saw them lying on the wall and beckoned. As they hurried to her, she saw questions and uncertainty in their faces.

"A boy," she said. "She had a son for Liam."

"My God, Grace, what's wrong?" Owen asked.

*He knows.*

"They died. Both of them—Brigit and the babe. She bled to death. We couldn't stop it. Oh God." She lowered her head to her hands and wept great wracking sobs that like Brigit's blood could not be staunched.

Owen took her, in her anguish, into his arms and said, "Let it out, love. 'Twill be better in the open than hidden within you."

She leaned against him, feeling the soothing strokes of his hand upon her head and shoulders and down her back. When no more tears would come, she looked up into his face. "One wide grave, Owen. We'll put them both with Liam, so they can lie together. Her mam wants that for them, too."

He kissed the top of her head. "We'll go now, lass, and begin. I'll be back for them as soon as we've finished."

# CHAPTER THIRTY THREE

While Mistress Fallon sat in vigil with Brigit and her baby, Grace waited alone in the main room keeping watch over Liam's body, praying to God for mercy on all and to Granuaile for strength to endure what lay ahead. The minutes slipped by, dropping away one at a time like beads of slow-falling water. As dusk began casting its long shadows, she heard the men return and went outside to greet them. They looked weary from their work, the strain of their efforts clear on their faces and their hands and arms and their soiled, sweat-stained clothes.

"If you're ready for us, we'll take them now. We'll carry Liam first," Owen said.

"We are ready," she said, "and so are they. But before you go, my thanks." She went up to Donal Burke and to Sean and Tim McElroy and kissed each man's stubbled cheek. "I'm beholden to you," she whispered to each of them in turn. She brushed Owen's cheek with her lips as well then paused in front of him. "Please tell me now. Where is Da?"

He smiled, just enough to warm his mouth and eyes a bit. "Where no one would suspect."

"And where would that be?"

"Beneath the Hanging Tree."

Grace gasped. The boldness of it! All these long months, Da had lain under Rushmount's very nose, under the unseeing eyes of the villagers, under the tree that had claimed him, under his memorial, his headstone, his last place alive on earth.

"No one ventured near the lane the day I dug his grave. I knew he would be safe there," Owen said.

"I love you, Owen," Grace replied.

A flush rose in his cheeks. He took her by the arm moving her away from the others. "There is no need for me to say the same. You've always known the truth of my heart."

Tears burned their way to the surface of her eyes. She had to hear what he felt or die. "Tell me, Owen. The sound of the words is that beautiful."

"*Ta gra agam thu.* I love you."

"Forever," she added.

As he went to speak again, the cottage door opened. Widow Fallon in her blood-smeared work smock, her face expressionless, plodded over to Owen. He met her halfway and embraced her, then taking both her hands in his, he murmured sounds Grace couldn't hear. But the comfort of his nearness she remembered. Her skin and hair still longed for that comfort.

As she watched, saddened to the soul, Widow Fallon pulled back a little from Owen and, hollow-cheeked, hollow-eyed, looked up at him. "Has Grace told you we agree as to the burying?"

"She has," Owen said. "You'll forego the churchyard for Brigit and her babe?"

"I will. Grace told me what you said. 'All earth is hallowed.' I believe with you that God created the whole of the round earth. Every speck of it."

"Aye."

"'Tis a comforting thought, Owen. They should lie together. If Father Joyce will say a prayer over them, so be it. If not, I will do so myself."

"I'll walk you to your cabin, Mistress Fallon," Grace said. "Then, if you wish, I'll speak to Father Joyce."

"Go to him, Grace. I'll stay here with Brigit until Owen comes for her."

"Ah, of course," Grace said, the burning tears ready to start up again. An idea seized her. "Come, please come, Mistress Fallon. I have something for Brigit."

"She needs nothing more, Grace."

But Grace drew her indoors and hurried to the small

coffer next to her pallet where she kept her personal belongings—her extra shift and waists, her ribbons and ties, the ancient copper combs, and on the bottom, ruffled and tucked, a bed gown of finest lawn. It had been Mam's years ago and a treasure for that reason alone. She'd been saving it for her own wedding night, but she handed the garment to Mistress Fallon.

"For Brigit."

*I've had my wedding night.*

* * *

The priest was eating his evening meal when Grace knocked at his door. Between sobs, she told him what had occurred. "We know Liam cannot be buried in the churchyard, Father, so we mean to bury them together under the Hanging Tree. But your blessing would mean a great deal."

He ignored his half-eaten food and began an agitated pacing. In his small cabin next to the church, he could not walk far before reaching a wall, a few fast steps to the left, a few to the right, no more than that.

Grace looked away from the black-clad blur he soon became. She'd not been in his hut before, and a cheerless space it seemed to her woman's eyes with its rumpled pallet, cold firepit and a crucifix carved of wood hanging on one wall. The body of Christ sagged on its nails, the torso contorted in agony, the head twisted to one side. The floor in front of the image had been worn down lower than the rest of the hard-trodden earth. Father Joyce must kneel there to pray, she thought, finding little comfort in the idea.

On the table next to his porridge bowl, a book lay open. A quick glance had told her it was not written in English. Latin, perhaps. He must have been reading his daily breviary before she came in. She shivered in the close evening air. He had so little to cheer him, no human warmth at all.

"Mistress Fallon does not object to a pagan burial for her daughter?" he asked.

She focused her eyes on the priest. He'd stopped

pacing and stood in front of her awaiting an answer. "She will have them lie together. That is what Brigit would want."

"'Tis not what the church teaches. The mother and babe should lie in hallowed ground. Your brother is another matter."

Above the frown on his mouth, his eyes held a troubled kindness and his voice softened. "You know the church's rule, child."

"I do, Father, but—"

"No buts. I have to obey it."

"But I do not."

With a will of its own, his hand came up poised to strike her in the face. For a moment, as time froze, they stared at each other. In the next moment, his hand fell back to his side.

"You are a bold lass," he said. "I well believe you are the poacher as rumor has it."

"I am, indeed, Father. Not my poor brother. His death is on my soul. That's the sin you should strike me for."

"Come, sit child." The frown on his face eased as he took her hand and led her to the bench by his table. He sat next to her, keeping her hand in his own for the first time she could ever recall, rubbing the back of it with his thumb. "Heed me carefully. Liam's death is no blot on your immortal soul. Don't go through life carrying that burden. His death will be weighed against Lord Rushmount for driving him to despair. And I fear at the final judgment, Liam's damnation will be the result of his own doing."

Grace lowered her head, letting her hair curtain her face from his gaze. "But if I hadn't gone for the deer, none of this would have happened."

"You had the courage to seek justice...and food." His hand dropped hers and reaching up to her chin, tipped her face toward him. There was to be no escape from his keen, blue eyes. "And justice was what you wanted more than meat. Is that not true?"

She nodded. "'Tis, Father."

His hand left her chin. "You had the right. Every man has that right given to him by God. But the odds, the forces, child, are against us. Though Rushmount has had his blood and may be satisfied for the time being, you cannot continue as you have."

He sighed, a sound fraught with longing, she thought, though it was not like Father Joyce to yearn for anything other than his God. "I wish," he began, "I wish..." His voice died away.

"What do you wish for, Father?" she asked.

"Ah, I'm a foolish old man, Grace. But I wish you could leave this place. I've heard tell of the New World beyond the ocean with land aplenty for the taking. A colony has sprung up there I believe would suit you well. It welcomes those of an independent mind. Providence, 'tis called. A Godly name."

"The New World! How does one get there, Father?"

"By ship, of course. I've heard they leave from city ports. Galway, perhaps, or Limerick, or Dublin. I'm not certain."

"Dublin, is it? So far away."

"'Tis, and the New World even farther." The priest got to his feet. "Listen to me, dreaming of a land I'll never see. I'm daft, child. Daft enough to say a prayer of blessing over your family, a prayer that will hallow the ground they lie in."

"Thank you, Father," Grace said.

Out of respect for his kindness, she didn't tell him what she knew to be true. All earth was hallowed. If that could mean the tormented earth of this Old World, then surely it must mean the fresh earth of the New World that lay, like a dream in the mind, a vast ocean away.

# CHAPTER THIRTY FOUR

This time Owen hadn't smoothed the earth flat or concealed the grave with moldered oak leaves and scattered grasses as he had when he buried Da. The following morning, a mound curved high over the bodies of Liam and Brigit and their son, the loose, raw earth above them blowing free in the blustery winds from the Atlantic.

The mists will settle this place, Grace thought. They will sink the mound level with the ground and remove all traces of what has transpired here. Maybe that is the reason for the churchyard, after all. As long as the stones last, those lying under them will be remembered, and those lying here will be forgotten.

*Or will they?*

Grace stared up at the heavily-leafed branches. For so long as the oak stood, those who lay under it *would* be remembered. And as the druids knew full well, oaks lived a right long life. Comforted, Grace looked up to see Father Joyce approaching, and the villagers pressing in behind him.

He'd come vested as if for Mass, his cassock and alb covered by the funeral chasuble. The Doyle boys accompanied him as they did at St. Mary's each Sunday, one carrying holy water for the *asperges*, the other a book of Latin prayers.

God bless the man, Grace thought, to abandon strict church law for this one awful time, a time she feared would live on in her mind like an unending scream.

At the grave's edge, Widow Fallon fell to her knees. Stifling her sobs, Grace knelt next to her. From the sounds of movement behind her, she surmised the assembled villagers were kneeling as well.

"*In nomini Patris, et Filii, et Spiritus Sancti. Amen,*" Father Joyce intoned, his words accompanied by a little rain of holy water drops that fell on their heads with each thrust of his outstretched arm. "*Asperges, me, Domine...*"

So it began, and without the ceremony of the Mass or a eulogy of consolation, in a brief handful of minutes, it ended. After offering their awkward condolences, the villagers followed Father Joyce and, one by one, began taking their leave of Hangman's Lane.

How *did* one express sorrow? Grace wondered, for a suicide and a birth gone tragically wrong, except with a wringing of hands and a twisting of hat brims and a hasty word of sympathy.

A woman on each side of Widow Fallon drew her away from the grave. Dazed, she allowed herself to be led down the lane toward home. Brigit's half-grown brothers followed the women making a sad, straggling processional of their departure.

During the service, Owen had kept to the rear. Only when Grace looked about searching for him had she seen him kneeling behind the others, his dark head bent in prayer. When the mourners thinned out, he came up to her.

"I'll say good-bye to you now," he said. "Mary Burke will care for you this night."

"Mary?"

He nodded. "She has offered to do so. You should not be alone. Not tonight."

*Then you come home with me.* Her eyes, full on him, spoke the words, and his dark gem eyes heard her. She knew they did, but he shook his head. "'Tis Mary you need."

She felt a tug on her sleeve. "Let us go from here, love," Mary said, and like Widow Fallon, Grace allowed herself to be drawn away from the tree and its whispering leaves.

When they reached the cottage, they found it

stocked with loaves of bread and a pot of soft cheese, and a comfit made from wild berries. The sight brought tears onto Grace's cheeks. How had they managed? Someone would go to his pallet hungry this night. She could eat nothing, but Mary could have her fill for once.

Much later, after Mary dozed by the fire, Grace stared into the flames reliving the last few days. Only then did she realize she'd not seen Young Con at all. He'd not been anywhere in sight at the tree-side service, nor had he come to her in private since then with either a kind word or a harsh one. And he would not. He was too fearful, no doubt, to wed with a poacher.

Ah, sure and he wasn't the man for her at all. He never had been and never would be. She'd been foolish to think so for a single moment. If she never saw him again, she would be content.

Yet what did the future hold for her now? She couldn't manage the farm alone, and Rushmount would be after his rent as always. The bleakness of what lay ahead kept her awake for hours until, finding no solution except to run and fling herself into Owen's arms, she gave up trying for the night.

She rose from her place by the sinking fire and tapped Mary on the shoulder. "We'll both be sore in the morning if we don't stretch out a bit. Rest on my pallet, Mary, and I'll try to rest awhile, too."

Tomorrow, she felt certain, she would need her wits about her.

* * *

The next morning, Mary Burke had no sooner gone home to her family, her apron filled with leftover food, when Grace heard a knocking on the cottage door.

A visitor so early in the day!

She hurried to open the door. At the sight of Kath Mann standing there for the first time ever, she inhaled a small gasp of surprise. "Kath! Welcome. Welcome!"

"I'll bide a while, Grace, if I may. We must speak together you and I."

Grace held the door wide. "I'll stir the fire, and

there's food about. 'Twas given to—"

"I need nothing, Grace. Just a few words."

Kath carried a bundle wrapped in blue canvas. She laid it carefully on the trestle table before taking a seat across from Grace. "I've come with my husband Connor's permission," she began primly enough, "and with Young Con's."

Grace leaned across the tabletop and laid her hand on Kath's, staying her words. "No need to voice it, Kath, I understand. Young Con wishes to break our betrothal."

Kath nodded one time only. "I would have loved you dearly as a daughter. But the men say we cannot align ourselves with a—"

"Poacher?"

"That is what they say. For myself, I care not."

Grace took her hand away. She didn't respond to Kath's words. Let her believe the lie. But if Kath had to live the life of hardship the village women endured, she would soon regret her lost ease.

"Tell Young Con I release him gladly." He'd sent his mother to speak for him. Truly, he was not a man in full. "'Tis for the best, after all."

She could see the relief wash across Kath's plump face. "Connor sent you this." Kath put her hand on top of the covered bundle. "He wants you to keep it. You love it so." She unfolded the wrapping cloth.

*The English Bible!*

"Mine?" Grace asked, her voice choking with disbelief, her eyes refusing to credit what they were seeing.

"'Tis yours."

"How wonderful!" Truly, she loved the book as she'd never loved Young Con. Thrilled to her core, she got up and caught Kath in a tight embrace.

Kath stiffened. "You never embraced me the same way when you planned to marry my son."

Contrite, Grace released her instantly and stepped back. "If you say that is so, then it must be. I'm sorry if I did not. But I thank you with all my heart for this wondrous gift."

Kath got up from the bench without answering and left the cottage in silence, quietly latching the door behind her. Grace stared at the closed door then down at the book, a great treasure, indeed.

As she ran her fingers over its cover, she realized that in her entire life she'd never felt so utterly alone.

# CHAPTER THIRTY FIVE

In a raging sea, Owen cut through the broiling surf, his strokes sure and steady, but the challenge of the swimming failed to soothe him as it normally did. Grace had been with Mary last night and safe enough. But what of tonight? What of tomorrow? And of all the nights after that?

Every lad for miles around would soon learn she lived alone. He doubted any would harm her, but who knew for certain? And in a few days time, Rushmount would want another tenant to care for Liam's land. Harvest was only a few weeks away.

If Young Con had any sense at all, he'd take her home with him and keep her by his side until...

*Oh God.*

Owen swam farther out, pitting himself against the swelling waves. The desire to continue on and on until he had no strength left to return nearly overwhelmed him. *But that was a coward's way out of pain.*

He dove beneath the water, reversed direction, and came up to the surface. Pacing himself, he swam back more slowly, conserving his energy as the fury left him.

The memory of her white face, her hair blowing about in the wind as she knelt by the grave, still haunted him. God how he loved her. No other woman in the world could match her. As beautiful as an angel and blaming herself for what had happened. He'd seen that as clearly as if the words *mea culpa* had been emblazoned on her forehead.

'Twas not her fault, but that bastard Rushmount's. Castrate a man and you might as well slit his throat and be done with it.

On the shore, he stood and retrieved his clothes. No beautiful lass waited for him with her heart in her eyes, her lips parted with longing. Alone he was and always would be.

*Get used to it.*

She would be married soon and forever out of reach ...but if the whiskey plan succeeded...the chance of a better life glimmered before him for an instant...but no, he rejected the idea and the false hope it promised. Rushmount had shown his true colors. A scurrilous, untrustworthy bastard he'd proven to be.

Now that he'd taken his blood payment, the distilling plan would no doubt go forward. But ultimately, what chance at a better life did the villagers have? Their only bargaining tool was to guard the McElroy's secret method as if it were the Holy Grail. Could they? Liam's fate must have Sean McElroy pissing his breeches with fear.

Owen shrugged into his clothes and tied on his boots. Sean was the weak link. He'd go to his farm and try to put some iron in his spine. But if Sean gave the secret over to Rushmount, then what?

*I'll kill him. And Rushmount as well.*

*And such an act will help absolutely no one.*

God in heaven, there had to be a better country on earth than this beautiful, hopeless land of his.

\* \* \*

On the McElroy acres, the rye blowing in the breeze stood tall, the grain sheaths full and plump when Owen tried one with his fingers. A few more days of this sun and they could begin harvesting. Even the McElroy's rocky fields had produced well this year. Perhaps, despite all, their luck had changed for the better.

Sean's face when he called out to him said otherwise. Dour as always, this time he didn't respond to the sound of his name with so much as a half-hearted smile. Nor did he drop the turf spade and hurry to shake Owen's hand and offer a word of welcome, or a drop of the spirits.

*He was weakening already.*

"A good evening to you, Sean." Owen forced warmth into his greeting. No need to borrow trouble by mentioning it.

"Evening." Sean kept up a relentless digging.

"Are you on your way to China?" Owen asked.

"It's a new well I'm after, closer to the cabin."

"Ah, a fine idea, but could you lay the tool aside for a wee bit?"

Sean let fly with another shovelful of earth. "There's no need for you to be here, Owen. I've told Tim I'm against it."

"Against what?" Owen asked as if the answer would come as a great surprise.

"Your plan." Sean struck the spade into the ground, then of a sudden let it go free. Held by the earth alone, the shaft wavered between them for an instant before falling at their feet. "I won't do it."

"I see."

"In God's name, I hope you do. Look at how they savaged Liam. We'll be next if we don't tell Rushmount how we run the still."

"Has he asked?"

"He's about to. He sent Young Con here earlier. He wants Tim and me at the manor house tomorrow morning. What other reason could he be having? Calling for us two and no one else." Sean swiped his shirt sleeve across his forehead before reaching down for the spade. "Connor must have told him we're the brewmasters."

"That may be. Or he may want to talk of the rent. You're overdue, you said."

"For that he would send Connor to harass us, not waste his own time."

"Where's Tim?"

"He walked off in a huff. I told him I'll not hold out if Rushmount puts the screws to us."

"Tell him I'll come with you tomorrow. I'll stand by you. No matter what Rushmount says, we'll—"

"Forget that, Owen. You have no more clout than we

do. What good can you do if he's out for blood?"

Owen felt the rage begin deep in his gut. It came pounding up to fill his mouth, and he spewed it out in a vow. "I'll threaten to kill him if he tries to force the method from you."

"Jaysus, man, we'll all be strung up."

"Will he hang the whole village? Every man and lad of us? What of his fields, then? No, my threat will be subtle. I'll tell him he might have an accident when he's out riding the chestnut he's so proud of, or a hand might come over his mouth when he sleeps, or a drop of poison might fall on his meat. I'll put the fear of God into *him* for a change."

"Forget it, I say. I'm for telling him what he wants."

"I can not." Owen spat out the words. "This is our only hope. If we let this chance be taken from us like everything else, we'll truly be slaves. No more than that. We would be better off dead."

Sean shoved the spade back into the earth. "Life is too good to wish for death."

"How can you be sure how good life is? You've only known hell."

The shoveling began anew.

"Tell Tim I'll go to the manor before you do tomorrow. You need not be with me when I speak to his lordship." Owen spat on the ground at his feet. "Lordship! Lordship be damned. That word belongs to my God and to Him only."

"We can't prevent you from going," Sean said his eyes on the dirt.

"Did Young Con say when you were to be there? Sure and not at cock's crow."

"Before the noon meal is all he said. His mind was distracted."

"Oh?"

"He was on his way to the uplands to help his brother drive Rushmount's cattle back from the summer pasture. A shame it had to be now. What with the feasting and all."

"What feasting? There hasn't been a feast in the village since Christmas last."

Sean shrugged. "He asked for a jug to take to his da. A bailiff from two counties away has come to look over the dairy. 'Tis admired far and wide, he says." Sean gave the spade a vicious shove into the dirt. "And he told me something more as well. He's broken off with Grace. They'll not be wed after all." Sean paused to catch his breath before going on with the digging. "The Manns cannot stand on the side of defiance, and if it's true, as the lass claims, that she's the poacher..."

\* \* \*

When Sean looked up, Owen had already left him, hurrying with his clumsy gait across the fields that had begun to darken as gloaming turned into night.

# CHAPTER THIRTY SIX

By the time he reached the edge of McElroy land, Owen's breath began to come in ragged gasps. For once, no breeze blew in from the sea. The air was as thick in his throat as clotted cream.

*The fool. The bloody fool and a weakling to boot. To forsake her for her courage alone. That was what set her apart, made her a treasure beyond gold or jewels. Not that he'd seen either one, but he knew of them, and he knew her. God, how he knew her! Aye, her courage paired with that cloud of hair, and her silken skin, and the imp in her eyes, and the smile on her when she would have her way with him.*

He quickened his pace. He knew what a poor figure he must be cutting with his shoulders dipping in haste, the hurry exaggerating his gait. Many times over when the urchins mimicked his walk, they'd shown him all too well how he appeared.

Well, the devil take the leg. He would give it no more than a passing thought. He truly was more than his leg, and as long as the lass believed that nothing else would matter, not ever again.

He scrambled over a stone wall. On the other side, lay Liam's north field. Without giving the sheaths a single curious glance, he wove a hurried path through the ripening grain. Two more acres to the cottage clearing. As he drew closer, a sound out of place in those fields came to him through the thick air making him stop his urgent haste and stand still to listen. Aye, he'd heard aright. There it was again. A horse, impatient for a run, snorting and pawing the ground. Speaking to its owner it was, and that could only be one man.

Rushmount had wasted no time. Anxious to remain in his good graces, Connor must have scurried to him with news of the broken betrothal. But Christ, by doing so, he'd abandoned Grace to an evil fate. There had been no mistaking the lust in Rushmount's eyes when he spoke of her. An Irishman, be damned. Connor's loyalties went deeper than his blood. He was an Englishman now and forever.

Owen slowed his step, moving silently as he drew nearer to the horse. If Rushmount had abandoned his mount, there was only one place where he would be. Owen's jaw tightened, but he would not let the rage overtake him.

As he expected, the chestnut, loosely tethered to an oak branch near the clearing, stood alone, saddled and ready for a run. No wonder the steed was impatient. He'd been left saddled. Apparently, his master didn't plan to take long at his dalliance.

The blood raced through Owen's veins, pounding in his temples, turning his hands into clenched fists.

"Rushmount!" he shouted. "Rushmount!"

The horse reared up ready to flee from danger, but the reins held fast.

"Rushmount!"

Owen tore across the clearing, the leg hardly hampering him, his fear for her rising with each passing second. He burst through the cottage door, but the main room was empty.

*The second room!*

He slammed open the door, then stopped, frozen at the sight revealed by the lamp light. At the far wall, Rushmount held Grace crushed tight against him, his fingers wrapped like snakes around her throat. "Come any closer," he said, "and I'll snap her neck."

Ignoring the pounding of his heart, Owen stayed unmoving just inside the bedroom door. "And if you snap her neck, what good will she be to you then?"

He shifted his weight from one leg to the other, forcing his ragged breath into a careless, conversational tone as if he were in the center of the village having a chat with one of the lads. "Of course, there's a rumor about that your preferences are warped. 'Tis said you can't take a woman in the normal way. That you have to resort to twisted means."

He moved a step closer.

"Stay back," Rushmount ordered.

"Let her go, and I will." Owen's voice dropped into a confidential whisper. "Those twisted means now, they're too ugly to bear repeating. But you know what I'm speaking of."

"I do not. You're insane."

Owen inched closer. "Mad, am I? Tell me, your lordship, is it true? The infant daughter, Elizabeth, a right regal name she bears. Well, be that as it may, is it true, she's none of yours?"

"How dare you!" With a vicious shove, Rushmount threw Grace aside. As she fell against the bed, he lunged for Owen.

His legs braced, Owen was ready. He took Rushmount's weight without staggering and balling his hands into clubs, he aimed for the Englishman's jaw. His right fist met it with a solid thud that sent Rushmount reeling. He recovered fast and came back, his legs pumping, his arms up and flailing, eager to strike.

With his left fist, Owen hit him in the jaw again. As Rushmount went to straighten up, Owen's right fist smashed into his gut, and the left, at the ready, rammed back at his jaw. The impact sent him sprawling to the floor where he fell, spread-eagled, onto his back. A soft sigh escaped his lips, before his eyes closed, and his lashes fluttered down to rest on his cheeks.

Owen looked at Grace and grinned. "He sleeps."

She ran to Owen and flung her arms about his neck. As his breathing slowed to normal, he held her in an embrace as tight as Rushmount's had been, but as different from it as day is from night.

"How did you know?" she asked.

"When I heard your betrothal had ended, I knew

he'd be after you."

Grace looked down at Rushmount's still form. "Now what will we do?"

"First *we* will put that knife in your hand to good use."

"*Kill him?*" Her eyes flared wide.

"You're tempted."

"'Tis true. But I won't, not now. If you hadn't come, though, I would have plunged the blade into him. My hand was in my pocket fingering it."

"You're a marvel of a woman, Grace O'Malley. I believe you would have done what you say, but I'm glad you saved some of the pleasure for me." Rushmount groaned, but his eyes remained closed. "Still, I'd rather not repeat my performance. Do you have a rope about the place? And a cloth to bind his mouth?"

"I do."

"Fetch them, would you, love? We'll tie him while we decide what to do next."

As she pocketed the knife and went to carry out his request, she brushed against him. He caught her to him. With her face in his hands, he kissed her, his lips soft and gentle on hers, his breath warm. Too soon for both of them, he let her go. "Hurry, before he wakes."

In short order, they secured Rushmount's hands behind his back and tied his ankles together. He groaned as Owen twisted the rope about him, but remained unconscious.

"Now, love, we must talk," Owen said. "You know we can't stay in Ballybanree, not after this."

"No, we must leave this very night."

"Leave for where? Shall we become wandering tinkers without a home to call our own?"

"Not at all." Her eyes shining, she said, "God is watching over us, Owen. I know of a place we can go. 'Tis a vast distance, but what matter if we're together?"

"Together. It sounds like you have heaven in mind."

She smiled. "Not yet, God willing, nor for many years to come. 'Tis a place in the New World called Providence. They welcome men of independent mind. And women, too, I warrant."

"Ah, you've been talking to Father Joyce."

"You know of this Providence?"

"Only what he's told me."

"He wouldn't lie."

"Not at all. But tell me, Grace, how do we earn our passage on the great ship that sails there?"

She slumped onto the bed and stared at her empty hands. "We have no coin, 'tis true."

"None at all." Despite his words, he smiled. "But we do have something to bargain with."

"What?"

"The harvest. 'Twill be ready for reaping in a few days."

"I don't—"

"Help me drag his lordship to the door. The three of us are going to call on the Manns this night."

\* \* \*

The chestnut heeded Owen's voice and the stroke of his hand and trotted calmly enough up to the cottage door. While Grace held the reins, Owen heaved Rush-mount to the saddle and flung him across it like a sack of grain. His eyes fluttered open and closed again.

"He should be awake by the time we get there," Owen said. "Now, love, make up a bundle that we can carry. Only your most precious things."

She ran back inside and flung open the top of her coffer. Onto her da's old shag mantle, she laid her woolen shawl, her extra shift and waist, her moleskin brogues, the copper combs and on top, the English Bible. Heavy though it would be to carry, she could no more leave it than she could a part of her body.

Finished, she hurried out and handed the bundle to Owen. He tied it on in back of the saddle and they set off without another minute wasted.

\* \* \*

Light flickered through the Manns' cottage window and out the open door. Laughter and talk from within masked the noise of their arrival until, with the chestnut's reins held tight in his grasp, Owen pounded on the door frame. "You have visitors, Con."

A stool fell over as Connor jumped to his feet. "Jesus, Mary and Joseph. Is that you, Owen? At this hour of the night?"

"'Tis. And I'm not alone. Are we welcome in your home?"

Profiled against the firelight, Connor stood in the doorway. "As always, my friend. Come in, come in!" At the sight of the chestnut looming outside, with Rushmount spread over the saddle, he lurched to a stop. "What's happened to his lordship? Is he dead?"

"Of course not, just dead weight, and awake, I see. Help me get him down."

Connor hurried to do Owen's bidding. "Is he injured? Dear God!" His voice trembled. "He's bound. And gagged as well. What in the name of heaven?"

"Not now, Con. Let's get him inside." After tying the reins to the door latch, Owen gripped Rushmount's leather belt and pulled him from the saddle. Before he could fall to the ground, Connor caught him, and together, they half dragged, half carried him into the cottage, and sat him, still bound, on a stool by the table.

Kath, her face reddened by the fire and a drop or two from Sean McElroy's jug, sat at the table with a well-fed man of middle years, a stranger to the village. At the sight of Lord Rushmount tied and gagged, her hand flew to her mouth. "Holy Mother above!"

To the stranger, Owen said, "Keep your seat, sir. We have no quarrel with you." The man nodded, his eyes round and startled, but he made no move to leave his place. Owen took the candle from the table and held it close to Rushmount's face. "You're awake? Nod if you can hear me."

Rushmount's head jerked down once then up.

"I'll have Con remove your gag, but you'll keep quiet and listen once it's removed. Nod if you agree."

Again the jerked head.

"Jesus, Owen," Connor said, "what's this all about?"

Owen upped his chin at Rushmount. "Take it off him."

With trembling hands, Connor went to release the gag, but the knots were too tight for his fumbling fingers.

"Here, let me," Grace said. She approached Rushmount with the knife in her hand. At the sight of the weapon, he began a frantic twisting against his bonds. Owen grasped him by the shoulders.

"Afraid of the knife? No need. The lass is going to cut the cloth, that's all. Sit still and let her do it."

One swift stroke and the gag fell to the floor. Rushmount exercised his jaw moving it gingerly. He winced, the stab of pain rekindling his defiance. "I'll see you hanged for this, O'Donnell."

"Our aim is not to harm you, Rushmount. Or to hang." Owen allowed himself the hint of a smile. "We're here for payment."

"Payment! You'll get that all right." Rushmount swiveled on the stool searching out his bailiff. "Take these ropes off me, Mann."

"Ah, now that Grace has put aside the knife, you've found guts again, have you?" Owen asked.

"Leave off, Owen, for God's sake," Connor said.

"Soon, very soon. But first, tell me, Con, would you be having paper here, and a quill and ink?"

"I do, but—"

"Fetch them."

"I give him his orders, not you," Rushmount said.

"Hand me the knife, Grace," Owen said. Taking the weapon, he stood behind Rushmount and held the point against his throat. "We await your orders, my lord."

Connor sputtered, "Your lordship, I—"

"Shut up, Mann, and do as he says."

Rigid with fear, Connor didn't move. Owen pressed the knife to Rushmount's throat. A tiny blood bead showed red against his skin.

"Now, you fool. Now!" Rushmount shouted.

Spurred into action by his master's enraged voice, Connor hurried into the other room.

Owen pulled up a stool and sat facing Rushmount. "I have another business proposition for you, but this one will be, ah, what is the word in English? Consummated tonight."

"I have no business with you. Not any more."

"You're mistaken. That chestnut out there. Grace will accept him in payment for her crop which is now ready for harvesting."

"You're insane. The chestnut's worth ten crops that size."

"Is he now? He's a pretty beast, I admit. But it seems to me he's paltry payment for, let me see..."—Owen held his hand up to the candlelight and began counting off on his fingers as he spoke—"for murdering a man, for driving another to suicide, and for an attempted rape."

Kath's quick, in-drawn breath was the only sound in a room suddenly gone quiet. Then Connor shuffled back with a sheaf of paper in his hands and an inkwell stuck with a feather quill. He put them on the table.

"Ah," Owen said. "Con's brought us the tools for writing a bill of sale. What say you? Have we struck a bargain?"

"I don't bargain with trash. Get these ropes off me, Mann. That's an order," Rushmount said.

Connor took a tentative step forward. After the single step, his eyes darted about the room looking for an escape, but finding none he stood stark still.

"Untie me, I said," Rushmount ordered.

"Sir, I cannot. I fear for your life."

"For God's sake, he's a cripple. You're two against one. There must be a knife about the place. Get hold of it."

Connor looked over at his guest who shook his head and refused to meet his eyes. With a sneer, Rushmount swung his attention back to Owen. "They're both useless." He shrugged. "For the time being, at least, it seems I have no choice."

"That is correct. Grace will cut the ropes from your hands. When she does, make no false move. Who knows? She might forget her Catholic upbringing."

Grace grinned at him.

*Enjoying herself she was. No fear in her at all. What a woman!*

Rushmount didn't answer. Owen ignored the gleam of hatred beaming from his eyes. Nothing could diminish this night. Nothing. The exultation he felt pulsing through his body was completely alien to him until he recognized it for what it was, his first full taste of freedom. With a flash of insight, he realized he'd been waiting for this moment his entire life. No one and nothing would ever take it away from him again.

"Cut his hands loose, Grace. He'll need them to write the bill of sale."

"I'll write nothing."

Owen bent down bringing his face on a level with the Englishman's. "Look at me, you viper. Tonight I give the orders, not you. You'll write what Grace tells you to write, or I'll brand you. Do you understand? With this knife in my hand, I'll carve an R into your face. Think of how grand you'll look wearing that."

How he could ever lift his hand to carry out the threat, Owen didn't know, but even to his own ears the words carried menace.

"You won't get away with this."

"Write."

His hand trembling, Rushmount picked up the quill, and with many flourishes and dips and curlicues and much curved underlining of his name and title, he wrote out what Grace dictated. When he finished, she picked up the paper.

As the ink dried, she read what he'd written then turned to the stranger. "Can you write in English?"

Reluctantly, he nodded.

"Would you kindly sign this, then, as a witness to the sale?"

"I don't think—"

"That's right. Do as the lady says," Owen commanded, "and add the name of the estate where you work. Bailiff is what you are?"

"Aye," came the sullen answer.

"Add that as well."

After scratching a few words onto the parchment, the man flung down the quill. Grace eyed his signature then gave the document to Connor. "Your name, Con, as a witness." When he finished, she read what had been written, folded the parchment, and tucked it into her skirt pocket before turning to Kath.

"Can you spare some cheese and bread, Kath?" she asked. "My husband and I will need food for our journey."

"Your husband, but when...?"

"A long time ago, Kath, in a cave by the shore."

"But—"

"Speak to Father Joyce if you have a mind to. He'll tell you what you need to know."

"Christ, Owen, what have you done?" Connor asked.

"Stay out of this, Con. It has nothing to do with you." His eyes narrowing with intent, Owen turned to Rushmount. "You understand that, don't you? Con Mann had nothing to do with this. We came here for the document so you can't set the dogs on us. Now the steed belongs to Grace free and clear."

"Like hell."

Owen grabbed a fistful of Rushmount's shirt, launching him off his seat to the sound of ripping fabric. "Listen to me, and listen well. There are to be no reprisals against the Manns or the villagers. When the McElroys come to you in the morning treat them decently and you'll profit by it. Treat them ill and there's no telling what accident might befall you...or when...or where."

Owen tightened his grasp on the fistful of shirt. "If all men are your enemies, whom will you trust?" He glanced over to the room's dark edge. "Except Connor there. He's your man in full, but he alone can't protect you, as you see here tonight. News of any vicious behavior will be sent to me." He could, he realized with a flash of amused awareness, lie with great conviction.

"These fools can't write."

"You're wrong. Every villager can make an R. That's all the message I'll need. And marking takes only a minute—like gelding."

Rushmount's eyes, pools of hatred and fear, darted over to where Connor stood covered with nervous sweat that was cooling in the night air causing him to shiver.

"You bloody—"

Owen let go of Rushmount's shirt. At the sudden release, he fell back onto the stool, his bound feet tripping him in place.

"Enough," Owen said.

Silently, her round face pale and anxious, Kath gave Grace a packet of food.

"I thank you kindly, Kath. For this and for all your goodness to me."

Kath nodded but didn't break her silence.

Owen grasped Connor's hand and clapped him on the back. "Sorry for tonight, Con, but I saw no other way."

"Just go," Connor said.

\* \* \*

The chestnut whinnied as Owen untied the reins. "You know me, boy," he said. "And you will get to know me better." With an agility that surprised Grace, Owen rose into the saddle and held out a hand to her. "Come, lass, up here in front of me. I'll hold you on."

"I've never been on a horse before."

"You'll love the ride. Come."

She stood on her toes and reached out to him. Owen grasped her hand and, with one quick move, pulled her up and into the saddle in front of him. Once she was settled with his arms about her, he flapped the reins over the chestnut's mane, urging him forward.

"Before we leave the village, we have one more stop to make," she said over her shoulder.

"Where is that, lass?"

"Father Joyce's cabin."

He laughed, the sound floating free on the dark night air. "You're a marvelous woman, Grace O'Malley. I'll be the happiest man on earth to have you as my wife."

"May you always think so," she said.

"I will," he replied. "I'll love you always."

She nestled against him as he led the chestnut out of the clearing toward the village road. "Owen, I've been wondering something."

"What is that, love?"

"Are there kings in the New World? And queens?"

"I truly can't say for certain. But I've heard there is more land there than any king has measured."

Her voice took on a dreamy musing. "Wouldn't it be a wonderful way of things? To have a New World with more land than anyone can measure and no kings or queens at all?"

He held her in a tight embrace. "Except for one, of course."

"And who on earth would that be?"

"The beautiful Queen of Ballybanree."

As they rode on, their laughter floating free on the sea breeze, another laughing voice, as clear and happy as their own, sprang into life and began swirling around them.

'Tis Granuaile, Grace thought, her heart swelling with joy.

*She will be with me forever!*

## Coming Soon!

Turn the page for additional adventures in the life of
Grace and Owen.

*In the Lion's Mouth*

From Jean Harrington

Available from Highland Press Publishing

2008

*The Barefoot Queen*

*Jean Harrington*

# In the Lion's Mouth

Grace cupped her eyes against the glare, the better to watch the tall man stride along Claddagh dock. Even as their boat pulled away, she kept staring at the shoreline. Only when their vessel rode the tide into the bay and no sail followed did she breathe a sigh of relief and relax in Owen's arms.

"That's Rushmount back there, Owen. I swear it is."

"I think you're right, lass. The man's treading the wharf like a cock o' the walk. Few Irishmen have such an arrogant strut."

"Did he see us, I wonder?"

"He may have. Whoever it is peered out to sea."

"You think he'll come after us?"

"If he does, he'll see me hanged. But before I let that happen, I'll kill him. You know that, love."

Still intent on the dock, Grace said, "If you don't, I'll kill him myself." At the sound of her own words, she tore her gaze from the receding shore and looked at Owen with dismay. "Listen to us. Talking murder and meaning every bit of it." Dropping to the rough plank deck, she covered her face with her hands. "Dear God."

Owen sank next to her. He put an arm around her shoulder, drawing her close to his chest. "We are not murderers. We're decent people forced to the edge of a cliff. Should we leap to our deaths or fight for life?"

She lifted her tear-streaked face and grinned up at him. "Fight, of course. As long as it's not with each other."

He grinned back. "We're both stubborn and bound to disagree from time to time. 'Twill add to life's excitement, I'm thinking." Still smiling, he stood and held out his hand. "But we'll not argue now—not on this day. Come, love, let us watch Galway fade from view. 'Tis a sight we may never—"

A shot rang out, the ball whizzing by his head, singeing the hair over his right ear. As it flashed past, it grazed the mast, sending shards of wood flying about the boat.

Owen dropped to the deck. "Stay down, Grace. 'Tis Rushmount."

Hearing musket fire, the captain came racing along the deck. At the sight of the splintered mast, he stopped in his tracks. "'Twas a bloody ball! I cannot believe it. Who would shoot at us?"

"An Englishman," Owen said. "He was aiming at me."

"Why you?"

"He wants her...my wife."

In the same instant, both men looked down at Grace lying quietly at Owen's side.

"Oh my God." The words were as close to a scream as any Owen had ever uttered. "Grace! Dear God, Grace."

Blood ran from her temple down her cheek trickling into the corner of her mouth and along her neck. Already the stream was soaking into her bodice, staining the linen wine red.

"Grace. *Mavourneen.*" Owen lifted her quiet form in his arms searching for the blood's source. His hand trembling, he brushed her hair back from her forehead. A splinter of wood, sharp and lethal as a spike, had pierced the flesh above her left eye. He looked up at the captain in horror. "It nearly took her eye. Thank God, it went in no farther...it must be removed."

*Now, before she awakens.*

Just enough of the wood jutted out to give him a purchase. One fast pull only would he allow himself.

Ordering his hand not to tremble, he hesitated for a moment, then with fingers of steel he pulled—hard. The shard came free and with it a fresh gush of blood.

Grace lay against him without moving. He had to stop the blood!

"Wait," the captain said. "I've something 'twill help." He hurried below deck, soon returning with a jug, a tin cup and a soiled piece of cloth. He waved the jug. "'Tis *uisce beatha*, a cure for everything under the sun. Dab some on her wound. 'Twill staunch the cut, and the sharp feel of it will bring her round."

Owen poured a little of the whiskey into the cup, his terror mounting with each second Grace remained unconscious. But he shook his head at the cloth the man held out.

"I have a cloth, sir." From his breeches pocket, Owen took out his greatest treasure, the square of embroidered linen Grace had given him the summer last. A gift from her heart it was, and now her heart's blood would be on it, making it more precious than ever.

Carefully, he dipped the linen into the whiskey. His hand above her face trembled. This would cause her pain. How could he?

How could he not?

Dabbling the wet cloth on her temple, he pressed it to the wound. At his touch, she moaned, rocking her head back and forth as if to escape the sting. He lifted his hand. The bleeding had slowed. Again he pressed on the wound, his touch lighter this time. After what seemed an eternity, she rewarded him with a flash of green eyes. "Owen," she murmured. "What are you doing?"

"Tending to you."

"What happened?"

"Rushmount shot at us. He aimed for me, but missed."

"I can see that," she said, a little smile lifting her lips.

He helped her to sit against the side of the boat. To his relief, when she raised her head, the bleeding showed no sign of increasing. Gradually, the trickle slowed to a few drops beading the gash. He dabbed at it again as gently as he could, but still she winced.

"Sorry. So sorry." All the anguish in the world shown in his eyes.

"Don't be sorry, Owen O'Donnell. He could have killed you."

"He could have killed you!"

"But he didn't. And here we are as right as rain, alive and loving each other more than ever. What have we to feel sorrow for?"

"Will you always be so wise?" Owen asked. "Throughout our entire lives?"

"Aye," she said, her chin firm, her eyes asparkle. "And 'tis glad I am you know it."

He laughed, and tossing the whiskey in the tin cup overboard, he poured a fresh tot from the jug before easing down beside her. "Sip this, love. 'Twill do you good."

They passed the cup between them sipping slowly, warmed by the *poteen* and the sun overhead. When Grace dozed, her head against his shoulder, Owen scanned the horizon. It was possible Rushmount would board another vessel and give chase. But no sail hove into view. A good thing, he thought. Grace had gone through enough already and the day not yet high noon. She had no need to see her husband kill a man before sunset.

# ℰ𝒜bout the 𝒜uthor

A Rhode Island native, Jean Harrington
taught writing and literature at Becker
College in Worcester, Massachusetts, for 16
years and was a visiting lecturer in the
Adult Education Program at Providence
College. Earlier, she wrote promotional
copy for Reed & Barton, Silversmiths, and
then, with the help of her husband, John
('we've been married forever'), brought up
their two children. Jean and John
now live in Florida.

*The Barefoot Queen*

# *Also Available from Highland Press*

*The Barefoot Queen*

*Rebecca Andrews*
# The Millennium Phrase Book
*Chris Holmes*
# Blood on the Tartan
*Deborah MacGillivray*
# Cat O'Nine Tales
*Leanne Burroughs*
# Her Highland Rogue

# *Upcoming*

*Anne Holman*
# Dark Well of Decision
*Holiday Romance Anthology*
# Romance Upon A Midnight Clear
*Holiday Romance Anthology*
# Love Under the Mistletoe
*John Nieman & Karen Laurence*
# The Amazing Rabbitini
(Children's Illustrated)
*Isabel Mere*
# Almost Guilty
*Chai/Ivey/Porter/Young*
# Mail Order Brides
*Candace Gold*
# A Heated Romance
*Romance Anthology*
# No Law Against Love 2
*Eric Fullilove*
# The Zero Day Event
*Jannine Corti Petska*
# The Lily and the Falcon
*Romance Anthology*
# The Way to a Man's Heart

*Jean Harrington*

*Romance Anthology*
## Love on a Harley
*Romance Anthology*
## Dance en L'Aire
*Lance Martin*
## The Little Hermit
(Children's Illustrated)
*Brynn Chapman*
## Bride of Blackbeard
*Sorter/MacGillivray/Burroughs*
## Faith, Hope and Redemption
*Anne Holman*
## The Master of Strathgian
*Romance Anthology*
## Second Time Around
*Jannine Corti Petska*
## Surrender to Honor
*Romance Anthology*
## Love and Glory
*Sandra Cox*
## Sundial
*Ginger Simpson*
## Sparta Rose
*Freddie Currie*
## The Changing Wind
*Molly Zenk*
## Chasing Byron
*Cleora Comer*
## Just DeEtta
*Katherine Deauxville*
## The Amethyst Crown
*Katherine Deauxville*
## Enraptured
*Don Brookes*
## With Silence and Tears

*The Barefoot Queen*

*Linda Bilodeau*
# The Wine Seekers
*Jeanmarie Hamilton*
# Seduction
*Diane Davis White*
# Moon of the Falling Leaves
*Katherine Shaw*
# Love Thy Neighbor
*Jo Webnar*
# Saving Tampa
*Jean Harrington*
# In the Lion's Mouth
*Inspirational Romance Anthology*
# The Miracle of Love
*Katherine Deauxville*
# Eyes of Love

*Cover by DeborahAnne MacGillivray*

LaVergne, TN USA
27 December 2009
168197LV00002B/43/P

9 780980 035667